OKAVANGO GODS

OTHER TITLES BY ANTHONY FLEISCHER

CHILDREN OF ADAMASTOR (Robert Hale, London, 1992; David Philip, Cape Town, 1994)
'His authorial voice is a whisper rather than a shout and all the more powerful for that. Altogether this is a novel of integrity and eminent readability.' Frances Coburn, *The Star*

VAGABOND FLAG (Macmillan, London, 1971)
'Here is a writer with some of Hemingway's uncanny knack of projecting human beings in a crisis of action ... An impressive book.' Sir Francis King, *Sunday Telegraph*

GARIBALDI'S SKI-BOAT (André Deutsch, London, 1961)
'It is difficult to pin-point the extraordinary attractiveness of this story ... He proves an unpretentious confidence and skill lacked by many more famous European novelists.' Robin Denniston, *Time & Tide*

FLY AWAY PAUL (Andrée Deutsch, London, 1963)

THE SKIN IS DEEP (Secker & Warburg, London, 1958)

ANTHONY FLEISCHER

OKAVANGO GODS

DAVID PHILIP PUBLISHERS
Cape Town   Johannesburg

ACKNOWLEDGEMENTS

The author wishes to acknowledge reference to the following publications:

The Epic of Gilgamesh – An English Version with an Introduction by N K Sandars (Penguin Books, 1972).

The Hambukushu of Okavangoland – An Anthropological Study of a South Western Bantu People in Africa. D.Phil. thesis by Louis Lourens van Tonder, 1966.

Basutoland Medicine Murder – A Report on the Recent Outbreak of 'Diretlo' Murders in Basutoland. HMSO Cmd. 8209, April 1951.

ABRACADABRA the Magic of Medicine – Wellcome Institute for the History of Medicine. Arnold, Baldwin, Mack, 1996.

Further information to be found in the Appendix.

First published in 1998 by David Philip Publishers (Pty) Ltd, 208 Werdmuller Centre, Claremont, 7708, South Africa
© Anthony Fleischer 1998
ISBN 0 86486 385 3

Typeset by User Friendly, Cape Town
Printed and bound by the Natal Witness Printing & Publishing Co., 244 Longmarket Street, Pietermaritzburg, 3201, South Africa

CONTENTS

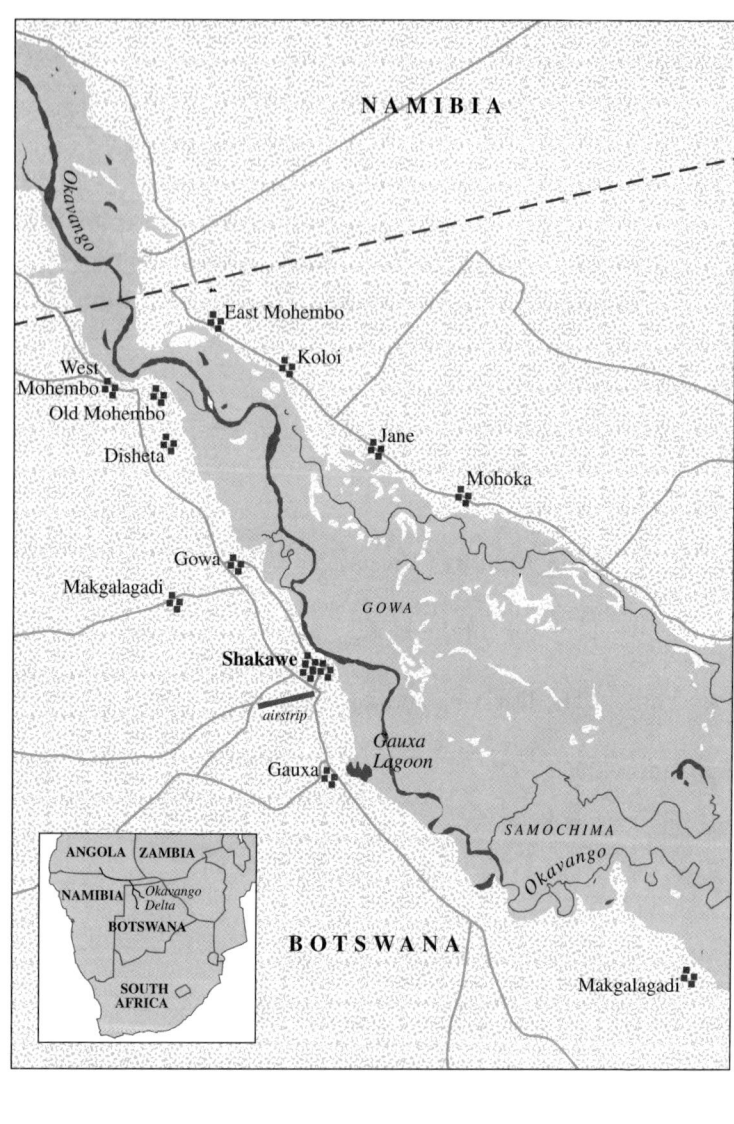

PART ONE

AT THE MOUTH OF RIVERS

'Thus it was that the gods took me and placed me here to live in the distance, at the mouth of rivers.'
– *THE EPIC OF GILGAMESH*

1

On the old washboards in the bottom of the boat lay a tassel of dry papyrus. The stiff brown fibres moved slightly but rhythmically. Pula stared at two insects caught in an embrace amidst the fibrous head of papyrus from the swamp. There was some aura of urgency about the ritual mating, a pulsating promise.

Pula hung over the wooden plank which was the front seat in his father's boat; he knelt there on the washboards, his hands hugging to his chest his most recent wooden creation, an intricate carving, a weighty and elongated figurine with a flat head.

He stretched forward, eyes wide and very close to the insects in the papyrus, studying them. In the shadow of the prow, on top of the old anchor rope and its short length of chain, hidden in a crown of swamp papyrus, the ancient pattern continued. Pula could sense the coming violence.

The bigger insect, the female, lay still while the male busied himself above her. He was well connected, Pula noticed, and he knew that the triumph would not last long.

'Good god,' he said quietly into the bottom of the boat.

The connection was well secured, the purposeful male clung to his partner's back and the papyrus fibres moved, ever so slightly, a wild bed for mating gods. Pula willed the god to mate, willed him to continue his natural purpose.

As Pula watched the pulsating performance, his own excitement grew, he felt himself to be part of all natural action. He too could mate one day, glorious, part of nature around him, throbbing, existing forever like the swamp itself.

Pula saw a slow and sinister movement of huge and scissor-like talons. The female moved to grasp the man above her. Pula tucked his long wooden carving closer to his chest, leaned forward to watch. He could feel the flat head of his god-model hard against his ribs. He clutched the slender form of it, the hard wood, *moselesele*, felt like steel in his fingers. He lifted one hand away from the carving, stretched towards the mating insects.

He was about to poke the big body of the female with an outstretched finger, when it seemed that the male asked him to stay his hand. Wait, the insect said, this is my glory.

Pula slowly withdrew his hand, hugged his carving. He did not disturb the gods again. He only watched as the small but determined male pulled himself higher on to his partner's back, dragging her connected tail upwards as he did so. The two bodies formed a curve now, their tails stuck like sucking mouths, the male holding on for dear life or dear death.

His moment came and Pula noticed it, understood it. He felt a deep sympathy for the victorious man, a connection to all creatures, a warm wish for life for himself. He knew how the end would come but he was pleased that he had not disturbed this little god, doing his godlike duty. It was over.

No! It was not over! Those big talons moved again, the sinister scissors. They grabbed the head of the exhausted mate, clasped it between sharp teeth. Then the woman bent her head to one side and began to eat the thing which she held in her claws. She chewed her mate's eyes, his very head, so that the rest of him jerked feebly, losing control. The big female jaws moved voraciously in their own triumph, chewing strongly so that pieces of her mate slobbered on to the papyrus. She was enjoying her meal, moving both mandibles in huge delight, even moving her legs on the papyrus as if to walk away now that the ritual was done, the final service performed, the new cycle begun.

Pula sat back on his haunches, away from the primitive scene. He still knelt on the washboards, holding his carving in his lap. He heard the water slap lightly against the side of the boat from his own movement. He lifted his hands together, touched the head of his god-model to his lips, praying like a mantis.

In sudden anger Pula thrust out a hand and grabbed the eating creature and its awful meal, the papyrus head too, and he threw the whole mess into the swiftly flowing river. He saw the fibre raft and its hottentot-gods float away with the stream.

Confused, somehow frustrated, Pula sat down to wait for his father. He took his small knife out of his pocket, began to work on his god-model, making tiny snicks below the eyes of the old man's face. He then turned the elongated figure in his hand, holding it level so that its sculpted form revolved slowly. He carefully checked his handiwork. On one surface was a young man with a young body and a young face, but a flat head as if the top of his skull had been sliced away. On the other surface, slowly revolving into view, the man had grown old, but still with a small flat head. Linking the old and the new were the twisting forms of a chameleon and a lizard. In a single turn the young man was an old man, the lizard and the chameleon as witnesses.

Pula worked on the old man's eyes, cutting deeper lines, stark contrast to the smoothness of the young man's eyelids. He chipped with the tip of his knife at the chest and the long legs, using it like a chisel. The hard wood flaked away in dusty shavings. He cut flesh from one side of the leg so that the muscle was older and harder, in contrast to the powerful smooth muscle of the young side. He examined the whole carving once more, rubbed the flat Mbukushu head with his thumb.

He stood up in the boat and stretched his arms to the sky.

He saw his father limping along the path to the river. In one hand he was carrying the red tank of petrol against his thigh; the other hand steadied the new engine on his shoulder. This was a new burden, this new engine, heavy for him, but cherished.

'Have you cleaned up from yesterday?' his father asked, as he stepped into his boat. Carefully, he laid the tank of petrol in the bottom of the boat, then he slipped the clamps of the outboard into place over the transom. He tightened the clamps, hooked a short length of chain to a bracket on the new engine.

'I have cleaned up,' Pula answered. He lifted other bits of papyrus from the washboards, picked lengths of grass from the round cork float attached to the anchor rope, flicked the debris over the side. His father tightened the clamps one more turn, checked the retaining chain. He connected the fuel lead from the red tank, squeezed the bulb, set the throttle. The Yamaha started on the first try. With a skipper's nod to Pula to push away from the bank the old fisherman's day began.

Soon they were out in the mainstream of the Okavango River. Pula moved from his wooden seat to lie on the prow, his favourite position now that they could travel fast in the centre of the river and not creep along the bank in a *mokoro*. This was the way to move across the water, flying along, pushed by a new engine. Pula lay on his stomach with one arm stretched out, his hand flat, level with the water, pointing forward into the wind. He raised the tips of his fingers, ever so slightly, like finger frills at the end of a wing. His hand was lifted up and away. He flew that way, his moving hand arching smoothly into the warm air. Lying there he breathed a Tswana word to the wind and to the water below him.

'Puuula!' He said.

He was saying 'Peace!' to the wide waters. 'Rain!' he was saying, greeting the great swamp itself, which could never be drained away.

Pula saw below him a crocodile swimming in clear water like a big flat fish. A long and powerful tail forced a huge body fast through the water. The creature's snout was the tip of a deadly arrow, shooting through shallow water, hunting tiger-fish. Pula was thrilled to see below him such a monster moving so fast. He turned his head from his prone position in the prow of the moving boat and called in excitement to his father.

'He swam past us! He moves faster than we do!'

'Some gods are swift.'

Pula looked down again into the clear water of the Okavango

River. The crocodile had disappeared and now below him, also swimming fast under the boat, was a school of tiger-fish busy with their own hunting. They flashed over the sand bank and then were lost as the light colour of diamond sand sloped away into deeper water.

To Pula it was all diamond sand, the clean white strips which marked the direction of the current, even the sun-dried patches above the water on which the skimmers nested. All diamond sand. The vast stretches surrounding the swamp, the dry road to the Tsodilo Hills where he was born, the horizon of the Makgadi-kgadi, all shimmering diamond sand, his home, the home of the Hambukushu, the people of wild grapes.

His father twisted the hand-throttle of the new outboard, a little hesitantly. He reduced speed as they entered the channel. The exhaust of the outboard bubbled and smoked beneath the surface of the water. The bow where Pula lay settled lower. The papyrus on either side of the channel rustled as the waves disturbed the big reeds.

The old boat with its new engine made its way slowly up the channel. Sparks of brilliant colour burst out of the reeds in front of the moving boat. Squacco herons and bee-eaters rose from the papyrus. A few yards ahead, below the swamp birds, in a muddy slipway between reeds, lay a big, dry crocodile. His eyes were open, watching, but he did not slither away into the water as the boat passed his basking-place.

'He is very old, that one,' Pula said, moving back to the seat in the bow. 'Older than you.'

'Some gods are swift, some are old.'

'He could be dead. He is so still.'

The idle crocodile slowly swung his heavy head towards some new disturbance in the river. The water churned ahead, as if over sudden rapids. The crocodile rose slowly on stubby legs. Then, with incredible speed, it galloped to the water's edge. It slithered down the muddy slipway and plunged into the water.

'Never say that a crocodile is dead. He lives forever like an ancestor, like the god he is.'

'Like *seremapetlo*, the hottentot-god?'

'He too.'

'Do they all feed upon themselves?'

'Yes.'

Pula's father said this in all seriousness, and Pula thought of water and life and the cycle of both. There was some kind of swirling in his mind, a dust devil or a whirlpool of doubt about these gods around him. At great speed, at the very edges of his understanding, he was being drawn into the presence of eternity. His father was old too, one day he would go.

Pula reached for his carving, looked again at the old side, frowned slightly, uncertain of the old eyes. He turned it round to smile at the young side, satisfied. He touched the fine lines of the young man's face, then he lifted the carving as if it were a weapon, held the long legs. He tapped the flat head on the gunwale.

Pula's father touched the throttle back even further, too much. The outboard died. The boat drifted to the new sound of sudden rapids.

'Listen! The barbel are moving!' Pula's father called, his one hand pointing towards the churning water ahead.

The huge school of migrating barbel was attacked as it moved. Both old and young were vulnerable, like any creatures migrating. The snapping of predators from the papyrus island and the cries of excited birds filled the air. The papyrus fronds waved from the noisy action at their base and there was blood in the water. The savage slaughter continued in a cacophony of carnage, small birds swooped for food, a crocodile rose with a *vundu* in its teeth. It flipped the big fish once, as if it were a morsel to play with, then closed its teeth on it. The tail-fin flapped once more in the air, then it was gone.

Pula witnessed this second slaughter, considered again the circle of life. The water came down from the mountains in Angola, it spread itself wide across the diamond sand only to be sucked up into the sky by the sun, to rain again in the mountains. For this the *mugrodi*, the rain-mother, produced children to be sacrificed?

'Rain is close to the gods,' Pula said to his father.

'So are you.'

'Because of the *mugrodi*?'

'I have told you so many times. Always you ask!'

'I never knew my mother, there has only been you. Will you tell me again?'

'Tonight maybe.'

'You hid me in the bushes so that you would not be alone?'

At that moment the water was stilled as if by a godly hand. All was suddenly quiet and the human voices lingered loud in the natural silence. Pula and his father sat still, now close together, and they sensed some power in the sky, heard its presence. They both looked up and saw a fish-eagle high above them, calling. The sound of his call was very clear above the silence of the stilled water. The eagle folded his wings and dropped from the sky, falling straight towards the small boat on still water.

It was as if the fish on the surface knew of the new danger; they sank deep as the eagle swooped down. His wings opened in controlled stall, gliding him to a single target: one barbel still on the surface. He hit the water very close to the boat, talons open. He hit his prey but could not immediately lift it. His huge wings now beat above the water so that a patch of the still water was again disturbed for a moment, ruffled by his slipstream. The eagle clung to the back of the large barbel, talons digging into his food, then he collapsed into the water, like a crippled aircraft. His head switched in unfamiliar indecision as he sat on the water like a pathetic duck, first to look at Pula and then to look at the papyrus so close by. He swam then, sweeping his way across the surface of the water with his wet wings, rowing himself in feathered scoops towards the papyrus. When he reached the reeds he rested a moment, his body still shuddering from the desperate movement of the fish in his claws.

The fish-eagle looked directly at Pula sitting in the boat and Pula saw distinct appeal in the eagle's diamond eyes. He felt the entreaty in the piercing eagle eyes as if the bird had spoken directly to him, as if a proud creature – made so ridiculous for a moment – had stooped to ask for understanding. A magnificent eagle of the air, wet in the rough papyrus, a god brought down, had appealed directly to the young man.

'Pula!' Pula said very quietly, but his father heard him. He smiled for love of this son who was born in the shadow of the Tsodilo Hills, at the mouth of rivers, who spoke to eagles.

Pula raised his long carving in salute, waved it like a wand over the water, willing the bird to fly. He too would fly one day, he would see from the air all the places which his father talked about, even the Tsodilo Hills, the Makgadikgadi. The Hills were sacred, sacred rocks thrust out from the diamond sand in celebration. Pula would fly above the sacred place, above sand, above diamonds, above the water too. He would fly with the gods. He would hover like a kingfisher, plunge down like an eagle, swoop close to the water like a skimmer.

The fish-eagle was not frightened by the waving god-model. It move awkwardly in the papyrus, dragging its prey.

Pula did not see the ears of a hippo flicker above the water, very close to the boat, but his father saw them and acted at once. He stood up quickly, moving purposefully as if he were a young man. He reached for his son and pulled him away from the bow of his boat, telling him to hold on to the low gunwale. He then turned in a great hurry to start the outboard; in too much of a hurry. The engine caught at once, the tiller swung as the propeller thrust his old boat forward towards the papyrus island, and Pula fell over the wooden seat, backwards into the boat. As he reached out to grab the tilted gunwale, he dropped his carving over the side. His father was also off balance for a lurching moment – he stumbled and fell over the gunwale into the papyrus.

The fish-eagle, now startled by the sudden action of the boat, released its prey and rose at once into the air. The engine roared and the boat scraped higher, on to the papyrus island. The papyrus fronds were all about Pula's head, he was trapped in them like an insect. He flailed his arms to escape from them and switch off the terrible noise. He stepped over the wooden seat, scrambled to the stern, twisted the throttle of the new engine to close it.

It was very quiet after the sound was shut off. The fish-eagle, even the barbel, had gone. The water was still, there was no sign of his father. In sudden alarm Pula looked downstream and searched the expanse of moving water. The angry hippo had also disappeared beneath the surface of the water. Dry papyrus heads, loosened by the action of the boat, were scattered on the water. He saw his long god-model caught like an ordinary log amongst them, floating away downstream. The young side was facing the sun.

Pula stepped on to the wooden seat this time, prepared to dive into the water to fetch his carving. He sensed a tickle of fear in the pit of his stomach, it held him back for a moment, as if his feet had decided to disobey his will. He hovered there above the water, saw his god-model twist away in the current, spin out from the clutch of the papyrus, and float fast with the river.

At that moment he recalled the shape of the simple piece of *moselesele* on which he had worked with his knife, and he was suddenly deeply guilty. It was only a piece of wood. Watching it float away, he had forgotten his father.

He heard another movement near the boat and saw his father sitting on the papyrus island where he had fallen. He sat there in shallow water, a bit like an eagle brought down. The papyrus was flattened where he sat and Pula shouted out in sudden relief and love, held out his hand to help his father aboard.

'You are still learning this machine,' he said.

O GODS — B

2

Pula and his father continued on their journey upstream, along the main channel towards the village of Shakawe. Pula's father motioned to him to take the tiller while he squeezed water from his wet shirt. The boy hurried to do this favourite duty. He opened up the Yamaha, thrilling to the speed on open water. He raised his flying hand again, fingers pointing towards Shakawe and the mainland, straight into the wind. He lifted his fingers into the air as they sped along. His flat hand was again swept up and away. Despite the great noise of the roaring outboard motor behind him, Pula knew that flying was silent. He would fly like a bird, quiet, the wind whispering through outstretched wings. At the very end of his wings feather frills could be moved like guiding fingers. He rose to his feet in the stern of the boat, feeling the wind about his face, feeling it sting his eyes. His father told him to slow down and to sit down. The old boat could not take such speed.

As soon as the pilot stepped into the boat Pula knew that he was a man who could fly. The man was just what he imagined a flying man should be. He wore a leather jacket with an eagle on the pocket. He carried a camera and Pula knew that the flying man took photographs of what went on below him, he could see all the diamond sand, even the Tsodilo Hills. Through the lens of his precious camera, he could see the world below him, record everything that happened in the swamp. This was the pilot who liked to fish, who flew a huge machine through the clouds, but who also came down from the clouds to fish from John Barotse's boat.

The pilot settled himself on a yellow cushion in the middle seat, near the fishing-rods. Pula's father now took control again, turning the boat into the stream to return to the migrating barbel, fast with the current of the Okavango. There would be plenty of tiger-fish along the papyrus island, plenty of game fish for his flying client, the pilot.

The pilot saw a fish-eagle high in a tree on the mainland bank. He signalled to Pula's father to stop, and raised his camera to one eye. The boat drifted in the mainstream. Pula knew this eagle too, it always waited near Shakawe, high in its tree. Pula took a small fish from the bait box. He thrust a length of dry papyrus into the fish's mouth.

'Wait!' he said to the pilot.

Pula stood up in the bow of the boat and whistled to the waiting eagle. He saw the eagle's head move, saw that its eyes were already on the fish he held. He liked to be fed this way, this eagle, to show off to visitors, to perform before cameras.

Pula knew that the eagle was watching his hand, the same hand that could soar like a bird. When he saw the eagle's shoulder shrug, he knew that it was about to fly. He glanced at the pilot, checked that he was ready with his camera, and threw the fish with the dried reed in its mouth, high into the air.

The fish-eagle dropped from his perch and swooped down, talons open. It plucked the offered morsel from the river. There was no need for the dry reed, the bait had no time to sink. The fish-eagle hit it in one perfect swoop and rose with it on huge wings.

'It was too quick for me,' the pilot said, with some embarrassment.

He took a picture of the eagle eating, high in its tree.

'You can also fly,' Pula said to the pilot.

'Not like that. So silent, so swift.'

When they drew level with the papyrus island Pula fixed a thin wire trace and an Abu spinner for the pilot. Soon the pilot was in action, happy, fishing.

He had ordered this, he had asked for John Barotse who lived near the Fishing Camp and who knew the river better than any other Mbukushu. The Hambukushu were all fishermen, but only John Barotse used the tribal surname of swamp people further north. He claimed affinity with all water people. He owned land near the Tsodilo Hills, and he claimed that the 'John' came from John Mackenzie, missionary amongst the Kololo tribe, friend of the great Khama III. John Barotse was also a rainmaker.

The first tiger-fish came in. Pula lifted it from the water and he shouted out to the river and to the sky ... 'Puuuuula!'

He, Pula Barotse, would shout out loud, his own name and his own ambitions. He would fly too, fly with the pilot just as he was now fishing with him. He would wear a jacket with an eagle on the front and he would fly over the water, even over the Tsodilo Hills to the land of diamond sand where he was born. His father might not believe it; anyone who saw him fishing for tiger-fish, who knew his father's old boat, might not believe it, but it would happen. A man such as this one in a leather jacket could teach him to fly, just as he himself was taught to fish.

A horse-fly bit the pilot's white leg and the man slapped at it, hard with his right hand, still holding the flick-rod in his left. The fat fly fell on to the washboards, its legs still moving.

'Could that be a tsetse?' the pilot asked with some concern.

'A tsetse is much bigger,' Pula Barotse told him. 'It can kill an ox in two weeks.'

'And a man like me?'

'You would get sleepy and more sleepy, then very sick! But that is only a horse-fly.'

Pula reached out with his foot, squashed the fly on the washboard. He should have squashed *seremapetlo*, the hottentot-god.

'Even an American like you could die of the swamp sickness.'

'We will get rid of the tsetse,' the American said.

Later, Pula listened very carefully as the pilot, drinking beer from a can, told his father how he had flown his big aeroplane into many wild places in Africa, often to help the people. This time he had brought scientists and the engineers and all their equipment to Shakawe. The scientists from South Africa had a scheme to kill the tsetse and the engineers had come from the salt mine in the Makgadikgadi. Soon, cattle could graze in the swamp.

'That would be terrible,' John Barotse said, but very quietly. 'Cattle in the swamps!'

'There could be great development in your country. The water and the salt of the Makgadikgadi will make you rich.'

'Rich? We cannot sell salt. We cannot sell water. We, the Hambukushu, we are the rain-makers but we cannot sell what we make. We have no such magic.'

John Barotse, who made rain, who lived on the water, had lost his belief in his own magic. He turned to look again at this white man talking about his swamp. No one could fish in a dry swamp.

The pilot put down his beer can and took up his fishing-rod. Pula pulled the scoop-net from its place below the gunwale and held it ready.

'How many have I caught?' the pilot asked.

Pula moved some of the reeds with which he had covered the fish lying on the washboards. He also moved two separate pieces of *moselesele* and placed them on the wooden seat, out of the way. He touched the head of an unfinished sable for a moment, considered his god-model floating away, never to be completed. He was not happy about losing that model, he was also not happy with the curve of the sable's horns. He left the unfinished carving and the other piece of hardwood on the seat and counted the fish.

'Thirteen,' he said.

'That is unlucky.'

'It is enough,' John Barotse repeated. 'Enough is a good word.'

'Did you make that?' the pilot asked, pointing with his chin to the unfinished model of the sable.

'It is not finished,' Pula explained.

'I will buy it. How much in pula?'

'The horns are not right.'

'How much for it as it is?'

'Ten pula,' Pula said, very quietly, almost talking to himself. He was talking about money with new audacity.

'I will buy it.'

That night under the stars, around the fire outside his hut at the Fishing Camp on the edge of the swamp, John Barotse smoked a pipe and repeated the things that the pilot had said, almost as if Pula had not been in the boat himself. He also talked about the days when men could live alone in swamps, moving quietly in *mokoros*. He talked quietly about the old magic, how it had disappeared. Now, there was power much greater than a man in a *mokoro* with a pole: aeroplanes for example, Yamahas on the river. Too many people, not enough water.

He talked of African people spreading over the land, of his own Barotse and their Kingdom, of the Lozi, the Aluyi, the Kololo, of the Kongo further North. He talked of riches in the desert, in the caves near the Tsodilo Hills. He talked of the powerful Bamangwato, of the Kalanga, Tswapong, Sarwa, Talaote and the Makgadikgadi themselves in their flat fields. Instructing his son, he talked of the Batswana on the other side of the border in South Africa, in an alien place which was once known as Bophuthatswana, the gathering place of the Batswana. In that country the white man had tried to carve out pieces of land for each tribe and also a big piece of Africa for himself. It had not worked, simply because tribes do not live in only one place. They live with their language and their customs. Like us, they may move between floods, or from the mountains to the plains.

He told Pula that wars established boundaries, changed names, but that the days of war were also over. The Hambukushu had learnt to avoid war, had not changed their name. A tribe's name was like a person's name, both could live within the whole world of other people, but both must be true to themselves. That way the world could find some kind of peace, with enough space for all, enough rain, enough water.

The Hambukushu could also have diamonds, and already Botswana was rich. Look at Orapa, Jwaneng, Lethlakane, all the people there, caught in a trap. They had walked into the trap, they had looked for work away from their homes.

Those pipes of blue ground which came from the centre of the earth so long ago, were like traps set in the desert. What could suck hot rock to the surface of the desert and then leave it there to trap people? Men should tread carefully over the earth, leave her secrets undisturbed. Instead, they rushed around like ants, in their thousands, because they were always searching for work, like ants. They stopped wherever they found the work, like ants around a dead body. When the dead body was eaten the people had to move on.

'When there are too many people they destroy everything,' John Barotse said. 'That is what will happen when the tsetse are killed. Basotho people will come with their cattle, then their goats will follow the cattle and then will come the desert. They will ask me to bring rain, but I will not be able to do it.'

'You will always be able to do it!' Pula said, a little confused by his father's reasoning. What, after all, was the work of a rain-maker, of a fisherman?

'Our ancestors were Basotho. It is in their hands.'

'Like Potlako Lereng?'

'He is from Thaba Bosiu, from the Mountain of Night, like Bubi. He speaks our language, but he is a demon, that one, he likes war. He does not yet understand our country, our swamp. He is using old Basotho beliefs to frighten the Batswana. He looks for power, not peace. He does not talk to eagles, not as you do.'

'Eagles have power! They can be cruel, they can fly!'

'Potlako is a scorpion. You must watch out for his sting.'

'A mantis can be cruel, it can fly.'

'Sometimes the truth is cruel. Maybe the swamp *will* die. Beneath the diamond sand are unseen rivers. These rivers join up with the salt lakes. Maybe our water will drain away. There will be no grass, no papyrus, no birds, no sitatunga, no letchwe. No fish or crocodiles. No Hambukushu, no hippos, no rain.'

Pula knew that his father did sometimes grow sad in the evening, as the sun set, and he had heard this story about the swamp drying up, many times before. Tonight the sadness was of a different order. It touched Pula in an unusual way, as if the pilot had been some kind of messenger from another world. A world where people flew.

'The surest way to kill the tsetse is to cut down the trees,' his father continued. 'When the trees are cut there will be no shade and no tsetse. But who wants to watch the trees die?'

'We will stop them!' Pula said with great conviction, to comfort his father. 'I will talk to Julia and we will make a plan to stop them!'

'Ah Julia! The little Portuguese girl who asked you to her birthday party. How old was she that day of the fight?'

'Fifteen.'

'You and Julia together will stop the world?'

'She can talk to anyone, even to scientists and engineers.'

'I see.'

'Her father is a doctor. He will know about the tsetse. He knows about everything, even the beginning of life. He says that life began at the mouth of a river.'

'So the doctor knows all about us?'

'About magic and medicine too. In Portuguese it is *feitiço*, that is what Julia says.'

'Ah! Magic! That is good. Magic and the people from the Mountain of Night.'

'Bubi believes in magic,' Pula mumbled and settled down beneath his single blanket.

'You have talked to Bubi?'

'I would like to talk to her. I would like to ask her about my mother.'

'But I have told you so often. She was the *mugrodi*, but she died after you. You are the only one who lives. The rest were sacrificed for the rain.'

'Why did you keep me? Why not let me go too?'

On the edge of sleep the hottentot-god which had been eaten, came to talk to Pula in hushed tones about the real meaning of his death and his glory: the swamp was the beginning and the end, it was eternity. Water was the beginning and the end, and the creatures which lived near it might wonder how the cycle might end for each of them, but the cycle itself would not end. For each insect and animal in the swamp was the first and the last. They were eternity, like gods. Eternity was magic, nothing else.

There were dust devils twisting Pula as he lay near his father, waiting for sleep. There were whirlpools, sucking him into a circle of truth. The hottentot-god was caught in one of the whirlpools, riding on a piece of papyrus. He raised his praying paws and preached to Pula.

There is only so much living available, only so much water in each cycle to sink into the deep tunnels under the ground, to be sucked up again from the Makgadikgadi in an eternal pattern. You are part of that eternity, part of the rain which your father made, like a god.

A pilot with his big aeroplane could think that he might himself be god, that he might escape the cycle, but there was no escape, even for pilots. Life did not belong, it was only borrowed, passed on from me to you, and that was the cycle which the pilot did not understand. That was why he would destroy himself. He had no god but his machine. And who could trust any machine, no matter how magic its flight might seem to be?

Never believe that there was no purpose in my death, never believe that any man can be a god, like me! You are growing up, but you will only be a man. You may be a very special man because your father saved you. You should have been buried with your head open to the rain, and you are lucky to be alive. But only as a man.

As you grow to be a man, do not deny any god his choice, any creature his dignity. I will look after you, Pula, man of peace and of rain who must live amidst the violence of both flood and drought. In turn you must look after that which you have borrowed. Use it well. You who might have been sacrificed for the rain, the child of a *mugrodi*. Do not listen to any man or woman who plays god, only to me.

'And Julia? What about *feitiço*, the things of medicine and of magic?'

Pula realised then that he had said these words aloud, even the Portuguese word, and that his father was not yet asleep. He looked at the dark form near the fire, saw an arm move beneath a blanket, the slow action of some creature settling to sleep.

'They are not of the swamp, like you and me,' his father answered, as if the question had been addressed to him, 'they have other gods.'

'She has only one god. I do not know about his magic.'

'All gods use magic of some kind.'

'Do you think I was left with some magic because you saved me?'

'There is magic all around us. Now go to sleep.'

Pula found Julia in the school-yard the next morning and he told her about the pilot and about the day in the swamp fishing with his father. He also told her that soon there would be no tsetse and that the swamp would be dried out by scientists and engineers from South Africa.

'They can never dry the swamp!' Julia said with great conviction.

'Maybe not dry it, but if they kill the tsetse the Kalanga cattle will come. They will eat up the grass on Chief's Island.'

'Cattle can't swim so far!'

'When the tsetse are gone, the cattle will be everywhere.'

'There is enough grass, even for cattle.'

'The miners will take all the salt from the Makgadikgadi and sell it.'

'Why can't they get salt from the sea?'

'We have no sea, only the Makgadikgadi. The water will drain away along the tunnels that join the swamp to the salt. The swamp will dry up.'

'Tunnels? You mean pipes, like diamond pipes. That is what they are looking for! Not salt!'

Julia knew that Pula listened to her, he was older, he was African but he listened to her. She liked that. Her father said that he was a wild man seeking something, that he was Enkidu, friend of Gilgamesh of old. He told her to be very careful with a wild person. He was like those who lived thousands of years ago, at the mouth of another river.

Julia said that Pula was very clever, he was not wild and primitive. He was sometimes a little arrogant, as if he knew as much as she did, but he was not dangerous. He argued with her sometimes, but usually she could put him straight. He argued about things they learnt in history class, even about Africa being discovered by the Portuguese! Julia told her father that Pula had actually laughed when she talked about the Portuguese discoveries, about the great mariners, about the men who found Africa. He even laughed at the missionaries, at the white man preaching.

He did not laugh at her. He was serious with her. He told her that there was a spirit in the swamp which was the original spirit of the world.

'*Feitiço*!' she had said, in Portuguese.

'Original man came from the swamp,' Pula had persisted.

This time too, he was serious. This time he would say that she did not understand the Hambukushu and the swamp.

'You don't understand the swamp,' Pula said.

'Aha! Only Hambukushu understand! Is that it? Only Bubi and her bones, only those who were born in the Tsodilo Hills, on the slippery slopes. A little white girl only thinks about diamonds and new clothes!'

She turned away to walk purposefully back to her classroom, but Pula caught the sleeve of her white blouse, as she knew he would.

'Wait,' he pleaded, 'I told my father that you would help us.'

'How, Pula? How can I help you, knowing so little about the swamp?'

'You must come with me. To listen to Bubi. Then you must ask your father about the pilot.'

'This is ridiculous. What can Bubi do?'

'She is also a doctor. She uses magic to cure people.'

'My father is a proper doctor.'

'She knows the gods. Cured people believe, so she is also something of a god herself.'

'You mean she plays god!'

'No. It is not like that.'

'There is only one God.' Julia said, pulling her arm away from Pula. His thumb and forefinger, which had held a tiny but precious piece of the cloth of her sleeve, stayed pinched in the air, forlorn, hesitant.

'That is not true!' Pula whispered. Julia hardly heard him but she turned to see him standing there with fingers pinched as if he were grasping for something just lost. He looked so pathetic, so African, so wild.

'Actually he is Three,' she said, facing him again. 'God the Father, God the Son and God the Holy Ghost.'

'Now you are playing.'

'My father says that doctors can produce new life in a glass. Can Bubi do that?'

'This is serious!' Pula said with some annoyance. 'It has to do with the future of the swamp and all that lives in it.'

3

Pula whittled with his knife and this time he was carving a heron from the horn of a buck. He showed Julia the shape of it, turning it around before her eyes so that she could see quite clearly that it was a heron with a long neck.

'You carve such beautiful things.'

'I lost my little god. I was making it for you.'

'Your birds, your insects and crocodiles. I like them all.'

'Sable sell.'

'Your hands talk to me. They don't argue.'

Julia reached for the carving hand to stop it working and to take it into her own. Pula closed the small knife and put it into his pocket. They walked along the narrow path that led away from the road to Namaseri Camp towards Bubi's hut. Even tourists took that narrow path sometimes, to have their fortunes told by Bubi.

The path was first a game path, made by buck walking through the bush, but later people had followed the path. Where many feet had trodden, the earth was packed hard, no grass grew, and Julia looked back to the more familiar road. Pula stopped ahead of her, pointed to the skull of a monkey placed on a pole.

'She will be here,' he told her. 'Not in her cave.'

Julia followed further until they came to a single low hut. On the roof of the hut were more skulls in a disorderly mound at the base of a huge pair of sable horns. The black horns themselves were so graceful, arching up to the sky, the pile of lesser skulls below them so ugly, pitted and cracked, with broken teeth in jaw bones, bits of putrid flesh still attached.

Pula pointed out the curved sable horns, his hand swept above the roof of the hut in an arc, shaping the beautiful horns. The adornments above the low doorway disturbed Julia. She stopped outside the hut, let Pula go in alone. She noticed wisps of smoke rise from the top of the roof, seep through the rough thatch-grass.

Pula came out again at once, pulled on her hand, told her to mind her head as she entered.

Bubi sat beside a small fire inside her hut. As the young couple entered she threw a pinch of powder on the coals. Flames rose up in a great thud of light and Bubi smiled at her visitors.

'Come in, children,' she said, 'sit down.'

Pula and Julia sat down on the dung floor, close to the fire because there was not much room in the hut. Pula spoke quietly to Bubi, while Julia rubbed her stinging eyes, tried to look up to the place where the thatch was black, where the smoke escaped. She herself thought of escape; she sniffed the air, held her fingers to her nose. She saw shapes in the thatch, small bodies, hanging gourds, the long skin of a snake. Tied to rough rafters of the roof were rotting plants too, bulbs and roots and old bark tied in bundles with thin riempies, made from the guts of a buck. She shivered, reached out to touch Pula's hand.

Pula placed a ten pula note on the floor, the one the pilot had paid him for the sable. He spread it flat with one finger so that Bubi could see quite clearly what it was. This time he would do the talking and the paying.

'Doctor Bubi,' Pula began. 'They want to dry out the swamp. There will be no water and no trees for the birds.'

'Who wants to do this?' Bubi asked, angrily but in English.

'White people.'

'Is that true?' Bubi asked of Julia.

To Julia the simple question coming so clearly from an old black woman in a hut, sounded like an accusation. She wanted to run from the hut. She saw that Pula was watching her, waiting for her to answer. She took another breath of acrid air, was about to get up and go, when she caught the appeal in Pula's eyes. He was asking her to be serious about this thing! She felt a sudden chill, but knew that she had to say something. When she spoke her voice seemed to her to be thin, weak, childish.

'Pula says that the pilot brought engineers and scientists to the swamps in his aeroplane. He is worried that they are planning to drain the swamps. I told him not to be ridiculous.'

'Is it ridiculous to come to me?'

'Pula thinks you can help.'

'And you? What do you think?'

'Nothing can drain the swamps, not even underground rivers. They have been there since the beginning of time. My father says so ...' Julia was silenced by Bubi who raised a skinny arm, thrust an open palm towards her.

'Enough!' she commanded. 'You do not know anything about life. You know nothing about the Hambukushu, about the diamond sands. The Hambukushu diamond is a big stone shaped like a pear. I say it is the shape of water in the desert.'

Pula pushed the ten pula note a fraction forward towards Doctor Bubi, his finger firm on the piece of paper. He felt Julia's finger join his, pulling back.

'Also about the tsetse,' Julia demanded, recovering her composure. 'The scientist is going to kill the tsetse so that the cattle can come in.'

Bubi saw the two young fingers on her ten pula note and she looked fiercely at this growing white girl who made demands on her. She was headstrong, this white girl. How close was she to Pula? And what might that mean in the future? This white thing was close to child-bearing. What might that mean in the future?

'Which is it to be, Pula?' Bubi asked, 'the water or the tsetse? These are different questions.'

'Both,' Pula said at once, 'throw the bones for both.'

Julia lifted her finger from the note and Pula slid it forward.

Bubi did not take the note, she only shuffled a moment on the floor by her small fire. She pulled out a skin pouch from the folds of her sitatunga skirt. From the pouch she lifted a soiled cloth in which were wrapped eight bones, two sea shells and two rough diamonds. The diamonds were unpolished and dirty. She spread out the square of cloth by her side and then she talked to the things which she held cupped in her hands. She spoke to the bones and the sea shells and the diamonds, blowing lightly on her fingers as she did so. She told the shells to fall this way or that way, open or closed; she talked to the bones about children playing in the river, about seasons of drought and seasons of flood. She talked about the Hambukushu and about necessary sacrifice for rain.

At this talk of sacrifice, she stared at Pula for a moment, and said quietly in her own language that a cycle had been broken, that the child of the *mugrodi* had not been sacrificed, it had not been buried at the corner of a field with its skull sliced open to catch the early rain.

Pula held her stare. He repeated in his own language that the last *mugrodi* had died in childbirth, that the child had been saved.

Bubi returned to the bones in her cupped hands, blew on them once again. She mentioned tsetse in the shade of trees and water birds in the air. She talked about change, about the war between the spirits and the diamonds, about duty and service and about sanctity of life and the flesh.

She shuddered when she spoke of flesh, of the medium of the Basotho, and she said to the bones that she did not need flesh on them, only that they should fall the way they chose. She wanted to have nothing to do with the vision of flesh.

Then she threw all the bones and the shells and the two diamonds on to her cloth and she studied how they lay.

Pula and Julia studied too. They saw Bubi's gnarled finger turn one cowrie shell so that it lay on its back, open. The finger shivered as it moved a knuckle bone to lie near the open shell, a mate. Then Bubi reached for the note which lay at Pula's knees. She was disturbed, there was something in her bones which she did not like.

She reached behind her and brought forward a small portable

radio. She set it firmly on the cloth, near the bones, slipped the ten pula note under it so that it was held firmly. She moved the shiny aerial of the radio, swung it round once so that it pointed to Julia.

'I thought I would find some darkness,' she said, in a thin voice. 'We are all related to the Basotho. They have a mountain which gives much water. Diamonds as well. They trade in flesh, and the only way is to sacrifice. If you wish to save the swamps you must sacrifice. That is what the bones say.'

'Potlako!' Julia exclaimed, with sudden concern. She reached for Pula's arm, held it tight.

'What do I sacrifice?' Pula asked, calmly.

He knew the word well enough, it was part of his understanding of the swamp and the rain, of the *mugrodi*, the rain-mother. He knew what it meant, he knew that a *mugrodi* used to sacrifice her children, but what did one sacrifice at a time like this? A fowl to Okavango gods? A beast to still the waters?

Julia imagined a man on a cross, a stone slab on a mountain, a prophet with a knife in his hand.

'The Basotho use human flesh, cut fresh,' Bubi said with a glance at Julia, who was now silent. Bubi was pleased about that. The white girl was silent, even she could be made afraid of mysteries. How did such a girl think that she might understand the son of the rain-maker, one who should himself have been sacrificed? She would need to be taught about sacrifice.

'Rain-makers like the Barotse have to make sufficient sacrifice,' she said, 'otherwise the seasons will become confused. We could all die.'

Bubi looked towards Julia again, wished her to be troubled by her words. She saw her edge closer to Pula, clutch his hand.

'Later you will make the real sacrifice. This time you need only find a young, living bird. You will stop it flying, sacrifice it.'

'Thank you,' Pula said, squeezing Julia's cold hand in his, hoping that Bubi did not notice.

'They showed one Msotho,' Bubi said, very quietly. 'Is there one in your life, white girl? One Msotho from the Mountain of

Night?'

'Potlako Lereng! He lives across the river.'

'So do the sitatunga and the letchwe and the tsetse. The spirits too, and stones. Now you must go, I do not like this thing.'

Bubi slipped the ten pula from beneath the portable radio, swung the aerial again so that it pointed in a different direction. She folded the note twice, then dropped it into her skin bag. Business complete, she shooed the young clients from her hut. She got up from the spot where she had consulted her bones, bent but determined. She pushed old fingers into the small of Julia's back, urging her out.

Pula turned at the low door, saw that she did not put the rough diamonds back into the pouch. These she popped into her mouth. She sucked them for a while.

4

On Friday afternoons Pula worked in the Shakawe Garage, where battered Land Rovers and other four-by-fours were repaired or overhauled. The foreman found that the eager schoolboy, working for pocket money, was very good with a panel-beating hammer. After only brief demonstration, the boy could shape old metal as if he were modeling. He seemed to respect the smooth curves which he was able to produce from twisted metal. He would reshape a fender, return it to its original form as if the damage which had been inflicted on it had been something of an affront to the original form. Even the square frame of a twisted window above a battered door was worth restoring, with this boy at work.

The shining surface of a machine-ground fender reflected the splashing sparks of a welding machine nearby and bits of hot metal rolled about the floor where Pula stood. There was little charm about the place to call for artistic attention from Pula with a hammer. He tapped lightly on the door panel of a Mitsubishi. His eager modeling echoed under the high tin roof of the work shop. He was absorbed in his repair work, in a studio of some kind.

At one end of the workshop, behind a rope protecting the space around it, was a most remarkable mechanical creature quite unlike the battered vehicles on which Pula worked. It was a metal bird of some kind, and only the foreman worked on it. Pula sometimes went up to the rope to stare in fascination at the unlikely micro-light with its huge wings, like those of an eagle above the swamp.

As Julia came into the workshop from the heat outside, she felt for a moment that she may be trespassing. She wanted to be with him, to talk to him, to tell Pula what her father had said about the tsetse. The fly was a scourge of Africa, like endemic violence, her father had said. For centuries man could not even travel along rivers nor walk through the bush because of the sleeping sickness. Portuguese people were the first to control the sickness, he said, but who would be the first to control the violence? The fly was one of those creatures that had to die if man was to live. That was the violent rule of things in the body: for the body to live the enemies in the blood of it had to be destroyed, but only the enemies, not the friends.

She stepped into the busy and untidy place where others were working too and the foreman noticed her. He looked up from his time-sheets on his desk in his little cubicle and he was not pleased. This bright-eyed white girl knew too much, she was only fifteen but she talked like a teacher. Even though one was tempted to imagine her firm breasts expanding beneath a white school blouse and to consider the strength of her maturing thighs, her eyes froze you. She was also too white for his liking.

Pula sensed Julia's presence and he turned to face her, the hammer in his hand. She quickly took the last few steps to be with him, her hand to her mouth in an effort to control her laughter under the glare of the foreman and the glances of other workers. Pula reached towards her to touch her outstretched fingers, the hammer awkward in one hand.

'It is so hot. Let's go down to the river!' Julia whispered urgently.

The foreman shouted at Pula to get on with his work. Pula swung his hammer and the impact on the battered metal had lost its charm. It was now like the gong at the start of a new shift. He beat rhythmically against the form on the other side of the dented metal, regular clicks of shaping. The foreman returned to his documents.

Julia caught the handle of the panel-beating hammer as it was lifted and she restrained Pula's working hand.

'I have something to say about the tsetse!'

'I get paid by the hour.'

'You are not supposed to work here. You are too young.'

'I like it. I need the money. You must wait until I am off.'

'Off?'

'Off time. It will be soon. Wait.'

Pula glanced towards the foreman's desk and his hand moved the hammer it held to continue with his work. Julia smiled at him, then put a straight finger to her lips in playful silence. The foreman could not see the gesture which reduced Pula's resolve, made him drop his hammer and take her arm.

'I will come, but you must wait!' he managed to say. 'Wait there, by the door.'

When Pula finally left the workshop to join the white girl waiting, the foreman called after him. He came out of his little cubicle shaking a piece of paper in the air, saying something about next Friday. Pula did not turn back but he and Julia hurried on down the rough road towards Namaseri Camp. Pula held Julia's hand and pulled her along. She laughed and followed.

When they came to the short wooden bridge, Pula marched across it and took the path along the tributary. He noticed that the water under the bridge was higher than usual.

'You shouldn't come in when I am working!' he said at last.

'Don't be silly, you are still at school.'

'I have to work. School will soon be over.'

Julia considered this new mood in Pula, something which seemed to separate them. He with a hammer in a hot workshop, she with idle time on her hands, looking for something to do.

'And when school is over I suppose you will work here every day? In the heat?'

'Maybe. Later I will buy hammers and moulds, a compressor even, set up my own shop.'

'What sort of shop?'

'A workshop, a body-beating shop. I like the work.'

He had seen most of the essential equipment in the Shakawe workshop and was familiar with the jacks and clamps and grinding machines of the trade. He knew the prices too. The compressor and paint sprays were very expensive, as much as a new outboard motor.

'I spoke to my father,' Julia said with some eagerness, hoping to return to more familiar ground, to bypass their little disagreement. 'He says the tsetse must die if people are to live. It is a simple as that.'

'I spoke to my father too. He agrees that the best thing to sacrifice would be a small bird. It should be easy to find a small bird.'

They walked past tall red ant-hills into thicker bush and Pula searched for birds' nests. He told Julia that he needed a bird which had not yet flown. In it was all the possibility of flying, all the potential power of flight. The young bird would be a living thing. He would sacrifice a small bird, perhaps carve an image of it so that it might be remembered. He would sacrifice the bird and keep its image, something from his own hand.

In one lonely baobab tree which was festooned with monkey-ropes, they saw a hamerkop's huge nest. They stood beneath the tree, in its shade. Pula sat down and from the deep pocket of his working overalls, he produced his knife as well as the carving of a heron. He had made the heron's neck very long and very thin. He began to shape the fine long throat of the bird. Julia stood beside him, puzzled, looking up at the untidy nest.

'Everything you carve seems to live.'

'It is not living.'

'But it is, it lives in the form you give it. A bird with a long neck.'

'There will be young birds in that nest. Birds that have never flown.'

'The nest looks such a mess.'

'The hamerkop likes it that way. Big and comfortable for his family.'

'Well, I don't like it. And I don't like raiding a nest. Any nest.'

'Something young has to be sacrificed.'

'But why? It is all so barbaric!'

'Many people believe in sacrifice, even human sacrifice.'

They both heard the bush rustle, they heard twigs crack. They both turned together and both saw the four Basotho boys emerge from the bush. They were from the refugee camp at Disheta. They were led by Potlako Lereng. There was a fifth man, trailing well behind the others. He was a big Zulu whom Pula had seen before, at Disheta. He carried a calabash and Pula knew that they had been collecting honey. The Basotho approached slowly and Julia saw the thin sword in Potlako's hand. It was made of a bicycle spoke, with strips from the skin of a sitatunga wound tightly round the end which he held. Potlako had made her hold it once, forced her to take it in her hand. He had explained in awful detail how it was used. He had told her to watch carefully as he thrust the point into the base of a monkey-apple, slipping it easily into the soft flesh of the rump of the apple as if into the base of an animal spine. She knew that Kalanga cattle had died by such a weapon. They folded at their knees from one thrust under the tail, into the spine. It was an evil cattle-killing weapon, in evil hands.

Potlako Lereng was always trying to touch her. He was already a man. Julia felt a sudden vulnerability, as if she were naked beneath a baobab tree. Pula stood beside her, clutching his small knife.

Potlako came up to Julia and held out his hand. Two copper bangles on his right wrist clicked together. Julia remembered now that he always wore those bangles. She had once been made to touch them on his wrist. He had told her that they were very old. He had thrust them at her, they had clicked, just as they clicked now. They were carved crocodiles, mouths devouring tails. The crocodiles were fat, full of devoured flesh, Potlako had told her. In the circles was the devil's own order. Now she stared at the creatures which were thrust at her.

Potlako's friends watched and smiled as Julia moved her hands behind her back, clasped them together, out of the way.

'Let's be friends,' Potlako said, stepping closer.

Julia took one step back and Pula one step forward.

'Leave her alone!' he said.

Slowly, very slowly, Potlako Lereng turned his attention away from Julia to the Mbukushu nuisance. He saw the small knife in Pula's hand and noticed how the hand shook. He nodded, just a brief dip of the head, and his colleagues attacked Pula, wrestled him to the ground. The big Zulu took the knife from him. They all laughed then, the Zulu too. He grabbed Pula's carving. He held it in one hand and with the knife in the other he cut off the bird's head. He snapped the remains in half and threw the pieces up into the hamerkop's nest.

Julia was on to him like a leopard, claws out. The Zulu was taken completely by surprise, he dropped Pula's knife into the grass, lashed out with his fists, caught Julia low in the stomach. She crumpled to the ground. At once he dropped down beside her, almost apologetic.

Potlako merely smiled and he told one of his tribe to hold Julia's arms, the other her legs. He told them to pull her open from her doubled-up position so that she was spread out and he could look at her, open on the ground. The three boys all laughed again, one came to help hold Julia, one tightened his grip on Pula's neck. Their laughter was nervous and excited. Stimulated by the sudden violence, they felt the pleasure deeply, fun with the gang.

Potlako stood above Julia and stretched out a foot to touch her crotch with his toe. He tapped lightly through the cloth of her disordered dress.

'Get away from her,' he said to the Zulu, 'she is mine.'

Potlako pointed the thin sword at the Zulu's chest. The copper crocodiles clicked, the point of the rapier flicked like the tongue of a serpent. The Zulu moved away. Potlako turned back to Julia on the ground, thrust his thin sword firmly into the ground beside her. The rapier swayed from side to side, fixed to the earth by its sharp point, nodding to the action. Slowly Potlako removed his shirt, dropped it on the handle of his waving sword. He wagged a finger at Julia on the ground, expanded his chest, displayed his mountain muscle. He spoke like a scolding teacher, addressing both his gang and his captors. His voice was tight, he hissed in his excitement for the punishment to come.

'I will teach you about *diretlo*,' he said. 'I will tell you how a victim is chosen for her fine flesh, how bits of it are cut away while she is still alive, how her blood is collected in a bottle. I will teach you a mountain ritual.'

His friends laughed again but the Zulu was silent.

'I think Bubi must have offered you to me as a sacrifice,' Potlako said playfully. 'I must do what I have to do, properly, slowly. First let me feel you.'

He leaned down and touched her face, held one ear-lobe between thumb and forefinger.

'This piece must be cut away with some skin of the throat, a small flap of it so that the ear can be folded in it, presented to Bubi. She will know all about the power of it. She was also born in the mountains.'

He touched her lips.

'Such soft lips. These lips must be carefully cut from you before you are dead, dried in the sun, crushed with blood, made into good medicine.'

'Potlako!' Julia hissed coldly, with brave appeal to reason in her quavering voice, as if to calm a violent child, as if she knew that even children's games could get out of control. 'Enough! That is quite enough for now.'

'Enough!' the Zulu shouted in a booming bull of a voice, pushing Potlako away with a big hand. In his other hand he held a carved weapon, a figurine of wood. He raised the piece of hardwood as if to strike at his leader.

Potlako stepped back involuntarily, stunned by the sudden disobedience of one of his gang. He glared at the Zulu, deeply resenting this rebellion, this confrontation, this spoiling of his fun.

Pula could feel the black arm around his neck loosen slightly and he saw the Zulu raise the weapon which he at once recognised as his lost god-model. Julia's spirit and her calm words, his elation on seeing the symbol which he had been carving for her, the one he had lost to the river, somehow broke the spell of the tribe's dominance. Pula bit the black arm that squeezed his neck. He reached for his knife in the grass, slashed once at the Msotho's fingers which also reached for it. A line of blood rose quickly on the back of a black hand which was lifted away in sudden surprise. Pula sprang towards Potlako with the knife held straight.

The two boys holding Julia let her go and moved to protect their leader. One knocked over the ritual rapier, the shirt fell from it. Potlako turned to defend himself. The tableau was frozen there in the bush. The weapon had fallen beside Julia. She reached for it.

Julia felt the smooth hair of the sitatunga skin once again. She lifted the evil rapier in one shivering hand, saw its sharpened end flash like hope. She pointed it at Potlako's chest, holding the momentary advantage, trying to stay with reason.

'You once showed me how to use it. We are only playing games, aren't we Potlako?'

They all heard two clear shots from the bush nearby. Several guineafowl rose in a flurry from the grass, soared above them, making for cover. Potlako's friends turned away at once, ran to hide in the bush, leaving him with the Zulu. Standing next to the Zulu he smiled at Julia, held out his hand again.

'It is only a hunter,' he said, 'playing his own game.'

The hunter appeared along the path which led to the ant-hill. Two dogs trotted at his heels. He had one guineafowl hanging from his belt. He walked with his shot-gun held ready. He was a black man, from nearby Namaseri, and he raised a big black hand to the children at play.

'*Dumela Ra.* You should all get on home. The water is rising fast,' he said.

'They have settled again,' Potlako told the evening hunter in a secretive voice, a hoarse whisper. He picked up his shirt, took two easy steps towards the hunter. 'At this time they do not like to run, be ready when they rise at your feet!' he warned.

The hunter stopped near the ant-hill, the dogs nervous at his heels. Potlako pointed along the bush path. Julia held the thin weapon behind her back, smiled at the black hunter. Pula lowered his small knife. The hunter merely raised a hand to his forehead once again, moved forward along the path hoping for birds to rise at his feet, just as the young man had said. Pula, Julia, Potlako Lereng and the Zulu, watched the hunter step carefully along the path and away into the bush.

As soon as the hunter's back was turned, Potlako ripped his rapier from Julia's hand, faced Pula. He called to his friends. They at once re-appeared out of the bush, sprang into action. Two grabbed Julia. On Potlako's instruction one ran to the baobab tree, pulled lengths of monkey-rope from it, cut them free with a bush knife.

'We will finish our little game!' Potlako said to Julia, flicking his rapier like a swordsman at practice. He touched Julia's white throat with it, fencing a victorious end game, demanded that Pula throw down his small knife.

When Pula had dropped his knife, Potlako pointed his sword at the big Zulu's chest, touched his flesh. The crocodile bangles clicked.

'*Diretlo*,' he said, 'I will cut *diretlo* from a Zulu!'

'You are only a crazy Sotho from the mountains!' the Zulu replied, stepping closer. He jabbed the wooden figurine into Potlako's chest, hard, ignoring the steel weapon which the Msotho held.

'Enough. I have had enough of your madness.'

He jabbed once more, the old side up, then simply walked away.

Potlako screamed at his other friends to tie up the girl and to tie up Pula.

With the monkey-ropes, the boys bound Pula and Julia to the ant-hill, running in frantic circles around the termite pyre. Using the copious creepers of the bush, they wrapped their prisoners in leafy bonds to a sacrificial beacon. Potlako Lereng came to Julia, touched her again. He picked up the forgotten calabash, scooped honey with big fingers, offered it to her.

'So sweet!' he said.

He heard the Zulu call loudly to him, from way down the bush path. Another shot rang out from the bush, further away this time. Other birds rose into the sky.

Potlako dipped his hand into the calabash, raised the dripping mass to Julia's eyes and then spread the honey over her hair. She shook her head in useless resistance, and the honey spread to her forehead, over her ears. He stroked her shaking head with more honey, then he kicked the ant-hill so that the crust was broken. The disturbed residents hurried out to repair the damage or taste the honey. Laughing, the gang left their prisoners to struggle inside the rough web of primitive bonds.

The Zulu shouted again, a command this time. Potlako licked honey from his fingers as he departed.

Julia was the first to speak in the shocked silence of the bush after the departure of the gang. Her voice came from the other side of the ant-hill and Pula felt the binding creepers move as she called out to him.

'The honey is running all over my face! The ants are biting me!'

Pula did not respond at once but he tested his bonds. Long ago the Sarwa left their old to die on an ant-hill. Hyenas would eat them, even ants. Would the ants eat the sweet flesh of Julia beneath the honey? He moved his arms again, took a deep breath and expanded his chest, pressing outwards as hard as he could. Some of the creepers moved but he was still in their tangled grip.

His one hand was free enough to ease into the pocket where he always kept his knife. Of course it was not there. He recalled his own useless thrusts at Potlako, the mocking laughter. He saw the knife in the grass where he had dropped it. He squirmed and struggled. Were they to be sacrificed too, he and Julia together?

'There is a tsetse on my leg!' Julia screamed.

'Kill it!'

'I can't. It is biting me!'

Pula's feet moved against the ant-hill and he felt part of the crust crack just as it had under Potlako's boot. He moved his heels vigorously and the labyrinth of black holes beneath them began to crumble. He kept digging, exhilarated, digging with his heels, pounding at the surface of the termites' nest so that they hurried out into the light of danger, scurried out to mend the damage to their home. They found his leg and began to crawl over it. Pula beat at the crust with his fists too, moving them as much as he could beneath his primitive bonds. In one place the crust gave in and soon his hands were free. They sank into the holes they had made.

As his work loosened his bindings, he knew that he would succeed. Potlako's primitive prison was nothing! Pula felt a lift of the spirit as if he was about to fly. He saw a flock of carmine bee-eaters swoop down towards him as if to land on the ant-hill to which he was tied and from which he would soon be free. What were such beautiful beings doing here, they should be flying home?

The carmine bee-eaters did not land on the ant-hill but swept away to settle on the hamerkop's baobab tree. They sat still after their beautiful flight, so neat in a line, so brilliant in the evening light, true to their own order. Pula took them to be messengers of some kind which had come to free him. They were his intimate friends, these brilliant birds who liked to nest near water, they would be the agent of his escape from any bondage. Like his god-model, the one which the Zulu must have found on the river bank, they were hope.

The carmine bee-eaters lifted off again, together, when Julia screamed from the other side of the ant-hill.

'The tsetse is still there! It is drinking my blood!'

5

Pula was the first to release himself from his primitive bonds. He hurried to Julia to rip the creepers from her. The sun was about to set, little was left of the day. The carmine bee-eaters were no longer watching. Together they returned along the path towards the village, back to the short bridge over the tributary. Julia swept her hair back with an anxious hand as they hurried along, examined the sticky honey on her palm. She would wash below the bridge, wash away the memory of Potlako and the thin sword.

They heard the water before they reached the place where the bridge had been. The sound was too loud, an angry roar. At their feet, below a crumbling bank, the floodwater rushed wildly. Stark timbers jutted out from the opposite bank, vibrating, shivering in the current. Pula turned back, pulling on Julia's hand, urging her away from the edge.

'We will never get across that. We must find a *mokoro*,' he said. Julia followed, alarmed by Pula's urgency, by the rising water and the coming night. Flies stuck to the sweetness on her forehead and she longed to wash. She pulled grass from a tuft on the edge of the path and tried to wipe away the remains of the honey.

Pula hurried back past the ant-hill, along the game path which the hunter had followed. He made for the next bend in the tributary, towards a small creek where a fisherman sometimes kept his *mokoro* hidden in the reeds.

The creek was wider than he expected it to be but the *mokoro* was there, riding high. He helped Julia into the narrow craft and sat her down on a bundled fishing-net. She dipped her hand into the water to scoop some to her forehead.

Pula poled out into the stream, pointing the *mokoro* against the current, keeping close to the bank. The *mokoro* slid quietly past moving reeds, towards Mohembo and the border, upstream.

'We must go against the water,' he said. 'This all comes from the mainstream, from Angola.'

Pula knew where the carmine bee-eaters nested, in the red cliffs near the old transit camp on the island at Dichaube, not far from one of his father's fields, a *mosimu*, one which was flooded each year. Perhaps it was flooded already. If the mainstream was too strong to risk at night, he would make for the island. There they could wait in one of the abandoned huts, float back with the stream in the morning, with the morning light. He had no wish to meet the new flood in the dark.

Julia sat on the tangled fishing-net, bent forward, her head in her hands now, still feeling the glue gunge of honey which she could not wash away entirely. She tried to wish away the approaching night, thinking of the hunter and his dogs. Why had she not gone with him, away from the madness in the bush? She could still feel Potlako's finger on her lips, drawing its outline, talking of cutting flesh, of blood in a bottle. She also sensed Potlako's deadly rapier in her hand, could still see the sharp point of it, the point that would slip easily into any body, the body of a cow or the body of a man. Like the piercing proboscis of the tsetse, it could slip easily into any body.

She took her hands away from her eyes, shook her head, wiped away tears and felt the honey stick to her like memory. She looked at her hands as if they still held a sword, turned them over to examine the change in them. There was no blood on them as there might have been, only some honey and green streaks from the grass. These were on her dress too, she noticed, turning to one side. She smoothed the denim of her skirt, held her torn blouse close, felt a deep pain in her being as if someone had tried to rip her soul from her, show it to her as an organ of her body. This is you, white rubbish. With gentle fingers she touched the tsetse bite on her leg.

Then she put her hands together, as if she held the sword again. She looked at her hands in wonder: could she have used that thin weapon on Potlako? She lifted her eyes to Pula as he guided the *mokoro* along the reeds. He was working hard against the stream as if running away, uphill.

'Where are you taking me?' Julia asked from her perch on the Mbukushu net.

'To a place I know, upstream.'

'I must go home.'

'The only way home is by the main river, but at night we could be swept away, right down to Chief's Island.'

Pula continued to urge the *mokoro* along the bank of the river, glancing at his passenger each time he thrust with the long pole. He was calmed somehow by the action of moving against the rising water. He knew that he was doing the right thing, that he should stay upstream. He had not seen the transit camp on the island near Dichaube since the days when the miners came down from Angola, but he would find it. He would recognise the inlet which led to his father's field.

As he approached another inlet, where he and his father often fished for bream, he let the long pole drag in the water. Using it as a rudder, he guided the *mokoro* into the mouth of the inlet. He could stop here for a short while, talk to Julia. He would explain to her why he must head upstream, why he could not risk the turn, challenge the power of the deep river.

The *mokoro* glided quietly over green reeds. Water-lilies, which once covered the sheltered inlet like a carpet, now waved beneath the surface of the rising water, sunken ghosts. Pula laid the long pole carefully in the bottom of the *mokoro* and, with both hands on the thin wooden gunwales, he shuffled to the stern to comfort Julia. With the shift of weight the bow of the *mokoro* rose and water slopped over the stern. Pula sat back at once, steadying the flimsy craft.

'See how high the water is. We must wait somewhere. We must wait for light.'

'I want to go home.'

'I know a place where we can wait.'

'Can't we just float with the stream?'

'Maybe tomorrow. At night it is too dangerous, too many things floating in the dark. There is an old hut on an island near Dichaube, where miners from Angola used to rest. We can go there.'

'And do what?'

'Wait until morning. I will make a fire, get you some food.'

They both heard the sound of an aeroplane and they both looked towards Shakawe and the airfield. Soon the huge aircraft appeared as a moving shadow above the bushes, still climbing after take-off, wing-tip lights blinking. It passed directly above them, a grand silhouette against the fading light of the sky. They both watched the shadow and flickers of another world as they sat above the water-lilies in the fisherman's *mokoro*. The landing gear of the aircraft was still rising into dark holes in the wings. One locked later than the other and then the pilot and the day were gone.

The noise of the departed aircraft still roared in Pula's ears, like the noise of an outboard, mocking him. It angered him to be so useless with his long pole. Why should he be caught in the swamp with no kind of power?

Pula lifted the long pole again and thrust it down to ease the *mokoro* away from the rising water-lilies, now buoyed after sudden flood. He pointed the bow into the mainstream again, saw how the papyrus bent towards him, green stems waving like grass in a wind.

'It will be rough on the river tonight. There will be logs and papyrus islands moving.' Pula said.

'I would like to be in that aeroplane.'

'For now, you do not have the choice.'

There was an edge of annoyance in Pula's voice and Julia was reminded of the big Zulu. She shivered a little, imagined the sword again, Pula's small knife.

'What is *diretlo*?' she asked, quietly.

'You should never have heard the word.'

'Potlako said it to me and to the big Zulu. *Diretlo*! he said, as if it were a curse.'

'It is the flesh. It is a piece of a chosen victim, and the blood too. All *diretlo*. Something from the past.'

'Bubi is a *feitiçeira*. Would she know about it?'

'She would know. She saw it in the bones.'

Julia shuddered again. She felt a chill rise from the river, felt that they would be lost forever in the huge expanse of the living swamp. They were so close to Shakawe, so near the airfield, yet at the mercy of the swamp. She looked up into the sky, to the last light of the day.

From the level of the rising water the palm trees on each bank of the river still stood out in stark silhouette, retina images after the flash of the sunset. Julia closed her eyes for a dark moment, then looked ahead to the reflections on the water. The tiny waves from the bow of the moving *mokoro* caught the deep red of the darkening sky and played with it. Above her, making for the horizon, a final flock of open-billed storks flew towards Caprivi and their nesting place. Pula waved to the high birds, opened his mouth in an imbecilic grin, imitating the black storks which were so much part of his swamp. He could clearly see the open slits in the pointed heads of flying birds, as if they were swallowing evening stars. The whole flock was laughing.

'They are laughing,' he said to Julia.

'At us?'

After the flight of storks, vees of geese passed above them, and then white egrets flying low. These settled on a solitary tree on the opposite bank of the river and they set up a great noise as they fought for places on their traditional perch.

'It is not far now,' Pula told her, pointing to the silhouette of the tree which held the egrets. 'You will see that tree from the old camp.'

The flat line of the river bank rose to a red promontory in which there were the dark dots of nest-holes. Above the promontory a cloud of birds gathered like bats disturbed, growing more excited as the *mokoro* approached. Pula worked the *mokoro* close to the bank, beneath the swarm of carmine bee-eaters. Their perfect flying forms flickered in the twilight, a scintillating ceiling of colourful life from which came an excited twittering, a communal chatter. As the *mokoro* took them closer, Pula and Julia could see birds making for the holes in the red cliff, disappearing for a moment only to turn and fly out again to join the excitement. Outside each nest was a clear landing pad, ridged by the tiny feet of frequent entry and departure. Julia followed the flight of one bird, saw it rise above her, then swoop towards home. She lost it in the flurry of others, thought she saw it rise again, high above the main flock, making for the sky. It turned in jubilant flight, a carmine star of the evening.

'They work magic, those birds,' Pula said.

They passed under the cloud of birds and once the *mokoro* was beyond the brilliant ceiling, the water seemed to suck them into a hidden inlet in the red cliff. Pula guided the *mokoro* into the narrow channel. Behind the low hill, the water was quite still. The channel opened out and Julia could see an old wooden jetty at the end of the inlet. The birds were now left behind, they had settled in their holes. Here, more water-lilies grew and a green slime on the surface of the trapped water seemed undisturbed. Streaks of the slime stuck to the sides of the *mokoro* as Pula brought it towards the old jetty.

As they approached the jetty they could see that the inlet was larger than it had first appeared to be. It was in reality a curve of an old river course, cut off from the force of the main stream, but fed beneath the papyrus. The jetty stuck out from a hidden island and the still water had risen to flood its timbers.

'The miners used to wait here. They came from Calai in Angola and waited to be taken to Maun. It is a good place to wait.'

'Where were they going?'

'To South Africa to earn some money.'

'There was a war in Angola. Perhaps they were running away from the war.'

Pula brought the *mokoro* to the old jetty. Reaching out with the long pole, he pulled the craft closer. A plank crumbled under the pressure of the pole and Pula stumbled in the *mokoro*, nearly fell.

'It has not been used for a long time. We must be very careful,' he said, recovering himself.

'It will soon be pitch dark.'

'I will get a fire going for you. Soon I will bring you grilled fish for supper.'

Pula stepped to a more solid plank of the jetty, tested its strength, reached out a hand to help Julia alight. When she was on the firm earth of the island she looked beyond the low jetty for the first time. The earth rose to a smooth mound where two tall trees grew, dark shadows. Under the two trees was a small mud hut, with a thatched roof which seemed to shine in the late evening. Dark reeds grew around the hut, even in the walls. Creepers and vines had entered the thatch from the bush. What was once a path from the jetty to the hut was now a line of dark green weeds, more dense than the surrounding grass. Against the tallest tree, a gnarled and eternal fig-tree, leaned a simple ladder, firm in its outline.

Julia stopped near the hut and turned to Pula in sudden alarm. In the doorway of the hut was a short spear, its blade embedded in the earthen floor.

Pula hurried past her, pulled the spear from the ground.

'It will be useful,' he said. 'I will cut a reed mattress for you. It will be a warm night.'

'Your knife? Did you keep your knife?'

'I picked it up from the grass.'

'Why a spear? Who stuck it there, in the floor?'

At first there was no moon. Julia sat on a log while Pula worked with a piece of *moselesele*, rubbing it rapidly in his palms, pressing into a dry log held between his knees. Smoke began to rise from the hole he was boring. He told Julia to place slivers of dry reed and blades of dry grass into the wisp of smoke. He had a small pile at his knees and Julia took pieces from the pile and set them against the moving stick. She was deeply conscious of the growing darkness around her. She shouted out when she saw a tiny red glow at the base of the rising smoke.

'It is working!'

Pula blew gently, his pouted lips close to the red spot. The tiny glow became a flame in what seemed to Julia to be a very bright flash, a miracle of light in darkness. She fed the flash with dry grass. Now she could feel the warmth of the growing flame and her confidence in Pula began to return.

He seemed to be perfectly calm in all he did, confident, slowly arranging larger dry sticks in a pyramid above the first flames. He then collected dry papyrus and bound the fronds together to make a long torch.

He came to Julia to help her to her feet. From the fire he lit the tip of the torch. Julia rose at once, the flame light flickering before her eyes. She could not fully understand her acquiescence to his purpose, but knew that for this night she was in his care. She took his hand, followed him along the path now lit up by the flare and went with him to the water's edge.

At first the flickering light was behind her and she could see her shadow on the water. Then Pula lowered the long flare which he held under his arm, pointing down. The flames rose as he moved the torch above the water. He stepped into the shimmering ring of light, leaving Julia in the dark on the bank.

Pula held the rusted spear in one hand, the long reed flare in the other. He swept the flames slowly over the water, standing still in one place, like a marabou stork. Julia could even see the shining bulbs on the stalks which tried to lift the lilies to their rightful place, flat and still on the surface of the water. The floats reflected the light of the flare.

Then, incredibly, she saw a fish move beneath a leaf. It moved out very slowly as if quite unaware of danger. Julia saw the splash of the spear and Pula let out a wild shout, flinging the bream onto the bank at her feet.

After supper they lay on the reed beds which Pula had prepared on opposite sides of the small fire, because Julia would not enter the hut. They lay with their feet near the central warmth, their heads in darkness, two opposite spokes in a wheel of chance. They spoke quietly to one another across the dying flames. Pula tried to comfort Julia, talked about creatures of the swamp sleeping around them, hushed her to listen to the song of a night-jar, the tinking rhythm of an anvil-bat.

Pula looked up at the stars and wondered when the dark clouds would come, when it would rain on the river. He again told Julia that all the water which now rushed downstream came from another country, from the mountains of Angola.

Above them the sky was crystal clear, the storm was yet to come. Pula thought of his father at home and wondered about the other Basotho back at the refugee camp. Did they also talk of *diretlo*?

'There are too many men like Potlako Lereng,' Pula said to Julia. 'They puff up their chests but they are cowards.'

'Those bangles! The crocodiles! His own *feitiço*.'

'He is a coward.'

'Do you remember, at my party?'

Pula considered that fight, and he thought of the stories of war between the Kololo and the Aluyi, the history of his ancestors, all the Barotse, the Balozi. When he thought of his ancestors, he asked them to protect him from men like Potlako Lereng, to look kindly on his actions of the day, to calm the waters, hold the flood for a while. He asked his own gods to accept that he had done a justifiable thing. The bridge was down, the water was rising, the day had run out on him. He asked them to bless the two of them on an island and to make sure that the swamp survived, that it was not flooded by storms, or drained away by anyone. Even by scientists and engineers. He asked them to accept the sacrifice which he yet had to make and he considered again what he should sacrifice; a small bird did not now seem to be sufficient.

The final sacrifice any man could make was of himself. He could die in a war, so many died in wars. So many joined small armies to fight for their land and their language, so many died. That was once the way to glory but now there was no glory.

'I fought for you, at your party.'

'He is still there. You will have to fight him again.'

'The Zulu was on our side. Did you see the weapon he held?'

'It looked like a heavy doll.'

'It was the one I lost, in the river. It was for you. He must have found it on the river bank.'

'The god-model?'

'I was making it for you.'

Pula rose slowly from his place by the fire and came to lie beside Julia. He did not ask her permission but he lay close to her and pulled her to him with his one strong arm over her shoulders. Then he kissed her on the forehead as she lay there, lightly, like a respectful elder brother. Julia was inordinately disturbed by the sudden crossing of the distance between them, and she felt her heart leap from the single kiss and what it might yet mean. She felt, once again, Pula's natural control over her in this circumstance, her own dependence upon him and upon his knowledge of the swamp and of their predicament. She did not like the dependence; she was vividly reminded of Potlako and his bangles, of the thin sword. The heart leap from a single kiss was terribly confusing. What would she do if Pula persisted, if he simply took over, took her, what point would there be in struggling, here on an island in the Okavango?

'You should stay on your side of the fire,' Julia said, pressing on his shoulder with straightened fingers. He bent down again, kissed her again, touching her lips with his.

'Good night,' he said, 'sleep well.'

He left her then, settled down once again, on his side of the fire. He was also disturbed by the leap of expectation which had made his body quiver when he touched her with his lips. He lay on his back looking up at the stars through the branches above him. Lusty images of flesh churned through him, he was tempted to rise and demand, felt the same stirring, considered the insects locked together in the papyrus. He saw the jaws working, devouring a little god.

From the other side of the fire, he asked Julia about her mother. He had never met her mother.

'You are always with your father. Where is your mother?' he asked.

'They separated.'

'How do you mean?'

'My father and my mother separated. They could no longer live together.'

'Just like that?'

'Yes. Just like that.'

'Do your three gods accept such things?'

Julia turned over on her primitive bed, disturbed by his questioning, yet glad to have the calm voice reach her from the other side of the fire. It was as if he lay there protecting her. His was a friendly presence on a dark night.

'Sometimes it just does not work. And your mother? Where is your mother?'

'I thought you knew all about her, about *mugrodis*, about rain-mothers?'

'I have heard of the *feitiçeira*, of the witches in the bush.'

'Just like that? They are just witches, the *mugrodis*?'

Julia could not reply. Pula's voice sounded less friendly now. Her use of the word in her own language now seemed to have been an insult, an unkindness which she had not meant.

'I do not believe that any woman can produce a child for sacrifice.'

'Even for rain?'

'Even for rain. The thought appals me. I feel sick.'

'Your God would not accept such a thing?'

Julia closed her eyes to sleep. She saw Bubi with her bones, she saw her with a knife in her hand. She opened her eyes again. She could see in the flickering light of the fire, the point of Pula's elbow above his eyes as he lay on his back, opposite her. A burning stick crackled from the fire, spreading tiny sparks. Julia looked beyond the leaves of the trees above her to patches of starlit sky. She thought of space and eternity, of some god up there who would be watching her in her discomfort. Her heart had not yet stilled, she was disturbed as if by new messages.

Perhaps this was the real church, out here on the ground where she could look straight up and see her own God more clearly. She wanted to believe, here in the real church, but she had so many questions. Why had she felt so close to Pula when he had touched her? They were alone in this real church and yet so far apart. Why had she pushed him away so quickly? What did she really want? Would Potlako Lereng take her one day, like a bull? Why had the Zulu come between them? Would they both become *diretlo*, she and the Zulu together?

Potlako would kill the Zulu, he would also kill her, cut her into little pieces, collect her blood in a bottle. She could sense her heartbeat in her temples, considered blood flowing.

Surely God never really supported that, the use of flesh, even the eating of it and the drinking of blood? Potlako was a coward, Pula had said. He must spread fear. It is done to terrorise, it is done for power. He must have some secret ritual which will ensure that everyone will be afraid of him, terrified enough to obey, to lie down, to be ravished. God had no need to spread fear, no need to frighten, no need for blood and flesh. Was it only His church which preserved the ritual, like Bubi in a hut?

The flood would come, Julia knew. The water would sink away into the sand. There was only sand, all the way from here to the Boteti River at Maun, all the way to the Tsodilo Hills and beyond, there was only sand. It absorbed all the water of a huge river, as easily as the sea. Sometimes the sand had diamonds in it. Or at least the rock which was under the sand had diamonds in it. That was the real world, the world of order and real diamonds, not this frightening world of the flesh. The real world was the voice of teachers.

Miss Julia Pinto, tell these stupid boys about the first white man to paint pictures of our people. Not a bushman painting in the hills but a white man, who was the first white man? And how much older are the paintings of the Sarwa? And who was mauled by a lion when he was staying at Kgatla, Miss Pinto? And who did he marry?

Livingstone was a doctor like my father, he married the daughter of Robert Moffat who first recorded the grammar of the Tswana language, Mr Sechele. A wife can be a great comfort if you live in the bush, Mr Sechele. He and Moffat used to work together. My father says that they both dealt in faith. Livingstone was a doctor and a scientist, a practical man, hoping to heal. Moffat sought to save men's souls. They were in the same game, the one tending the flesh, the other the soul. My father says that flesh and souls often go together, Mr Sechele.

Maybe Livingstone kept working with Moffat because of the daughter; he waited to marry her. He saw in her both flesh and soul, so he waited.

6

Just how many birds unseen at night can rest in one fig tree, in *Ficus Africanus*?

'A million,' Julia whispered to herself as she lay awake on her reed mattress, looking up at the dawn light through the branches of the big tree above her. The birds had woken her, queleas mostly, but also mossies and doves and a few tiny white-eyes. Julia could see the white-eyes watching through close foliage. It was such a peaceful awakening, such a peaceful sound from the tree. Julia stretched, sat up. She saw that Pula was not lying opposite her, he was not in the place where he had slept, on the opposite side of the fire.

She sprang to her feet, recalling the past day, suddenly remembering the rising water. She saw the spear standing in the ground near the charred reeds of last night's torch. She hurried down the green path to the water's edge. The *mokoro* had gone.

The water had spread way beyond the old jetty. She saw a loose plank of the jetty floating amongst the reeds and she saw a brightly coloured dragon-fly hover above the plank, then land on it, wings shimmering in the morning sun. The beauty of it was like a warning, a whispered reminder of danger. She felt a twinge in her bladder, an urgent need.

She squatted in the grass, away from the jetty, hidden by the reeds. She noticed that the sand beneath her was as white as sea sand, washed by the river, that the water was creeping through the grass, running over dry sand in encroaching rivulets. The island itself would be covered, only the big tree would stand out from a big lake! She would have to climb into it, join the millions of birds. She looked down at the foamy trickle of her own water, saw it seep away into the sand. The diamond sand.

As she stood up and straightened her skirt, she saw Pula approaching in the *mokoro*. He was coming straight towards her through the papyrus, which was now covered almost to the first tassels. The island was smaller now. As he approached he reached into the bottom of the *mokoro*, held up a bunch of fish threaded to a length of papyrus.

'Breakfast!' he called. 'With duck's eggs.'

He leapt from the *mokoro* on to the island, proudly presented his catch to Julia, showed her four eggs in a crude papyrus basket. The long pole lay inside the *mokoro*.

Julia ran to him, shouting his name as if he had done something dreadfully wrong, as if she were a mother or a teacher or an aunt, scolding.

'Where have you been?' she demanded.

'Fetching breakfast. You were so fast asleep.'

'You should have woken me! Told me where you were going!'

'But why? You do not know about nets, where to place them in the early morning.'

Pula built up the fire again, looked for some utensil for the eggs, told Julia to look inside the hut. 'We should eat, then go,' he said, 'The current is very strong in the mainstream.'

Inside the hut in which she would not sleep, on top of the mud wall, below the thatch, Julia found some bits of cardboard, old identity cards with names on them. There also a faded paperback with a red cover, a metal badge. On the floor she found a rusty billycan, a reed mat. She gathered the badge, the billycan and the little red book and hurried out of the hut. She took these things back to Pula by the fire.

'What sort of people lived in that terrible place?' she asked as she shook dust out of the billycan, picked away dry leaves that clung to the bottom of it. 'I found a schoolbook for you, and a medal.'

'We can use the billycan.'

'The miner's companion,' Julia read, beating the little book against the palm of her hand.

'What does it say to a miner?' Pula asked.

While Pula prepared breakfast Julia read from the little red book, which was really a dictionary, a simple miner's dictionary. She read with heavy ridicule in her voice, a school teacher again.

'Did you catch *sikisi* fish, or only *fayif*?'

'It is Fanakalo, the miners' language.'

'Air: *Ntambo ka lo smok, tonel ka lo moya* – the rope of the smoke, and the tunnel of the air! There are three pages of A's.'

'They had to learn the language. Air is important underground.'

With a teasing smile Julia flipped through the faded pages, provoking more defence from Pula, as if this were his language too.

'*Skul!* S - K - U - L,' she read. 'Had none of them been to school?'

'The food is ready. We must eat and go.'

Julia flipped a few more pages, held the book out to point to the word for food.

'*Skof*,' she said, scoffing.

'Look up "danger". That is a word the miners soon learn.'

Julia turned a few more pages, mumbled a few strange words, came to the letter 'd'.

'Dagga, dagger, dam, damage, dance, danger!' she recited. '*Ngozi!*'

She closed the little red book with a flourish. She put it down by her side, took the food which Pula offered on the leaf of a water-lily. The bream was crisp and brown, an egg broken on top of it, a yellow dressing. He passed her a delicate two-pronged fork, and a sharp sliver of *moselesele* for a knife.

'When did you make these?' Julia asked.

'Julia Pinto cannot eat without a knife and a fork.'

'It looks delicious.'

Pula picked up the little red book which lay at Julia's side. He also flipped casually through the worn pages, fingered by grown men eager to learn.

'This language is spoken underground, even in the diamond mines. It is the language of work in Africa,' he said.

He picked up the metal badge by the safety pin welded to one side of it, turned it over.

'For bravery,' he read. He passed the medal to Julia, then looked up another word in the small dictionary. It was a word from Zulu originally, now used by all Africa, even Batswana and Hambukushu used it. He looked under 'A' after the fold, where Fanakalo words were translated into English. '*Amandla*,' he read, 'Power'.

'The word for "power" is "*amandla*",' he said.

'You people are always shouting it.'

Her voice was provocative, as if the words of the working language were something playful, little children's toys. To Julia the awkward words reflected only the pathetic noises of the inarticulate, they were really too ridiculous to be spoken by a teenager. Pula noticed the tone, reacted to it with rising anger. He was offended by the distance of 'you people', the presumed supremacy, the scorn of a primitive language. The mechanics in the garage used phrases of the language, phrases like '*fanakalo*' itself, 'like this'. You hold the panel-beating hammer, *fanakalo*. You must tip the grinding wheel at an angle, *fanakalo*.

'You should not laugh about Africa,' he said.

Pula still crouched near the fire, removed a piece of fish in his fingers. He lifted it to his lips. He nodded as he ate it, savoured it, savoured the sweetness while something nagged at his senses, some foreboding, some concern about the sharpness of Julia's voice, her vulnerability mixed with her arrogance. Why should he listen to her?

'Are you ready?' he asked.

'I look forward to a hot bath,' Julia said, licking bits of fish from her lily. She moved her feet, scuffed some sand on to the ashes of the fire. 'If you are ready, I am,' she said.

Pula sprang to his feet in sudden alarm, ran down to the water's edge, splashed through the now flooded grass.

The *mokoro* had gone. It must have been lifted out of its reed trap by the rising water, sucked out to join the mainstream.

In his excitement to bring breakfast to Julia, he had merely pushed the craft into the reeds, and had not secured it. He had left the long pole lying inside it. He cursed this lapse of discipline, silently blamed Julia, but hurried back to her.

'We must use the slide!' he told her with new urgency.

'The slide?'

'A slide across water. A miners' thing, something they made long ago. We must use it at once, leave this island.'

'The *mokoro*? What about the *mokoro*?'

'The road is perhaps two miles away on the other side. There are other huts there, away from the island, on higher ground. The Angolans used those huts too, when the water was high.'

Pula hurried her towards the simple ladder against the big tree and instructed her to climb it.

She hesitated, not yet aware of the depth of his concern, now that they were surrounded by water, but without the *mokoro*.

'Julia!' he urged. 'Move!'

The ladder took her to the open bowl of the huge tree. Birds scattered out of branches, flicking into open air. Above the open bowl, short lengths of rough wood were nailed to the main trunk of the tree to take her higher, to the next fork and to a small platform carved into the lower branch. Pula pushed Julia up to the platform, came after her, stood behind her, a firm hand on her shoulder.

They looked out through an opening in the leaves across a flowing river to another big tree. Connecting them, connecting one tree to the other, was a long loop of cable. Julia followed the line of the cable and saw that it was suspended from a spot just above her head, secured to the tree trunk behind her.

'Is it strong enough?' she asked, still uncertain.

'It was made by miners. It is very strong. This rope could carry buckets full of rock if it had to. I will show you.'

Pula pointed to the clamps which held the cable to the trunk of the tree on which they stood. He reached up to move a length of one-inch metal piping which was wedged into the clamped ends of the wire rope. The twisted cable ran through the piping and Pula moved the length of pipe up and down to show Julia how it worked. The pipe still waited for slide-riders. It shed rust as Pula moved it. Julia saw deep grooves inside the metal pipe.

Pula wedged the piece of piping back into its locked position, under the end of clamped cable. He looked down again at the water below him, saw that it had risen almost to the position of the lower end of the cable, approaching the tree trunk on the other side of the rising river. There was still a short length of dry path before the tree. Soon this would be covered too.

For a moment Pula turned to Julia standing hesitant next to him. He felt a pang of guilt that she should be caught like this by the water, that he had allowed the *mokoro* to float away. He looked at her face so close, he noticed the pure white line of her neck, her throat, the darker suntanned lines of her arms as she reached for the pipe above her. He felt again that sudden stab of desire, that will to possess. It was mixed with some anxiety, some anger.

'We will fly over the water, both at the same time,' Pula said, a dryness in his throat, emotion and urgency mingling in sudden bewilderment.

Carefully, he arranged Julia's hands on the pipe so that there was also room for his own. The four hands were firm on the pipe, the two bodies close together, high in a tree.

'It is scary,' she said, standing in front, looking down at the rushing water below.

'We will fly over the water to the path on the other side.'

'We could hit the water!'

'Not if we go now. See the loop down there, it will slow us, take us to the other bank.'

'All the way across?'

'Yes, like the miners.'

Pula edged closer to her body from behind her, his knees

positioned to hold her. Julia turned her head to touch her forehead on Pula's outstretched arm, just for a moment. The touch ran through Pula's body like the pain of fire. He dropped the touched arm to hold her around the waist, hugging her body to his. They stood like that for a moment. Julia still held the pipe with both hands. She stood on tip-toe, ready to spring.

'I can do it,' she said.

Quickly Pula held with both hands, knuckles tensing around the pipe, disturbed by her closeness, loving her firm words, the playful bravery of this disturbing girl. They should hurry. The flood was coming.

They left the launching pad together, four hands firm.

They sailed slowly down the long cable, rust from it rising to mark their passage through the air. They dangled like limp puppets in the morning sun. Julia was exhilarated by their unusual journey across water, away from the island. She was excited by their sudden escape. She began to move her legs in the air as if already running on the land on the other side. She had no doubt that Pula knew what he was doing, that they would sail above the floodwaters, land safely. Together they descended the suspended cableway, approached the rising water.

They did not reach the path which led to the base of the far tree. Their weight dragged the cable lower and the floodwaters were too high this time. Julia, in front, still running, felt the sudden splash of cold water on her moving legs and she lost her grip on the moving pipe. She was quickly washed away with the stream. Pula was raised a fraction above the water by the cable which now carried less weight, but he saw Julia's arms flail in the turbulence of the torrent and he too let go, dropped into the water to follow her. They were both dragged by the rip of the current towards the mainstream.

'Go with it!' Pula shouted as he swam as best he could towards Julia. She did not hear him call, she only felt the utter futility of her efforts to swim against the flood and towards the mainland.

Then the river caught them with even greater force, and they were swept away from the island, downstream. They were both dragged to the centre line of the current where they were tumbled along with other debris from the land, like bits of damp rag. Pula stretched out a hand as he reached Julia, caught the cloth of her blouse, held on.

'I will stay with you!' Pula tried to shout to Julia but water came into his mouth. He saw that she was shouting too, and he thought he heard her.

'Crocodiles!' was what he heard as he came closer to her.

'Too fast,' he screamed, and then he saw that they were catching up with a tree which rolled clumsily in the current. The heavy base of the tree swung towards them, and Pula put his one arm over it, pulled Julia closer. He held on to the trunk of the tree as it rolled closer; the morning sun touched its slowly rolling form and shone through the spray of its moving branches. Pula saw a short stub of branch on the tree, guided Julia's hand to it.

Julia held on to the log as if it were salvation. She closed her eyes for a moment, felt the pain in the back of her head once again, the tremor of continuing fear.

She was afraid of the moving water and of the crocodiles which she believed lurked in it, but she was deeply conscious of Pula beside her. This was his element, she was in his hands, he would see her to the other bank, to dry land. And yet she could not help thinking of creatures deep beneath her. There were crocodiles in the swamp, hundreds of them, and they gorged themselves at flood time. They fed on the animals that were washed down with the flood, they devoured the sitatunga meat, the waterbuck and sable, Kalanga cattle. They snatched a body from the current and hid it under a ledge in the bank of the river. That is what would happen to her. Africa would get her.

She closed her eyes against the splash and anger of the flood and hoped that she was still in touch with her God. She asked for His help. In the original water of the flood she made a direct appeal to Him. Then she called upon her ancestors as the man beside her would be doing. She wished to appeal to ancestors with Pula, to the Pintos and the Barotses of the past. She shouted for her father, for the man on the land to hold out his hand, for her own God to pick her from the flood.

'Oh God!' she screamed, and she sucked water into her mouth.

They were carried together by the big river. She knew that Pula was trying to make her as brave as he was in the water. She could hardly expect him to share her fear, to understand how her mind was racing with the adrenalin of her terror. She lifted her legs for a moment, bundled herself on the surface but Pula stayed with her. She kept moving but knew that her legs were dangling below her threatened body, that she was like some floundering creature in the water, so unnatural, so ungainly, a wounded something attracting attention. Those legs might have taken her running along bush paths, but moving loosely in swamp water they were only bait for crocodiles. She imagined those crocodiles, like devils, looking up from the depths beneath her, preparing to devour her as they would devour any available flesh. Africa would devour her.

She stretched one leg down, straight, pointing her toes, imagining some firm ground to touch, but she was only tumbled along by the water, now part of the reed-raft which was building up against the tree to which Pula held.

Struggling in the water with Pula she knew that devils would cut her body into little pieces, make *diretlo* of her. They would use her for their own dark purposes. She would be disposed of in ugly pieces, fuel for their power, food for them. They would use her body, count her only as another victim, to be consumed, eaten by evil. These were the devils, seeking her. The crocodiles were waiting for her in the swamp.

She felt Pula's arm tug at her more forcefully, drag her. She kicked her legs to help him move her. She felt the papyrus all about her, sensed that they had slowed in the water, that they were staying with the log and the moving papyrus raft, that the tree was now becoming part of a drifting island, it had attached itself to a floating mass. It was not land, it was not salvation, but it was hope.

7

Dr Sergio Pinto waited at home, sitting on his verandah in an old reed chair, reading. His reading was an important part of his life, and he had on occasions reasoned that it was the Latin which had originally attracted him to the medical profession: the Latin discipline, the necessary order, or even the symbolism of service, the caduceus of his calling. Perhaps he should have become a classical scholar rather than a doctor! Now where would he be? Researching old texts in Coimbra library, confirming his belief that his own people were the real Discoverers? Did Africa really begin at the Pyrenees?

He waited for Julia, was sure that she would be back before the sun set. As it set, the sky blushed pink, bands of red farewell streaked the horizon, high clouds glowed golden. He moved inside with his book, put it down on the small telephone table in the hall, rang the party line. He turned the handle urgently in one long and demanding call of no recognised sequence.

He asked anyone who was listening whether or not they had seen Julia, first in tentative enquiry and then more urgently. Two voices eventually responded. One was the Tswana girl on the Shakawe exchange, the other was the foreman from the garage. The girl on the exchange said she would ask around, the foreman said he had seen her with Pula Barotse. They left his garage together, but he had not seen them since.

Dr Pinto walked out of his gate and into the village, again asking if anyone had seen Julia. He talked to everyone he saw. He knocked on doors, went down to the river and was shocked to see how high the water had already risen. He hurried home and rang again. When the girl on the exchange answered with no news, he asked her to raise Sergeant Molefe at the police station.

He was told that the sergeant was at the clinic, in the morgue. Dr Pinto knew the small room at the clinic which was sometimes used as a morgue, so he went straight there. Sergeant Molefe was standing with the only mortuary assistant, looking down at a cadaver on the slab. The sergeant welcomed the doctor with a clap of his big hands.

'Ah, the Doctor!,' he said heartily, 'just the man we need!'

'I was looking for you. My daughter has not come home.'

'Probably with her boyfriend. See this big Zulu here. I need an autopsy. He was brought in dead, but look at him! Not a mark.'

'You must send the word out, get your people to search.'

'Your daughter knows her way around. Give her time, time with her boyfriend. Such a warrior and not a mark on him. But look at this.'

Sergeant Molefe beckoned to Dr Pinto to examine the meagre belongings of the deceased. Placed carefully on a folded blanket was a wooden carving. It had no wings, but its twisted form was the very replica of his caduceus, the symbol of Hermes, the badge of his demanding profession.

'Maybe some kind of fetish. I need an autopsy,' the sergeant said.

Dr Pinto understood well enough what was required of him, but he was inordinately disturbed by the sergeant's casual mention of his daughter 'with her boyfriend'. Now there was this evocative shape of the carving lying on a blanket which belonged to a Zulu. The twisted images of animals and man disturbed him further. The images were young and old and eternal. The top of the carving was a head cut off just above the eyes. The old eyes offered a demented stare, a plea to be released from the creatures which wound around the body.

Dr Pinto picked up the carving, turned it in his hand. He saw the old man turn into a young man. Holding the thing in two hands he twirled it to see again the old side. He noticed that the lizard and the chameleon moved. Twisting together, they moved with their messages.

'This is the boy's work,' he said to Sergeant Molefe.

It was as if he had just touched some mystery that might bring him closer to Julia. A shudder of guilt and premonition shook him as he considered what might have happened. What chance did Julia have in the swamp of lingering African conflict? How could she ever step across cultures, how could she ever understand the *feitiço*?

Should he have been more forceful in discouraging the relationship between Julia and the young Mbukushu, the wild boy? Should he have warned her more explicitly of the dangers of wandering across cultures? Had community health come before the health of his own daughter? What message throbbed to him through his fingers as they turned the heavy figurine?

'I need an autopsy,' Sergeant Molefe repeated.

'Why now? On whose authority?'

'Military. Botswana Defence Force. My own. Do it!'

Dr Pinto turned to an unpleasant task. He would make the sergeant watch. What was the sergeant's hurry and what kind of bureaucratic harassment was this? Were the police testing him, as if he had nothing better to do with his skills? One look and he would probably be able to confirm ritual murder again, more unacceptable evidence of a growing resort to the traditional power politics of their cousins, the Basotho from the Mountain of Night. Did they really care about the disease which walked its way into Shakawe clinic? The Slim Clinic, the paramedics called it.

Also the eye disease, the malnutrition, the ugliness of unattended wounds, the stillbirths. Why do these people wait so long to bring the mothers to the clinic? Why do they only come when the complications are beyond the skill of local midwives?

Because they still trust their own methods, their own symbols and their own magic? Is that it? Trust is based on evidence of past performance, and the only past performance for which there is evidence is that of the bush doctor. All that dried mud, that mix of grass and dung! What really happens in those far-away huts, what Okavango gods rule us all? *Feitiço*, ancient or modern, the amulets and horoscopes of the past, the nails driven into idols, the demonic interventions, magnetic healing, the Fountain of Life. It is only human to love life, fear death. It is only human to seek protection, or to provide it if you can encourage belief. That is what any doctor must do, build up the evidence of his effectiveness, encourage belief.

'Well?' Sergeant Molefe said beside him, 'Don't you have to cut him open?

The body was much bigger than that of the average Tswana, much stronger, a powerful specimen, cut down in his prime. This was not ritual murder, no *feitiço*, no fetish or sign left on the body. There were the obvious facial cicatrizations, he was a Zulu but also Mzingili. No other facial scars, no scratches, eyes intact, ears and genitals too, thank god, no ritual trophies this time; throat, cranium smooth. Externally from the front nothing to remark about except the physical perfection.

Dr Pinto signaled to the mortuary assistant. Sergeant Molefe stepped aside.

From the back too, broad and powerful shoulders, straight spine, narrow waist, one old wound near the waistline, no new marks. The broad back of a Zulu warrior. Proud man cut down by what sort of evil?

Dr Pinto noticed a streak of dried blood across one buttock, only the outline of earlier ooze. He examined with both hands, opening the cold lobes and saw it: a tiny hole at the base of the spine, like the mark that a professional lumbar puncture might leave.

Then he knew, he could indeed confirm. He had seen the same thing in Qacha's Nek, even in Baragwanath. It was the thin sword, the cattle killer. A rapier fashioned from a bicycle spoke, used so often and with such skill as a murder weapon.

What else would this awful day produce? This dead man was not from the district, he was from the refugee camp, like many others. There had once been all sorts in the camp – Xhosa, Sotho, Pedi, Pondo, Swazi, Shangaan, even this Zulu. The camp would soon be empty, thank god, the diaspora was over. They would soon return home to South Africa to build their own promised land. Soon, they would leave the Hambukushu alone.

Dr Pinto knew that many of these refugees carried with them a deep grudge against their fellow beings, as if they had recently been robbed of some utopia. Some glory which was their due, something which had once appeared rich and shining before their eyes, a glory promised, had been taken away from them. Freedom had robbed them, someone had stolen their toys. The token of tribal victory, the badge of total triumph, had eluded them. Now there was nothing to play with. They were merely useless soldiers in a forgotten war. They had not yet learnt to be anything else.

But a Zulu? A warrior as perfect as this one? Had he been wandering like Gilgamesh in the forest in search of everlasting life only to be stung by some coward? Was he killed because he was a Zulu in Tswana country?

Dr Pinto pressed a thumb against the tiny hole in the powerful body, felt the coccyx move. A body was a body was a body. How dare he think in ancient terms of tribal conflict since time immemorial, of wild men in search of immortality?

Dr Pinto despaired as he examined the neat hole in the big body. He thought of *diretlo*, of the close relationship between the Sotho and the Tswana people. He thought of the product of conflict, wounded people, bodies on a battle field. He thought of the power of a fetish, of Pula and Julia. Again he despaired.

His despair heightened the enormity of the crisis which he faced. He was searching for his only daughter lost in the swamp, but the swamp was also swallowing him, dragging him down into its depths, so that he was helpless, incapable of action, like a chosen victim of ritual murder. He was becoming confused by the immensity of his folly, paralysed by fear of what might be true. He had indeed failed his daughter.

'Why the military?' Dr Pinto asked of Sergeant Molefe, 'this is very recent murder: clinical, neat, with stealth, probably while sleeping, at least lying down, resting in the shade this afternoon. That would be my guess. He is foreign, too big to beat in an open fight.'

'Come with me,' the sergeant demanded.

When questioned by an army officer, Dr Pinto confirmed the possibility that the mortal wound could have been caused by a sharpened bicycle spoke, confirmed that he had seen such wounds before, in South Africa, in the Malutis, in Lesotho. The officer made no note of the reference to Lesotho, ignored it. He was obviously pleased with the doctor's work, happy with the confirmation so soon after the event. He wished to keep this death a civil matter.

Dr Pinto asked the officer of the BDF to organise a search party to look for his daughter. He was told that the army could not help him, that such a thing would be the job of the police. Sergeant Molefe was the one to arrange such a thing.

How can I address you, Sergeant Molefe of the Shakawe police? I am familiar with the gut feel of anxiety, the ache for the daughter I love. I am familiar with the issues of human crisis, a familiarity common in Africa, our continent. I am also familiar with the issues of survival, I have seen people die. I have seen ill-health destroy both people and land. I have tried to do what I can to help both, the first Pinto doctor for generations. Senhor Serpa Pinto gave his name to a town in Angola, Senhor Silva Porto did the same thing. He was a Portuguese slave-trader who studied the Barotse! Other descendants were traders and hunters, like my father. My father traded in skins and ivory, the remnants of slaughtered animals. You might have known him. He established Botswana Trophies Industry – BTI – built a substantial trade with Japan. Small hunters came to seek large animals. Stuffed trophies returned with them – kudu and buffalo heads, whole leopards mounted on logs, elephant feet made into fancy furniture, even fish-eagles with varnished claws. For their wives they took crocodile skin handbags, maybe a kaross of black-backed jackal, snake-skin shoes, narrow, narrow, in narrow boxes. All from BTI, which paid my tuition fees for six years!

Wits! The University of the Witwatersrand. Baragwanath! The teaching hospital near Soweto. Six months in Bara trauma unit taught more about man's inhumanity to man than a year in a field hospital. And the tropicals! Old Professor Bostock, was it, and his Department of Tropical Medicine? Where I met the Afrikaans girl who was to become Julia's mother. I had such hopes, I thought we would make such a wonderful mix, the two of us, dedicated. But some tropical diseases are diseases of the spirit. I am truly sorry, Julia. Even after such a history I should have taken you away from Africa, back to Portugal.

Sergeant Molefe, we did not run to Canada, or to Australia, or to Britain, nor even back to Portugal. We stayed on, Sergeant Molefe. We need more resources for community health in Africa, Sergeant Molefe. Julia helps me in the clinic. She is my only child, Sergeant Molefe. Please take some men and look for her, now.

She is an attractive girl aged fifteen, nearly sixteen. Find her, Sergeant Molefe, find her and ask her all the questions you wish. Find Pula Barotse too. I do not know him well, but I have seen him at the school, I have even seen him with Julia. Occasionally she brings the wild man to our house on the river-bank. I know that he is good with his hands, that he carves in wood, making images of gods.

A hundred years ago your people sought protection from the British Crown, Sergeant Molefe. That is where your uniform comes from, your warrants for arrest, your due process. You wanted the British to protect you from the other whites, from the Portuguese and the Boers. Well, now I must seek your protection, I am in your hands, only you can help me in my despair.

'Will you please find one Portuguese girl lost in the bush. Find her before it is too late?' he asked in some desperation.

'If I were you I would seek out John Barotse, Pula's father,' Sergeant Molefe said kindly, 'the water is rising and he knows what that means.'

At first light the next morning Dr Pinto set out to enlist the help of Pula's father, John Barotse, the fisherman. He took the sand road to Namaseri. He knew the road well, followed the sandy track which leads to Sepopa. It has its own speed, he told himself, trying not to hurry. The sand has its own speed, the drier the slower. Wheels sink deep in dry desert sand and they spin, get too hot. Damp sand makes a good road. Flooded sand becomes a river, no road, no dust. Flood time is the best time, when the big trees stand out in a huge lake, when the fish come to feed where cattle once grazed, when even the sitatunga float down south on papyrus islands. Dr Pinto listened to the tyres in the sand, not to the turmoil in his head.

John Barotse knows all the channels and pools and he can float above them, Dr Pinto told himself. He can sail straight to Sepopa on a swift current, Hambukushu travel. He can even make it against the stream. With his new engine, he can make it.

Hambukushu time could come again, time of the flood, time of the kingdom. Dr Pinto knew well enough that the Hambukushu, of all people, could live between the floods and droughts of nature. A child could sleep on his mother's back as she works in water, just as he could sleep in the desert. For centuries these good people survived in their kingdom of the flood plain, they could survive as long as water itself. John Barotse would know what to do.

When he approached Namaseri he was surprised to see that the water was well over the drift, that the road was impassable. It was not a draining of the swamp that might be the danger this time, but the flood. In a flood, Hambukushu travel might be the only way. Perhaps Pula had taken Julia on the water in a *mokoro*, perhaps they had been caught by the flood? They were waiting somewhere, waiting for the flood to pass.

A man in a *mokoro*, knowing that there might be some traffic to the Fishing Camp at Namaseri, waited near the drift. He stood up in his slender craft and held his pole high in welcome. Doctor Pinto parked his Land Rover a good way from the water, on higher ground next to a police vehicle. He opened his door, stepped out on to dry land, but remembered his black bag in its usual position on the front seat. He pulled it closer, opened it to examine it.

Dr Pinto's fingers ran easily over the small bottles and phials, the ampules, ointments and dressings. He touched the canisters of powerful insecticide, tsetse spray, two of them. He picked out a box of pills which were plastic-packed in orderly rows – a week's agonising treatment for bilharzia. Attached to little brackets in the lid of his medicine chest were a few instruments: a syringe, scalpel and scissors, his stethoscope. It was a traditional doctor's bag, square and black, packed for Africa, but what did 'traditional' medicine mean on this journey? What beat did one listen for, what First Aid did one offer to Africa's shattered immunity systems? And if one found only a corpse, a blood-drained body, neatly carved for medicinal purposes, what use was any doctor?

Dr Pinto closed the box, lifted in out by its familiar worn handle, and slammed the door of his Land Rover. He was about to lock the door when he remembered something else which might be needed. He reached for a folded blanket on the back seat and slung it over his arm. He locked the car door and walked towards the boatman.

Dr Pinto could see that the water was creeping up the dry road, rising further above the drift. He looked up at the few clouds in the sky. The boatman saw him do so.

'Not yet, *Morena!*' he called. 'There is time.'

'Yesterday the road was dry.'

'Yesterday. Today the water has arrived from the hills. Tomorrow it will be a big flood. Can I take the Doctor to the Fishing Camp? First the police, now the Doctor.'

'I am looking for John Barotse.'

'He is the one to blame. He makes the rain. He is one of us, an Mbukushu. We only use a pole because all the others use it. Here at Namaseri. The time for paddles is coming.'

The boatman patted the pole which was stuck into the sand of the flooded road, holding the *mokoro* in position, the bow near Dr Pinto's feet.

'Sit there.' The boatman pointed to a squat log wedged in the bow.

'You can bring me back after I have spoken to John Barotse?'

'Like a ferry. Quick, *Morena*.'

The boatman pushed away from the drift, placed his pole carefully along the length of his *mokoro* and took up a short paddle. Sitting on the flat seat which he had carved into the stern when he had fashioned the dug-out from a big tree, the Mbukushu ferryman paddled his passenger along the flooded road.

'Soon poles will be no good. Only paddles,' he said, guiding his craft along the road.

Dr Pinto could see the forward line of their route, the trees on either side flooded to the first branches. The alleyway of trees led into the distance; he was sitting on a blanket in a *mokoro* above the road. He sat in the road, in the middle of it on flood water, as familiar features passed. He saw the reverse side of a sign-post on a pole, knew that it warned drivers of the drift to come. It was a crude symbol shaped like a flat W. At the spot where the drift should have been, the trees were buried deeper in the water. A light cross-current made the ferryman point his *mokoro* into the stream. He moved his craft crabwise across the drift beneath, making for the clear gap in the trees which marked the continuing course of the road.

Dr Pinto sat on his primitive perch with his doctor's bag and contemplated his own dilemma in the face of the flood. How could he possibly find Julia if she had gone off into the swamp with the wild boy? What did he really know about people who lived in the distance at the mouth of rivers, today or yesterday? What did he really know about this particular ferryman and this particular journey?

The fishing camp consisted of a few rows of green canvas tents erected on flat concrete slabs. These slabs were on the highest ground above a bend in the river. A floating jetty was moored to the high bank, which was protected by a rocky outcrop of the mainland. Near the largest tent brilliant bougainvillaea grew.

John Barotse was on the grassy bank talking to a man in police uniform. The boatman pointed out John Barotse's old boat moored with the others, the one with the brand-new red engine. He also pointed to a round hut just outside the fence of the Fishing Camp. Near the hut was some rough scaffolding, a dump of sand.

'John Barotse is building a new room. For his son,' the boatman told him.

'That is the man I am looking for. John Barotse, the fisherman.'

'His son is lost in the swamp. I wonder if he will ever sleep in that hut which his father is building?'

Dr Pinto hesitated before stepping ashore, turning to listen to the ferryman, who allowed the *mokoro* to drift away from the bank. The ferryman was smiling at his passenger's indecision.

'John Barotse will go to look for his son. He is a powerful man, John Barotse, a rainmaker.'

'Can he control a flood?'

'Maybe. You must ask him, He talks to the water. Maybe he can save his son.'

The *mokoro* had drifted away from the bank. Dr Pinto had an awful and vivid vision of a drowned girl, her hair like water weeds, her face pale and swollen, like something deposited by the flood. He asked the ferryman to return him at once to the landing place.

'I need to talk to John Barotse,' he told the ferryman. 'As you say, he is a powerful man in these parts.'

'He is the spirit of the swamp. You should not talk too much, you should listen.'

8

I myself, John Barotse, father of Pula Barotse lost in the swamp, am part of the water. Like his hottentot-god, I came from water. The hottentot-god and the Hambukushu both first appeared at the time of the beginning of the world when the world was only water. First there was water and then there was the world. We were carried over the water by a bee who searched and searched for solid ground on which to deposit his load. The bee flew well but we were very heavy for that bee, *seremapetlo*, the mantis and the first Mbukushu. At last the bee saw a great white flower, half open, waiting for the sun to shine on it. The bee put us into the centre of the flower.

That was the beginning. The bee put the *seremapetlo* and the first human seed inside that flower. Then the tired bee died. The sun rose and warmed the flower. It opened with the hottentot-god in it, holding the first human being in its praying pincers, the original Barotse. He was Mbukushu. The hottentot-god told the Barotse that the world would dry up and the only thing that would listen to him was the snake. The snake once had six legs on which he walked to the edge of the water. When the world dried up, the moon took pity on snake and took away his legs so that he could slide easily across the sand. He works well with the moon, the snake.

I watched the world dry up, just as *seremapetlo* said it would. I watched the waters recede, I was the first person to see the water retreat, my desert is the oldest in the world. I rose out of Africa, someday everyone will understand this, that we were the first people, that the hottentot-god was just one of our gods. Do what you wish for any of your gods. Drink wine and blood, eat bread and flesh, lay out gifts for the sun, for the moon, sacrifice goats. Do all the humble things that mortals must do because they are mortal, but remember that my gods are of the water and of the desert. Water is the difference. Interfere with water and my gods will turn on you as happened once before. They will turn on you, fill you with disease, deform your future, nothing will be natural any more. Your bowels will not work, the ache in your belly will always return, your scalp will itch terribly. Your blood will clot, your heart will grow weak as the water rises. They will bring the final flood of disaster in which you will all drown. The last barbarians are those who cut all gods out of their souls, who stop the natural cycles. My hottentot-god knows all about cycles, from water to the desert.

All Africa knows *seremapetlo*. Some people call him *Thatabantwana*, taker of children, or *Twalambiza*, carrier of the pot. He carries a pot in his praying hands, he brings the water and the sun and the fire of life. He came from a heap of stones. He was a giver of good things, he carried a pot of luck, he was full of music.

I carry my own pot of luck. In it are all the things I need for rainmaking, the things of the sea and of the sand. In it are sea shells and thorns, fish scales and small white stones from their eyes, fish fins and powdered sitatunga horn, seaweed mixed with the bulbs of water lilies, strips of dried eel. One day Pula will have all these things. He will be the rainmaker.

Twalambisa may also have some of these things in his pot, but he also has fire. He stole fire from ostrich, he stole cattle. Let me tell you how he stole fire from ostrich, from under his wing.

Twalambisa said to ostrich that he knew of a tree which bore the most delicious plums. Ostrich had beautiful red wings, like hottentot-god, and together they flew to the tree, landed below its branches. Ostrich was delighted. He began to eat the plums which grew on the lower branches. Higher, higher, *Twalambisa* said, that is where the big plums are! Ostrich stood on the tips of his horny toes, spread his red wings to balance himself. As he did so *Twalambisa* snatched fire from under ostrich's wing.

Ostrich never flew again. He keeps his wings close to his side so that no one can see that he has no more fire in him.

That story is as old as my own, as old as the story of the Mbukushu and the Aluyi. From the Aluyi came the Barotse who have had their own kingdom for hundreds of years. The Hambukushu and the Barotse have never worried about boundaries. The only boundary of our kingdom is the line that water makes across the land. We follow that line, we can live in water and on land and our place is marked only by the extent of water's spread over land. We live from the lowest point of water, where the skimmers nest in dry sand, to the highest, where fish eat the insects which breed in cattle kraals. That is our territory, that is Pula's territory.

All men must know their territory. It must be clear in their minds as the place where they must live and die. If a man is a wanderer he will require a very big territory, like the whole world. Not everyone can have the whole world. If a man knows that he can live with all the others in such a huge place, he will need to protect some little space around him, carry it with him. He will have to carry his own world with him as he wanders the big world. Some can live separately with their own selves, but most people cannot manage that. They prefer a smaller territory defined by their neighbours. Most people wish for a smaller place where they can listen to their own gods and their own parents and then their own children.

Pula is my only son. Julia is your only daughter, Dr Pinto. We two fathers know the same thing, that we do not want the whole world, only a small territory for our families, like a cocoon.

There are many wanderers today; some may think the whole world is their territory but that thinking is not for most men, that is only for gods. For the gods this world is only one of many, their country is boundless and, for them, this world is a small one. Men who think they are gods, those who are not gods, will always get lost. It is not man's destiny to be god. Show me one man who is not lost in the whole world, who is at peace in such a large territory? He may claim the whole world in the name of some god, but he will not be at peace with it on his own.

Missionaries and priests, such people in the past, many of our own leaders, may raise their eyes to claim a larger territory as their own, but they cannot own it. That is why it is better to drop our eyes, Dr Pinto, know our own home, look for our own children.

Why did they come here those old missionaries, if they knew their own home, if they were looking after their own children? What were they trying to show us, telling us that there was another world, that ours was not the most important for us, that our gods, our ancestors, did not truly rule? Why did they come to tell us of their gods? Because their own people would not listen to them?

In our time many people have tried to make us become a part of something bigger, to join their world, but we have kept our own territory. There will always be someone who will want my son to join their army. Come Pula, they will say, join us! They will suggest that they will be stronger together, but the Hambukushu trick is to stay strong within himself. You do not need big territory, you do not need armies. That is the greatest mistake, to think that you need defend anyone but yourself and your own territory. The Hambukushu have fought. Kololo, Aluyi, Kololo again, they have fought! We will fight when the swamp is denied us, but not for other territory. We do not necessarily have the best in this world, this swamp, but it is the best for us and we know that. From here we can reach out if we wish, we can trade with all of our neighbours, learn what they can teach us, but do not ask John Barotse or his son Pula to leave the water.

It is a great privilege to have you in my boat, Dr Pinto. I had the pilot once before and he brought the engineers and the scientists to the swamp. He was a flying man, with a badge on his pocket and Pula saw him as a great hero. He was looking for fish, too many fish. Sergeant Molefe is looking for a murderer, he is looking for

Potlako Lereng.

We all know Potlako Lereng. He is not of our people. Lereng is a Sotho name. Many of us have Sotho names, we are all related, but we do not all believe in *diretlo*, the word the believers use for their medicinal flesh. Some doctors collect herbs and roots, some collect bits of flesh.

As a doctor you will know about herbs and roots, maybe about flesh. You have seen the wounds of its gathering. It is collected as other doctors might collect herbs, this piece of flesh for that fever, that piece of flesh for this desire. It is the flesh itself which is *diretlo*, the selected pieces, which must always be cut away while the victim is alive. You should know the word as part of your trade, but you should not think too much about this. You must not think about it because it is very much part of that wish to control others, like the messages of the missionaries so long ago.

Also, when you mention to me Sergeant Molefe, and the Zulu, and the carving which he held in his hand, I know at once that we should keep hope alive. We must not think of your daughter as *diretlo*, pieces of her; that would send us both mad. We need not talk of the *mugrodi*, of the rain-mother who must bear her children for sacrifice.

What else should we talk of, Doctor, travelling so slowly against the flood in my old boat with the new engine? You who have come across to our world, have you lost your own? Or are you able to live in the whole world because you live with your skill, is that it? Will Pula be able to live with the whole world because of his skill? Is that where John Barotse is finally to be proved wrong? I have no skill but fishing, and maybe that is not enough for a son. Those hands of his and the things they can make! Perhaps he has in his hands all the skills and the souls of his brothers and sisters who could never make the things he makes. Each man must know his home, and his skill, and a fisherman must find his home near water. It was there in the beginning, when it has gone, we will all go.

We will need to search all the landing places between Namaseri and the border at Mohembo, all the inlets where the Hambukushu set their nets. Maybe we will need to hurry because it must be raining very hard in Angola, I can smell the sky. Soon the floods will come, even greater than today.

Did you know that the crocodile is the one I fear most, Dr Pinto? He is the god I fear because I am the one who makes the rain. If I do not make it he will surely die, and so he depends on me. He does not like to depend on anything, only himself. He is all selfish people, all greed and grabbing. He rules me by fear and he despises me as I sit in a boat above him. That is the way of some gods, to rule by fear and to despise. Is it the way of your god?

I worry about Pula and Julia and crocodiles in the flood. The crocodiles will be waiting for creatures which have been caught by the flood waters, waiting in the new mud made by the flood. Look there, Dr Pinto, there is one, watching us in our boat.

Would I rather drive this boat from place to place in the swamp than stop to fish? From somewhere came a great liking for this machine. Maybe from the days when I worked with machines on the mines. Many of us worked together in the dark. The small lights we carried on our hats were like stars to guide us along dark tunnels.

We need something to guide us, right now. Maybe I am a machine man, not a god man. Maybe that is why I disobeyed, I let my son live. He can decide for himself, maybe become a rainmaker himself. It takes a big decision to throw away all the things that the tribe offers to a rainmaker. Maybe I am the first rainmaker who knows that he has no such power. Certainly my son was not to be buried as a baby, standing up, with his open skull collecting the first rain.

Can you imagine such a thing, Dr Pinto, as part of darkness? The top of the head has to be cut off cleanly and the body has to stand erect in its own grave so that the first rain will drain around it. Can you, a doctor, imagine such a thing? You try to save Tswana children, I know that. Could you accept such a thing, could your god accept such *diretlo*? He is Julia's god too, Pula has talked to me about him. What does your catholic god say about *diretlo*?

I know that he encourages people to eat the flesh and drink the blood, or is that only a trick of the church? And do your priests cut off a skinny tassel from a young boy so that he can become a man? Suddenly, the knife and the flesh make a man. What happens to that piece of flesh, that *diretlo*? Is it displayed by mothers in a bottle to prove that the tribe was obeyed?

You have used the knife yourself, Dr Pinto. You did it once for a young Kalanga boy. The boy came to you in order to avoid the anguish in the bush and you obliged. You dressed the wound and sent him on his way, a man. What do you do with all the pieces of person that you cut away, Dr Pinto? Do you throw them away with all the blood and rags and needles of your craft, or do you sometime keep them in a bottle? In the bottle is a piece of flesh, a specimen, evidence. You too have to decide which to throw away and which to keep.

There was some trouble about that Kalanga boy, I recall. The people said that you were interfering with the duties of others. I talked to Pula about that. I told Pula that it made me feel good, inside. You did what the boy wanted, not what the tribe demanded. The Kalanga boy soon threw away his dressing, and there he was, regular, like his mates.

I also told Pula that I should have asked you to do the same thing for him. I told him that I should have asked you, of all the doctors, to cut away that piece of flesh. Would you have done that for me, Dr Pinto, and for Pula? Would you do it for a girl? Bubi does that for girls, often.

It is such a tiny thing, that piece of *diretlo*, but small pieces of flesh can become ugliness. How can any of us honour all the things of the past? There must be things which you, even you, cannot accept today which you accepted yesterday. Is that not part of living, to change those things in which we do not believe? Pula was not born of a *mugrodi* to be buried in a corner of a field so that the rains would be regular.

No! He was made to rise out of the darkness of such burial and to live with me until he became a man on his own, and later a father. That is the most important thing for a man, to be a father. Like you and me. We fathers always have great plans for our children – sometimes that means that we must tell them to reject what is offered by the tribe.

I kept the necklace and the gourd. I met with my people when the drought was killing them. I pretended, but I did not believe. Is it not terrible, this dishonesty? This necessity to lie because of the repetition over the ages of the rituals of darkness. Truly terrible, both the repeating and the lie. I have tried to tell Pula this, to explain that some customs should continue because they help the people understand themselves, but that others must be thrown away.

The belief in the *mugrodi* must be thrown away, but some other things should be kept. *Nalikwanda*, the barge of the Queen of the Barotse should sail forever. Pula's hands must work on strange shapes, forever. He can create god-images in his mind and give them form with his hands. These things are of another spirit, another magic, things that should not be thrown away. Often things made this way, by a very skilled hand, even a painting on a rock, are linked to our ancestors and are forever.

Are there not choices for you too, Dr Pinto, and for Julia? Are there not customs and beliefs which you should reject, which your daughter should not retain? How else can you be a father but to help her choose?

My skill is only something to keep us fed, it is not a belief, it is not magic. But I wonder about your skill and about Pula's skill? Is his skill a belief, is yours magic? You saw his god-model, the one with the flat head. He sees images in a log of wood, in a stone, even in the Tsodilo Hills. He creates things from the shapes which form in his mind, and so many of those shapes are from the swamp, from his ancestors. He has to be very careful about what he rejects, or what he retains from the floods of the past.

Look there, Dr Pinto, at that big island, it is moving! The sitatunga which live on it have traveled further into the swamp although they may not know it. The water has risen underneath the island and it is floating away. There must have been very big rains in Angola. Those rains will make us all move, all of us who live by the water. At Katima Molilo, at Sesheke, Mongu, even at Kazangula, they will be talking about it. All the Barotse will begin to move as they have done for hundreds of years. Are we not clever, to have kept our own territory for so long, to have stayed near the swamps, one kingdom for hundreds of years?

You have a kingdom, Dr Pinto. The kingdom of your skill. Your people have been with us for a short time, you came with your language to Africa, you tried to make a home, up there in Angola where the floods are coming from. It did not work out too well but you still have a kingdom. Maybe you should have fought more for your territory, like the Kololo against the Aluyi. They beat us, finally we beat them. It was an old order, that fighting for territory. The new order is as I told you; we only need a small place, each of us, you with your daughter me with my son.

Mothers seem to know this, they are the best at recognising that the warriors cannot win, and that is why, amongst our people, the power runs through the woman. It is always easier to know for sure the child of a woman than the child of a man. A woman always delivers her own child, not necessarily that of her husband. It is a good system for us, this line of the family through mothers.

Our Queen floats down in a big barge and around her all the *mokoros* make a grand raft. We all move to higher ground and we all move together. The Hambukushu take themselves along in the world of the water, like those few people who can live in the whole world, we live between the land and the water. We carry seeds with us to plant in the soil of the new place. For hundreds of years we have lived this way because the spread of the water has been big enough for us. We have built strong families, a strong Queen, and you should know all about it, Dr Pinto. It was a Portuguese man long ago, who first wrote down some of our history. He lived amongst the Hambukushu and the Barotse, with Mr Livingstone. Do you not agree that it is a very important thing for a strong

Queen, to have the history written down so that it can remain the same for all to see?

I took a man fishing a short while ago. He was the pilot, I told you that. Pula looked at him as if he was a god. But he was only a pilot and he brought some men to the swamp who told us that the tsetse would disappear, that his engineers would take water from the Makgadikgadi. The Makgadikgadi and the swamp are joined by tunnels under the ground. Did you know that, Dr Pinto? Take the water from Makgadikgadi and you will take water from the swamp. That is the only thing which can destroy our Queen.

Look over there at that big tree rolling slowly towards us! That is from the bank near Mohembo. It should not be here. There is truly a huge flood coming!

The log rolling slowly, the one from the bank at Mohembo, which should not be where it was, held up a raft of branches and reeds and a clump of papyrus. John Barotse guided his boat away from the obstruction in the river. He gave the floating island a wide berth.

Dr Pinto watched the knot of logs and debris as it swept past. He saw something unusual amongst the floating papyrus, some human debris perhaps, a plastic bag perhaps or a piece of cloth, or perhaps the white underbelly of a struggling animal. It lay there at the base of the moving island. He called to John Barotse who turned to watch the back of the papyrus island, to see it slip away towards the Fishing Camp.

John Barotse wondered about the boats moored at the Fishing Camp, whether the floating debris would snag on the bend in the river. Sometimes, in a flood, big trees rolled along only to be trapped in a narrow place, making a temporary dam of a kind. Papyrus and reeds, other floating muck from the flood would build up against the quivering dam until it burst. The muck would then continue on its journey down towards Chief's Island, swirling loose until it hit some other obstacle. Sometimes animals were trapped in such moving islands, sometimes they escaped to the shore when the island was held up for a moment. John Barotse searched the knot of logs for signs of life.

He heard Dr Pinto calling to him, as he altered course very carefully, turning slowly away from the current, knowing that he would be whipped in the opposite direction as soon as headway was lost. Then he saw a body lying on the papyrus. Next to it a black arm rose into the air, the fingers of the black hand were splayed, hailing.

John Barotse turned upstream of the floating island, approached it with the current, new engine now only idling. The knot of them, the log, the papyrus island, the attached debris, the old boat with the fathers, and the victims of the flood, floated together, carried by the first flow of the biggest floods ever to hit the Okavango Delta.

9

Dr Pinto and John Barotse first pulled Julia into the boat. While Pula grabbed his father's outstretched arm and struggled aboard, Dr Pinto wrapped the blanket around his daughter and tried to lay her flat in the bottom of the boat to enable him to give her his kiss of life. He thrust her legs beneath a wooden seat, pulled her head back, bent down to put his mouth to her nose. Pula crouched in the stern, shivering and anxious. John Barotse swung the boat into the current, away from the floating island and hurried back towards the Fishing Camp at the bend in the river.

Pula shivered at his father's side, while Dr Pinto worked on Julia. Pula looked closely at his father sitting in the stern of the boat with his hand on the throttle which he now trusted, guiding the boat between debris in the river, hurrying home. His father did not look at him, not now, he did not even look at the girl lying so lifeless in the bottom of his boat. It seemed to Pula that the old man was praying. His father's lips moved as if he were talking to someone beside him, perhaps he was talking to himself. He stared straight ahead, his lips moving with his mind, worrying his way home, almost too fast with the current. Pula felt a deep warmth for the father he loved, it seemed to stop his shivering and he was for a moment elated over the realisation that they were saved, that Julia had not drowned.

When Julia groaned on the floor John Barotse frowned and glanced at her, bewildered and concerned. He saw his son reach out a hand towards her, a reassurance, a blessing perhaps, a loving hand. He looked forward again, to guide the fast-moving boat back home. He was bringing the children home, and the other father was with him. Two fathers, so far apart, but now brought together by a flood.

Water oozed from Julia's mouth as Dr Pinto compressed her lungs in desperate discipline, talking to her all the time, bringing her back into this world.

'This man has the greater skill,' John Barotse said to his son when he saw Julia's eyes flicker. He saw her chest heave. In huge relief he saw more muck from the river spill on to the floor of his boat.

Like running too fast downhill, there was still a great danger in running with the current of the flood. The slap of the bottom of the boat forcing ahead against the crests of waves, was now replaced by a slewing speed, which thrust the bow of John Barotse's boat deep into running troughs. The new engine was now idling so that the propeller itself could be used as a rudder. Too fast and too loaded, the rescue boat slithered away from the mainstream into another floating papyrus island.

On the island, flattening the papyrus where it lay, was a large crocodile. It rose on stubby legs to confront the intrusion into his own haven from the flood. It opened its jaw in an unusual display of teeth, snapped it shut on thin reeds. The reeds stuck out of the closed mouth, tassels shaking from the sudden movement.

John Barotse recalled his previous confrontation with the hippo, recalled his fall and Pula's hand helping him. His son had said that he had not yet learnt to use the new engine. He switched the clutch on the outboard and put the propeller into reverse. The stern swung dangerously away from the floating island. The current then caught the broad flank of the old boat and spun it in crazy circles towards Shakawe.

Julia groaned again as the boat swung, her father held fast to the low gunwale with one arm as he tried to steady her body with the other. He pressed her down, bracing himself against the wooden seat, and told her that the crocodiles would never get her. He told her that she was now safe.

When John Barotse tried to use the power of his engine to head back against the stream, to stop the swinging of his boat, one gunwale sank low and water poured into the boat, covering Julia where she lay. Her father lifted her shoulders then, clung to her wet body, hugging her in the water. The boat steadied and continued fast downstream, lower in the water.

The boat was now carried by the flood as a heavy log might be carried, and Pula, close to Julia but not holding her as her father was doing, moved to touch his father's hand on the tiller. He pointed downstream and they both saw many other logs caught against the bend in the river near the Fishing Camp. The logs were moving with the waves caused by the current and some spun out of the log-jam to be carried away, around the corner, deeper into the swamp. Father and son glanced at one another with the same thought: they must get to the other bank, otherwise the boat would be swirled that way, down to Chief's Island.

They looked up at the opposite bank and they saw a man standing on the high ground sweeping both arms repeatedly to his chest, beckoning them urgently. Pula then saw the police launch wedged into the papyrus, almost hidden there. John Barotse saw it too and he opened the throttle to turn the heavy boat in the stream to make for the opposite bank of the river. Slowly the waterlogged craft and its anxious passengers moved towards the hidden haven. Pula moved to the bow, took the tiller rope in one hand and prepared to board the launch tied to the papyrus.

John Barotse's old boat crashed obliquely into the side of the police launch and Pula jumped aboard with the rope in his hand.

The man who had beckoned from the high bank was Sergeant Molefe. He hurried down to his launch and ran across the planks which linked it to the packed papyrus.

'There is not much time,' he shouted. 'We must all get away from here.'

He held out a hand to help Dr Pinto and Julia on to the deck of the launch and then towards the line of planks across the papyrus.

'You found them!' he said, as he slapped Dr. Pinto's wet shoulder. 'We must take them at once to the airstrip. An aeroplane is coming to take us all away. My men will help you.'

Dr Pinto was off the boat, still carrying Julia. He felt her hand pull at his shirt. She was trying to say something. He bent his head to her to listen.

'I must say goodbye to Pula,' she whispered.

Dr Pinto looked back at the boat and saw Pula helping his father out of the launch. Sergeant Molefe was with them.

'The sergeant will bring him,' he told his daughter.

Dr Pinto hurriedly carried her towards the buildings of the Fishing Camp. Other policemen ran down to help.

Sergeant Molefe told John and Pula Barotse that a huge flood was coming, that the water had broken through above Namaseri and that it was beginning to flood the houses in Shakawe. He told them again that a plane was being sent from South Africa to rescue the people of Shakawe.

John Barotse stopped there on the walkway across the papyrus which was so close to the Fishing Camp and to the old jetty.

'No,' he said. 'I will not fly away, I will take this boat to Tsodilo.'

'There is no time,' Sergeant Molefe insisted.

'The petrol?' Pula asked, 'what about the petrol?'

'There is still some in the red tank.'

Pula stepped back into the boat, picked up the tank and tested its weight. A little petrol sloshed noisily in the bottom of the tank.

'We will tie up father's boat, and then we will come,' Pula promised Sergeant Molefe.

'I will send some men back. They can help you.'

Pula knew that it might be a long time before his father fished again. If the flood really came in all its potential fury, the only people who might be safe would be the Barotse and Hambukushu already in their craft, making for high ground. All of the seasonal plains would be flooded this year. This year the seasonal people might have to go as far as the Tsodilo Hills, but at least they would go by paddle-power.

Pula started to bail his father's boat with the tin which floated in the bilge. He worked rapidly while his father watched. Then he gestured to his father with some impatience, to help him drag the boat further on to the papyrus, to lift the gunwale to drain it. Complaining that it was useless, that boats should stay in the water if a flood was coming, John Barotse helped his son, who seemed to take charge.

Together they pulled the boat, with the engine still clamped to its transom, high on to the planks of the floating jetty. They tipped it, watched the water flow over the papyrus and then they dragged the boat towards the old jetty.

'We will tie it up, and then we will go,' Pula said.

Pula saw that one other boat rested on its side on the planks, that the jetty had already risen with the water. The grass hanging from the high bank now touched the timbers.

'You saved the doctor's daughter,' John Barotse said to his son, as they struggled with the boat. Pula did not reply, but dragged the boat, shuffling backwards away from the river.

'You are no longer a child,' his father now said, and Pula smiled as he too struggled with the weight of the boat. He wondered if he was no longer a child. He certainly could not rely on his father in the crisis which he sensed was developing so fast. They had to join the others before it was too late. He had to follow Julia, but how could he explain that to his father.

'But I am still a father,' John Barotse added with some authority, as if he had himself made the decision not to stay in his boat on the rising river.

Children? For how long does a father consider his children as children? They are always his children, but there comes a time when a father has to put away the idea that he is dealing with a child and face the man. It happens slowly, all along the road to manhood, but the arrival is sudden. A father accepts the new person that is growing in front of his eyes, accepts the differences, the uniqueness as a new person, he even tries to encourage the new person to grow in difference. If the father is a fisherman he has a deep wish that his child should be different.

All along, when the child is tiny, on first walking, experimenting, setting forth on those first adventures, the father watches his child with that wish. He will encourage adventure, encourage experiment, introduce danger with care but make his child afraid of nothing. He is to be different.

When the child starts to shape strange things with his hands, first lumps of clay into cattle which have fat clay horns, then finer shapes in wood, the difference becomes very exciting. Then the father begins to look out for odd shapes of roots from the earth, or twisted seeds from a tree. A shape that was not at first seen by the father, only through the hands of the son. There is so much that a son can show to a father, that he has skill and power in his hands, that he sees the world differently.

A good knife was a good present, expensive. In no time at all there were other beautiful things carved with affection. There were sable, buffalo, flying birds, moving insects, praying insects, a chameleon with one foot raised, a fish-eagle on a tree, a god-like living statue which you can hold like a weapon, which is a young man on one side an old man on the other. Creatures bind them together. There were even crocodiles.

How quickly these things were seen, how soon he became a man, how soon is the child only a memory. Perhaps the gods have spoken about this son, perhaps it is in their hands. Even the matter of the girl whom he saved, perhaps her future is in their hands.

It is too quick, the approach of the moment when I must forget the child. Some wish to hurry it, but not me, not John Barotse. When it comes, as it has come to me now at the beginning of the flood, I can accept it. The flood will change many things. It is like a huge wave of change which has suddenly hit my world so that it will never be the same again. I was born at the mouth of a river which flows out into the desert, my only son was born at the mouth of a river.

There will be mud, that is for sure, mud to dry when the water recedes, to become new pasture. And then again a hot dry season. The wind will sweep up the powder of the soil and carry it away in a huge cloud. From water to dust, dust to water, in the natural cycle there is very little change. A son will grow up. If he is very lucky he too will have children, those will grow up. I may even see them, his children, but then I will die and stop seeing them, some time in the cycle. Can any flood stop that? Even the biggest flood ever to hit the Okavango?

PART TWO

THE STORY OF THE FLOOD

Lay upon the sinner his sin,
Lay upon the transgressor his transgression,
Punish him a little when he breaks loose,
Do not drive him too hard or he perishes;
Would that a lion had ravaged mankind
Rather than the flood,
Would that a wolf had ravaged mankind
Rather than the flood,
Would that famine had wasted the world
Rather than the flood,
Would that pestilence had wasted mankind,
Rather than the flood.
– THE EPIC OF GILGAMESH

10

I, the pilot, do not belong to Africa but I have seen some very muddy floods. From the air I have seen rivers flowing out of Africa into the Indian ocean and the Atlantic ocean. The muck from Africa flows into a warm sea and into a cold sea, the debris of many floods lies on desert beaches. The Orange River floods and its brown waters still carry diamonds into the Benguela current. The Umzimkulu floods, the Umfolosi, the Umzimvubu, they all carry the soil out of Africa and into the sea.

When the Okavango floods it does not flow into the sea. It has deposited its muck into a huge valley for so long that the valley has been filled with sand. It flows not into a warm sea or a cold sea but into a desert.

I have seen many deserts from the air. In American aircraft I have flown food to starving people in Ethiopia, Somalia, Sudan. I have seen the desert encroach, wondered at the vastness of the Sahara, like a sandy sea whose shore expands gradually, drying up all the bush it touches. I have seen the tent towns, the long lines of people waiting in the dust. I have flown mercy missions, many of them, and I know that there is no god to grant mercy to Africa.

I began my mercy missions in Lesotho. They used to call us the Flying Angels. I flew medical men into remote airstrips in the Maluti Mountains. I remember one at Qacha's Nek where the strip was only a graded slope on a mountainside, on the very edge of the Drakensberg. At that time we flew un-American Brittan Norman Islanders, even squat Sky Vans.

As an American pilot working for WENELA I flew converted C130s, Hercules, carrying miners from Chileka to Jan Smuts. We used to take 136 passengers on each flight, we used to refer to them as our 'pax' for short. Like 'pix' for pictures. We ran a shuttle when the President of Malawi called all his citizens home. Before that I was on DC3s and DC4s to Francistown, Botswana. A senior pilot died in April 1974 when his Skymaster went into the ground at Francistown. Ground crew had mixed AVTUR with AVGAS in the same tank, and it blew the engines. Seventy-four people died in that accident, including the captain who was trying to bring the aircraft home. There was no mercy.

I know Shakawe airstrip at the head of the Okavango Delta. It was built and maintained by WENELA, to fly miners to and from South Africa. I have gone in there in many different aircraft, even a light jet, a Lear from Lanseria. It is a good surface. They drag a tree behind a tractor to sweep the runway. There is a wind-sock, sometimes a radio beacon. There is also a police station not far from the airstrip and a thatched hut inside the perimeter fence.

The Hercules was parked at Lanseria when the call came from Air Botswana. The water had risen to flood the village of Shakawe. Gaborone did not have any large aircraft available. Some of the people had taken to the water in their boats but the doctor at the clinic and his young daughter, a few policemen, and about eighty villagers had moved to the higher ground of Shakawe airstrip. There had been torrential rains in Angola, the water was still rising.

The C130 has a long range. With a skeleton crew I loaded at Lanseria. The engineer and the navigator could at least handle all electrics and radio. We took off from Lanseria over the Magaliesberg into storm clouds all the way to the border. The clouds broke over Serowe and we spoke to Gaborone. They welcomed us into their country. The thin straight line of the game fence and the road beside it was the only feature in the miles of bush that followed. That game fence has always offended me. It lies in the path of migrating wildebeest, a symbol of man's lack of an eye from the sky. His borders on the ground seldom bear any relation to the needs of animals and people, only to the plans of politicians.

The patterns of pans, windblown streaks of sand, stretched ahead to the Makgadikgadi, which was still dry. After the pan patchwork came Letlhakane, Orapa and Rakops, in that order at the base of the Makgadikgadi. Then we saw the Boteti River, the town of Maun. On our right at two o'clock we could see Chief's Island. The line of the river which marks the base of the delta was still very clear, the sun flashed on the water. Maun was not yet flooded.

We passed over Maun, saw a few light aircraft still on the ground, spoke to the tower. Tower! I have been into that god-forsaken operations room with only one window. The controllers handle mainly Cessnas flying tourists to swamp camps. They also welcomed us, told us that radio contact with Shakawe had now been lost, that we should go straight in, if we could, and pick up as many people as possible.

Normally, the pear-shaped area of the swamp hangs from a thin stalk which is the river. The twisting line of the Okavango attaches the shape to the rest of Africa. From the air the delta is really a most remarkable sight, a huge river emptying itself into the flat desert instead of into the sea. Just where the pear narrows, before the stalk, at the very beginning of the spread of the delta, is the settlement of Shakawe, beyond it the WENELA airstrip. I know the place, know its position, but this time I could see no thin line of deep river, only a vast stretch of water.

I recognised the Tsodilo Hills, ten o'clock, some fifty kilometres away, jutting out, dominant above sprawling lakes. Then I saw the airstrip with the people on it. Some distance from the strip were the dark dots of the few substantial roofs in Shakawe: the police station, the clinic, the WENELA houses by the river. There was no sign of the river bank, no sign of the huts and hovels of the village. The lower end of the airstrip was already under water. At this end, the end from which I approached, I could see the wind-sock on a pole, the small hut and a few vehicles. People were huddled around the vehicles and we could see them wave as we approached. They all seemed to wave, every one of them. The movement of arms held up to us was a ripple of life on the surface of all that water.

Beyond this pathetic island the water stretched not only to the Tsodilo Hills to the west but way past where Mohoka used to be in the east, into the Caprivi. From the air it seemed to me that a new wave of water was approaching slowly, moving down into the delta to cover everything, Namaseri, Xaxaba, Xugana, even Maun itself.

I banked over the water on a left-hand turn. We looked down at the island of people in a sea of floodwater. The navigator shook his head, pointing to the water creeping up the runway from the lower end. 'Even if we get in we will never get out,' was what he said. I was hoping that we could possibly land on what was left of the strip, turn round at once and take off the way we had come. We would not have much time to load. How long would it really take to get that lot aboard? And if the water came up to our wheels, how much drag could we take, how long before our fat belly was flat and floundering in the wrong element?

We had a few crates of cargo from South Africa. Some medical supplies, blankets, tinned food, sacks of mealie meal. We could perhaps drop them by chute but I had not planned to do that. I could hold a pattern at two thousand while we prepared the drop.

It was then that I saw a line of *mokoros* making for the Tsodilo Hills. Soon that would be the only high ground, the 'slippery hills' themselves. I resolved to go in.

Remember, I had been told about the white doctor and his daughter, about the few policemen and about the eighty Tswanas. While I was flying I was in charge, this was my aircraft. As we lost altitude I told my crew of my decision. It was my decision. I did not consult my navigator again, nor my engineer. It was my decision, and those *mokoros* making for the hills were part of it. If even the Hambukushu were afraid of the waters there was real trouble down there.

From the little ground that was left they would have seen the landing gear come down, watched the Hercules lose height, come in on another rescue mission. I suppose they saw us as salvation, a huge modern machine, a complex and powerful creation of today, something which could lift everybody away from the flood. I had thought something similar in the Sudan. After we passed the hook at Wadi Halfa we saw no more water, we flew over the proverbial miles and miles of bloody Africa, dry as dust. When we finally saw the line of people in the desert we realised that they were marking the strip for us, signalling salvation to its landing place. There were also a few vehicles on the ground on that occasion, a village of tents, and I recall a similar sense of despair. What about water? I thought in the desert. Here I thought about dry land, what about dry land? The contrasts of the continent were greater than anything I had ever seen, even from the air.

In the huge and efficient machine I felt quite helpless. I made for the remainder of the Shakawe strip with full flaps on every edge, with as much lift as I could manage, as short a landing as possible. If I had to I could still abort. I aimed to touch down at the very edge of the damp earth at the upstream end of the strip, away from the people. If I was too short, my wheels would be in the water, if I overshot I would be in the drink on the other side.

My eyes automatically swept across the instruments and in that moment, coming down, I had great respect for the machine I was flying. I had to accept that the skills which made it were the skills of other Americans, not me. Those skills had brought man to where he was, in the air. Skill would get me down again, would help me land, not just my skill but the skill of those others, those designers, those instrument-makers. The skill of staying in the air is of a survival order and I thought of people without skills as acutely vulnerable. As vulnerable as I would be without some training in the complexities of this technology, some experience. I was not necessarily proud of my own skill, I simply thought for a moment how I would be if I suddenly lost it, did not come up to the standards of the complex thing I was flying, was suddenly found wanting. Pilot error, they would call it. If I did not watch my instruments, use all the technology available to me, I would succumb. This time I could take a few other people with me. It was not a personal thing, this being the pilot, mine was only one skill. I respected all the others, all the abundance of skills working together to make something like this fly.

I approached that water with the conviction that I could complete this particular mission. My deep respect for all the intricate systems of the machine I was flying would help me win. On my side were the rules and laws and instruments and principles, particularly the principles. The theory of flight became the theory of human survival. Understanding and respect for the elements, the limits, the moment of lift-off, sustained flight, stall. Ignore them, ignore the limits, ignore the achievements of others, lose respect for what has been built so far – imperfect as it might be in relation to creation yet to come – and we end up in the swamp, in a canoe making for the hills.

The Hercules handles like a trainer sometimes, it is a remarkable American machine. I saw the sun flash from the water as I let down, I saw some big logs sweep against an island, other debris floating with the current. We hit the deck on damp sand, I saw the people move away from the far end of the strip, hurry to make space for us. One vehicle already had its wheels in the water.

Even if I say so myself, I think it was a perfect landing, the proverbial cat pissing on velvet, even in those conditions. We pulled up with fifty metres of dry land to spare. I used the taxi space to turn round and face the other way. I looked at the wind-sock on a pole, there was only a light breeze across our line of flight. I would take off downhill.

I asked the navigator to see to the loading and to count the passengers as they came in. We were big but we could only take so many, there were limits. Sensibly, he lowered only one set of steps, the forward one so that he might control any rush or panic. He did not open the big back hatch. I saw some women holding bulging blankets, standing in line. When the steps were down they broke their lines and rushed to the aircraft. They fought for position, stumbled on the stairs. The navigator stopped the first few at the top of the stairs, shouted at them above the noise of our engines.

A big policeman came to the bottom of the steps, waving a carved baton. He pulled the nearest woman down, clambered up the steps and tried to remove the others. He turned at the top of the steps to hold up his baton of authority. In a huge voice he called to his colleagues who, I now saw , were carrying a stretcher. They came at once, lifting the stretcher high to negotiate the steps. Behind them came a white man and a young Tswana man, who held himself very upright, as if he were a soldier escorting a wounded comrade. I presumed, correctly, that the white girl on the stretcher was the doctor's daughter. They lifted the stretcher to their shoulders and climbed the steps, keeping their patient level. The navigator told the bearers to place the stretcher on the floor between two rows of forward seats. The young Tswana took a seat near the stretcher. I turned to welcome them all aboard and recognised the young man at once. He was the fisherman's son, now so much older in appearance, the one from whom I had bought the beautiful carving of a sable. I remembered the fish-eagle too. Then the mob came in.

I was reminded of the loads from Chileka to Francistown. Seventy-four 'pax' in a DC4. I was reminded too of that fateful accident at Francistown, of the things that can go wrong on the most routine of flights. And this was hardly a routine flight, hardly a routine aircraft.

Our configuration was such that we could take four rows of passengers in the cabin up-front, two long rows on either side along the fuselage and tons of material centrally. The seats quickly filled up and then people began to settle themselves on the floor, sitting on their baggage. Again I thought of lowering the back hatch, the freight hatch. I looked out my window to see how many more were to come.

There was an argument at the foot of the stairs. An old woman wanted to take a goat with her up the steps. The big sergeant was very gentle with her, as if he knew her well. He urged her to climb the stairs, to leave the goat on the ground. Reluctantly she put the goat down and it skipped off towards the water. The other people began to come aboard and it seemed to me that many of them were Hambukushu, like the fisherman and his son. At least they were quite small passengers, quite light, but there were so many. I was alarmed to see how many still waited on the ground.

The navigator counted those who were already aboard. The tension was building in both of us. All this was taking too long.

Fortunately, our passengers carried very little weight by way of baggage, very few of them were heavy people. I turned to look at those that were still to come, to count them on the ground. There was a commotion at the back of the queue.

A fight started amongst the remaining men on the ground, perhaps because they thought there would be no room inside. Knives came out and I opened my side flap to shout at them to stop. I saw a man stabbed, saw the others kick at him as he fell to the ground. Sticks were raised, the men fought with their traditional weapons. These were not Hambukushu.

I pushed one throttle forward, full feather. The engine roared; the men looked up at me like guilty children and rushed to the steps. I closed my little window, ordered the steps to be raised, the pressure door closed. There were shouts from the people who were nearly left behind. One man was bleeding. I prepared for takeoff.

I could hear the babble behind me, saw the white girl raise her head on the stretcher, saw the young man reach out a hand to comfort her. The dignified and comforting action, the perfect raised head, the flash attraction of a girl's hair, the pale and anxious expression on an angelic face, drained the blood from my guts, left an empty core. I was spiritless, washed out, struck useless by sudden beauty.

My heart sank as I looked down the runway. The water had approached much closer, it must have reached a particular level to flood a long flat section of the strip. It did not look like enough runway to me, but I was committed. Throttles were through the gate, we were rolling.

On looking back on what happened afterwards, I think my aborted take-off saved many lives. I know that the aircraft sat in mud for a long time, that the enquiry found pilot error, but I still submit that the water would have been like a brick wall against our undercarriage. At near take-off speed we would have come unstuck very badly. I could have killed a lot of those passengers, particularly the ones who were not strapped in. As it was, some of them were thrown around, hurt a bit. There was no AVGAS mixed with AVTUR this time, but something else just as dangerous, just as African. I did not have a viable balance between land and water and air. The extremes were too great for me and for that beautiful Hercules. I regret that I did not try to complete the take-off, to try might have proved me right, but what else would it have proved? I know that we would have flipped had I continued at that speed into deeper water. Instead, we stuck in the mud.

11

We sat in the mud like a sick duck, and that is what we turned out to be, a sick duck. You might ask what use a grounded Hercules might be, what good is something made for flying that has its wheels stuck in the mud. Well, it can be a shelter from the rain, it can become a church, a court house, a hospital or a pathetic symbol of a failed mercy mission. I had flown in with such skill, a veritable Hercules with the troubles of the world on my shoulders, a made-in-America saviour of Africa, and now I was stuck in the swamp like a sick duck. A hollow duck with a wet belly.

First the church. The old woman who wanted to bring her goat on board turned out to be the most powerful witchdoctor of the district. The people said that she had come from Thaba Bosiu, the Mountain of Night. I ask you, the Mountain of Night!

One of the Ovimbundu claimed to come from Angola, said that he had been a priest in Calai. These two together became quite awesome at times and all the others in the plane were under their spell, including the police sergeant, Sergeant Molefe.

Besides these two who claimed to be priests of some kind, there were my fishing friends Pula and John Barotse, Dr Pinto and his daughter Julia and the Tswana policeman Sergeant Molefe. Apparently the Tswana policeman had been instrumental in persuading the reluctant fisherman and his son to climb the steps after the stretcher-bearers. In fact he had ordered them to join the others. Old John Barotse had wanted to stay with his boat on the swamp. I was very happy to have those two on board. To my mind

John Barotse, the dignified old gentleman, was one of the wisest of the whole bunch. He and Dr Pinto, the two fathers, seemed to have a realistic understanding of our predicament on this particular Noah's ark. We had the dimensions and the polyglot load of passengers, we could see a mountain, but we could not get to it. Noah found a mountain somehow, stuck on it after the flood. This lot were meant to fly: we could not even float.

There was also me, the pilot, and my skeleton crew, the navigator and the engineer. Theoretically, I was still the captain of the aircraft and therefore responsible for everything that happened to it – or in it. The rest were mostly Hambukushu. There were also a few Ngwato and Ngwaketse, six tall Hereros, three Kalanga, four Owambo, a group of Ovimbundu from Angola, led by their adopted priest.

The passengers all seemed to understand the Tswana language, but appeared not to trust one another at all. They soon separated into their tribal camps, quite naturally. Simple boundaries were drawn, with some class structure from floor to lateral seats. Almost First Class, Business Class and Economy, although the Hercules conversion was not done with that in mind. I made sure that John Barotse had a seat near the door.

Dr Pinto used a length of crêpe bandage from his bag to mark a barrier between the front rows and the rest, some sort of dividing line between his sick daughter and the rest, a simple demarcation of a sanatorium ward. He stretched the bandage across the aisle to isolate himself and his patient.

The Ovimbundu asked for more crêpe bandage to do the same, to put a dividing line between themselves and the Hambukushu, but the doctor's supply was limited.

Deeply concerned about his daughter, Dr Pinto suggested that I should order a military chopper with floats from South Africa to take her to hospital. He asked me to tell her that I would do so, that I would get her away from this place, from the awful predicament. She needed to be in a hospital, he said, and he led me to her make-shift bed. She was lying on her side facing away from us but she must have sensed her father's approach. She turned slowly on to her back, she moved a pale hand to the edge of the stretcher on which she lay and a faint smile greeted us.

'The pilot will get you out of here,' Dr Pinto said and all I could do was to nod my head in assent and smile back at her. Now I really was useless. Here was the pathetic embodiment of all my do-good intentions, here was a real person to rescue from a real predicament, but what could I do? Me and my useless bloody aeroplane. As if any rescue effort from the air or from the dizzy heights of good intention, was doomed from birth. And yet she was so serene. An innocent in Africa.

I looked again at that gentle face, at the striking pallor of eternity in the pale olive skin. I believed myself to be in a saintly presence. This was no girl lost in the swamp, this was a woman of purpose struck down by some terrible African disease. I could do nothing and I could say nothing. I was struck dumb, if you like, again struck by the beauty of her, by the touch of death perhaps, or by the faint and all-forgiving smile of eternal womanhood. Here, this saintly presence, this yearned-for virgin in white, this unexpected gentleness, in my aeroplane!

'I will try,' I managed to whisper to her, knowing suddenly how truly lost I was.

When the navigator tried to radio he was told that there was a new diplomatic hold-up in South Africa, some trouble across borders. I had thought, initially, that all the passengers would be lifted out in a day or two, or the water would recede enough to allow the strip to dry in the Kalahari sun, allow me to open the back hatch and let them all go home. I had not expected this emotional shock, this sudden and unwelcome revelation of my own vulnerability. Nor had I expected the African theatre to come.

The first time my Hercules became a church, I had to interrupt the proceedings when the ritual became too much like a nightmare. I had to stay with the real world. The ceremony started on the evening of the first day. I had ordered no more cabin lights. The engineer was not eager to use fuel running one engine just to charge the batteries; we had to stay in the dark. We would see by the light of day, sleep at night. Little fires were lit by the Hambukushu and my crew stamped on flames in some anger.

As we sat in the evening darkness on that first night, the priest, the one from Angola, called for silence while he lit a small oil lamp. I was concerned about the flame, but let him continue. A thin wisp of smoke rose from the tiny flame which he held at his chest so that his face was lit up – awesome, as I said. He placed the small lamp on the back of a seat and in the half-light he spoke to his audience in extraordinary English, as if he had been trained by the London Missionary Society. Indeed, he talked of David Livingstone as his brother, the first of his order ever to reach the swamps, to walk across Africa all the way to Luanda. Holding his little black bible in one hand, hugging it to his armpit, he talked of Moffat, of salvation. He looked up to where I was standing near the door to the cockpit and raised his voice, addressing me above the heads of his congregation. He asked whether any of the white people in the church knew of Livingstone or Moffat and of their work amongst the people.

It was Dr Pinto who first saw the point of this sophistry. The priest from Angola was insisting on an answer from some white person, preferably from me. He was trying hard to separate the few of us from the 'pax'.

Dr Pinto answered for me. He said, in the waiting silence of my church, that the great man of whom he spoke was the same man who set the example we should all follow, who travelled with Chief Sekeletu all the way across the continent to Luanda in Angola. He had freed the slaves of Africa.

At which the priest repeated the word slavery, slavery, slavery. He asked his audience whether they were released from slavery, whether they were truly free. He was perhaps using an old text, somewhat out of place. Who had to live in mud huts, he asked, while others flew through the air in machines such as this great creation in which we all found ourselves?

The question did not seem to strike a ready response; I don't think they understood much of this. Old John Barotse knew enough English and he said out loud that he would rather be in a *mokoro* as his ancestors had been, following the water wherever it might lead, than sitting in this useless thing listening to a man from Angola. There was some giggling from the Hambukushu women, and Dr Pinto immediately saw the danger of this. He clearly did not want the impromptu ceremony to end without dignity, did not want the priest to lose face.

Dr Pinto asked the priest to bless the whole gathering, to ask for deliverance for all of us, for his daughter too. I bowed my head too, I knew what deliverance we needed. On all the mercy missions I had flown I had not come across anything quite like this.

Strictly speaking it was not my Hercules. It was only an agent of one of many African missions that had been mounted over the years, but when I was in control of it, I looked upon it as mine. Just as I looked upon the country where I was born as mine, as the leading civilised country of the world. My country was about as disparate as this Hercules load, but it was more a white mix than a black mix, a European stew rather than an African stew, but with strong African flavouring. Even we had our own problems with tribes, so did Europe.

I hoped that my country would not one day prove to be as useless as my Hercules. All that technical equipment, that flying promise so close to takeoff, brought down.

What missions could we fly now, stuck in the mud like this? We were at least a priest's delight, a captive audience in trouble.

There was some order to the service, the priest seemed to have some kind of message, but I was not prepared for the next participant in the drama of the coming long night.

It was the old woman who had left her goat behind. Her name was Bubi. Everyone seemed to know Bubi. She stood on an aisle seat in the back row and screamed at the people in a very shrill voice. She waved something above her head in a frenzy, a sort of rough balloon which whipped through the air with a peculiar whirring sound, like a half-feathered prop. She loped down the aisle in her scraggy outfit, animal teeth hanging at her throat, weird bones in her hair, still screaming at everyone. I suppose she was shouting to her own converts, a competitive performance for those who appreciated this sort of thing after the English tones of the priest.

Right at my feet she threw some fire. How the hell she did it I do not know, but it startled me and I stamped it out at once. It was some kind of burning powder but I saw no match struck, nothing, just the sudden bolt of fire. Then she knelt before the tiny ashes which were now under my old flying boot, and she offered something else to me. In her hand she held her offering. It looked like a thin stick of biltong, or a piece of dark chocolate. I did not take it at first but she insisted. I then reached out my hand and took it. It was a human finger, skeleton bone covered in dry skin, but alive enough in its horror in my hand. I took it to be the finger of a woman. I imagined the pale olive skin of the beautiful girl on a stretcher, saw her hand minus one finger. I was lost again, in some limbo of disbelief which brought such unwanted images.

Bubi then produced a little bottle from the folds of her ochre skirt, removed the dirty cork and motioned to me to dip the finger into the opening of the bottle. She smiled the while, pointing to the neck of the bottle with her own gnarled finger. I heard the beginning of ululation from the women. The sound took over, it filled the big hall of the Hercules so that it became a witch's cave. First a church and then a witch's cave. I knew there was blood in that bottle, that I was meant to dip the finger into it. The body and the blood. I could not. I reached for a paper bag from one of the seat pockets near me, dropped the finger into it, and told the navigator to take the woman to her place in the back of the aircraft.

'Only the gods can help you fly,' the old hag shrieked as she was led away.

All was ominously quiet in the cave as the woman returned to her place. The ululating stopped. The gathering waited in shocked silence as if I had insulted their god, or at least the messenger of their god. I had sworn at her, committed sacrilege, sent her away. I could sense the growing hostility towards me. There had been no hostility to Dr Pinto when the other priest was in control. It was as if the Portuguese white man could participate legitimately because the priest was from some other church, not really of their belief. Bubi on the other hand was theirs and I had insulted her. I looked at Dr Pinto, saw that he had his face in his hands, he seemed to be praying still. He was leaning forward in his seat, almost in the brace position. His daughter was lying on her back, quite still on the stretcher, which had been laid across three seats as a sick-bed. Somehow I had offended her too, by the thought of that finger. Pula watched me and I felt that he knew of my utter confusion. I wanted to apologise to the people, I wanted to comfort the girl the way Pula did. I even wanted to take her in my arms and promise to take her away from all this.

I was quite disturbed, I can tell you. These sudden pale visions, the sense of loss and longing. I had also interrupted a primitive ritual, I was in very unfamiliar territory, the people were restless. I knew I had to take control again. I needed to restore household order, as it were, after the disturbances.

I raised my voice, spoke like an army officer, ordered Sergeant Molefe to interpret for me. I explained about the toilets at the back, their substantial but limited storage, explained that one set of steps would be deployed to the water, that the men at least should go outside that way. 'Who knows,' I said, smiling at John Barotse, to show that I knew at least one of their number, that I could talk to fishermen, 'maybe some of your Hambukushu friends in *mokoros* will come and visit us.'

This little speech was received with even greater hostility. A low hissing began and they began to move towards me. I saw Pula lift up the crêpe bandage barrier that marked the place where the suffering girl was being cared for by her father. He ducked under the barrier, stepped out to talk to the Hambukushu.

The general reaction was immediate. They watched his hands in the half-light, the flickering shadow of his hands against the bulkhead. He held them out, open, inviting them to listen. He explained to them what I had been saying, appealed to reason. Look, we are in this together, all of us. The people watched his hands as if in awe of them, as if they held some peacemaking secret.

He told them that the doctor's daughter, Julia, was very ill, that she had the sleeping sickness. He said that she needed her own kind of medicine, and that her father would look after her in his own way, just as everyone must look after their own in their own way. Bubi was right, only the gods would let the aeroplane fly, and there were many gods.

A low and rhythmic chant rose from the congregation and Bubi herself waved her wand above her head and slowly came down the aisle to touch old man Barotse with it and then to tap Pula's outstretched hand. I now seemed to have another ally, apart from the old fisherman and his son.

What I had predicted to my initially hostile audience, happened the next morning. I heard John Barotse calling from the open door. He was shouting excitedly to a group of people in *mokoros*. In the stern of each craft sat a man with a single paddle. The *mokoros* were heavily laden, they were low on the water. I wondered if this would be another tribe, bringing other gods, more trouble.

These people were also Hambukushu, John Barotse told me. Even their high land was flooded. They were angry, they accused him loudly of making too much rain, and of wanting to fly away from his people in a big aeroplane! There was something terribly wrong. Never before had this happened to them. Now the only dry place was the big aeroplane and they wanted to come aboard, to join the others, to escape this final flood which would destroy them all. They too wanted to fly away to some other land, find other resting places. They wished to abandon the river for the sky because some awful day of judgement was coming. It had all been predicted, long ago, there would be a great flood because the rain gods had been so offended by their earthly agent.

That was it, John Barotse had failed them. As their earthly representative he had failed them, now was the time for judgement. As far as I was concerned John Barotse was almost as important to me as his son was proving to be. These two were at least representatives of the majority, they were Hambukushu. They believed that the white girl Julia, who was so ill, had the sleeping sickness. They certainly knew all about the disease. What other diseases would come aboard with this new batch?

I thought again of lowering the back hatch, of allowing our new refugees to come in that way, but too many Hambukushu already huddled inside near the tail of the aircraft. They would make room for the others if I allowed them to enter in a single file, up the steps. One by one the *mokoros* came to the bottom of the steps, unloaded more passengers.

Pula told Dr Pinto of his belief that Julia was suffering from the swamp disease, but the doctor did not agree with this diagnosis. He had no arsenical compound, but he also had reasons for his doubt, medical reasons. Despite the general tribal acceptance of the diagnosis, he solemnly told Pula that there were contrary signs, that there was some clinical doubt, no one could be sure at this stage. He would collect all the evidence, before pronouncing on the fate of his daughter who was now so very ill.

'I was with her when the fly bit her leg,' Pula said.

'You told me. But there are other signs.'

'Bubi has seen signs too. She is a doctor. She agrees with me.'

'Signs, Pula? What signs do we all look for? Signs to guide us in our faith, a fetish to believe in? Some medical sign, some magic?'

'She is very ill. Even the pilot knows that.'

Pula Barotse looked at me and there was distinct challenge in his eyes, as if he had understood my own shock on first seeing Julia, as if he were the sole judge of her condition. That pallor between life and death, that poignant beauty so threatened, very life itself in fragile balance.

'Yes, I know that,' I said, 'I also know that she will survive.'

'By whose medicine?' Pula asked me, but Dr Pinto answered.

'I will be the judge of that,' he said.

12

The judge! The judge had no court, the pilot had no plane to fly. The engineer had only useless engines. The navigator had his maps but remained in one place. The passengers waited, going nowhere. And the doctor, Dr Sergio Pinto, could he indeed be the judge of his daughter's predicament? He had no laboratory, no hospital, only a suspect diagnosis. He was no Schweitzer in Africa, no Livingstone, no doctor playing God. Like all of us he faced the breakdown of order and, uniquely, the breakdown of his daughter.

On the morning of the third day, more *mokoros* arrived at my ill-fated ark. The refugee people all told the same story of flooded villages, no dry land. All that could be seen above the surface of the water were the tops of tall trees, some of the roofs of Shakawe and Mohembo. There was nowhere to go. Even for people who knew how to live in balance between the high water and the low water, there was nowhere to go.

The number of *mokoros* moored to the aircraft grew quite alarmingly. Each arrived with people and their meagre belongings, some food and some firewood stacked amidships. The firewood stayed in the *mokoros* but the people and the food came aboard.

Conditions in the cabin deteriorated further. Any crowded cave will begin to smell, this one was no exception. There was some disposal to the water outside but the natural detritus of crowded living began to accumulate, the odour of our slow decay was pervasive. We were decaying in isolation, the world had forgotten us, we were an abandoned garbage vessel floating nowhere.

I asked the engineer to take over the rationing, to plan for a further week as a minimum. The mealie meal was the problem. We now had only three bags in our storage areas, stacked along with bundles of blankets and useless tents and other emergency material. The passengers now numbered ninety-five; six hundred pounds of mealie-meal, less than a pound a day for each of them. Their own food would not last for long, they would look to us for supplies. They would insist that a big airship like this would surely carry enough supplies for all? If not, why had they come aboard? They needed food so the big ship would have to provide. That was how it would be.

The engineer kept aside a few special rations for our patient, Julia Pinto, but now she could not eat. I held a spoonful of warm soup to her lips and my heart lifted when she sipped. Her father told me that she complained of intense headaches. He suspected another bout of malaria at first but a few symptoms were inconsistent, he said. I knew all about malaria, I had carried it in me for years, knew the headaches.

Pula still insisted that it was the swamp sickness. He told us again about the time in the bush, when Julia had been bitten by a tsetse fly. He spoke of the fly on her leg. She could do nothing about it. She was bound there to the ant-hill, not far from the village. Even at the time it was all happening, Pula feared that the tsetse on her leg would carry the disease. Now that it was clear to every Mbukushu that she had the swamp sickness, why was it not clear to her father, to the doctor?

On the fourth morning, outside the aeroplane, John Barotse saw more *mokoros* approaching and he saw that the people in them had paddles, not poles. That was what made him think they were Hambukushu, that they might also blame him for the flood, blame him for the rain up-country. He looked up the steps towards the open door, called to me, but I did not hear his call. I was busy with the engineer, looking at a leak in the joint of the tailgate. The water was above the line of the main hydraulic lift, which was why we had not lowered it. The women heard the shout.

From the tail-gate mechanism to the open side door and the one set of steps deployed to the water, was a considerable stretch of fully occupied fuselage. The Hambukushu had cleared a rough path for us to walk between them, along the central line of freight clips, but we still had to step over people and belongings to return to the open door. The shout which I did not hear was heard by others nearer the door and one man called out to John Barotse at the base of the steps. John Barotse had seen the other *mokoros* approach, and he knew from the awkward way in which they paddled that the craft were not Hambukushu. I sensed some urgency in his words but I did not understand them. The engineer and I turned to move away from the tail-gate and we heard more shouting outside the aircraft and then felt the distinctive movement of men on the steps; a staccato drumming which reverberated through the fuselage.

First came John Barotse, who scrambled up the steps, scurried through the door in a great hurry. He lunged towards Sergeant Molefe, calling out to him.

'Police! Police!' he shouted.

Behind John Barotse appeared a man with an AK47 rifle. This man pulled the trigger, shooting wildly above the people in the crowded aircraft, hitting one of the women, puncturing the fuselage. There was screaming from the women and then there were three men at the door, three rifles. The engineer and I were half way down the centre aisle, stepping over the people cowering there.

I saw Sergeant Molefe respond to the old man's call. He rose to confront the terrorists, raised his elaborate baton, an unusual carving, just as the shots went off. Dr Pinto moved to help the stricken woman. Pula crouched down close to Julia, his body blocking hers. They both recognised the voice of Potlako Lereng.

'Sit down everybody,' the voice said, 'sit down in your comfortable aircraft.' He pointed his rifle at Sergeant Molefe in front of me, demanded that he hand over the baton.

'Where did you get that?' he asked and Sergeant Molefe stepped forward with it. He stood tall and defiant in front of the hijacker, authority itself.

'From a Zulu. The man you murdered.'

'Fat pig! Policeman! Give it to me!'

'Lereng! You are under arrest.'

Potlako Lereng jabbed the barrel of the AK47 into Sergeant Molefe's stomach and ordered his comrade to take the baton from him. Then he demanded immediate food and drink, as if he were raiding an African kraal, as if he too should be fed from our supplies. He wanted food and drink, and he wanted a doctor for an injured colleague who was lying in the bottom of a *mokoro* outside. Where was the doctor? His eyes swept to the white people first. He saw me, he saw Julia lying there, Pula crouching next to her.

'Ah! The beautiful Portuguese girl!' he said.

Stepping away with the god-model now in his hand, away from his second comrade who still covered the people from the door, he walked slowly towards the place where Julia lay. He looked down at her for a silent moment. The knot of women tending one of their number, the one who had been shot by a stray bullet, watched from the aisle. Pula rose to his feet to face Potlako.

Potlako reached down with the carving, flicked away the blanket which covered Julia. She lay on her back staring at him. Her father had dressed her in a white cotton coat, one of his working coats from the clinic. Now he saw that the cloth was too light, his daughter too exposed to this man. Her olive-brown skin was golden against the white cloth, the bulge of her thigh smooth and firm, no longer a child's shape.

Potlako began to stroke her exposed thigh with the young side of the carving in his hand. He ran the hardwood to her knees, then lower to her feet and toes. He transferred the baton to his other hand, took one big toe between thumb and forefinger and shook it, as if playing a game again.

'Once there were many Portuguese girls in Angola,' Potlako Lereng said. Pula leaned over Julia, stretched out, drew the blanket back to cover her. She raised a weak hand in acknowledgement and I noticed that the hand was shivering.

'Leave her alone!' I shouted.

Potlako let out a loud guffaw of laughter and his comrades joined him with great glee. All three men slapped the butts of their rifles as if at a given signal. They faced me then turned to the passengers, brandishing their loaded weapons, still laughing along with their leader, sharing his fun. One of them took a pack of cigarettes from his shirt pocket, giggling like an excited schoolboy. He offered the pack to his leader, took one for himself with his teeth. With a flourish he produced a lighter. When the two cigarettes were alight he stepped towards Pula, held the small flame of the lighter beneath Pula's nose, raised it to singe a little hair. The pungent odour of burning hair was immediate and menacing in the silent hall.

Potlako drew on his own cigarette, taking his time, holding his rifle in the crook of the one arm, tapping the barrel with Pula's wooden carving. He took in smoke deeply, contemplated the glowing end of his cigarette, then also stepped close to Pula. He drew smoke again, puffed it into Pula's eyes. He then thrust out his hand, twisted the cigarette into the flesh of Pula's neck.

'Is this pilot man your friend?' he asked.

Pula must have heard the copper bangles click, I know I did. In reflex he pulled his head away, brought both hands up to grab the hand holding the cigarette, but Potlako was too quick. He stepped back, laughing, raised the assault rifle again.

'I will do just as I wish with her,' Potlako said. 'Maybe I will cut a little line on that white cheek, put a little of my ash into it so that she will always carry my scar.'

Pula raised one hand to press the burn on his neck. Potlako shifted grip, thrust the weapon at Pula.

'The games are over!' Potlako said, his finger on the trigger.

Pula dropped the hand which was pressing the burn on his neck, slowly searched in his pocket, drew out his small knife, closed.

'Remember this, Potlako? This little knife. With it I made the god which is in your hand. With it I will kill you.' Pula opened the knife, deliberately, watching his enemy. He stepped closer to Julia.

'Do you not feel the spirit of the Zulu burning your hand?'

Perhaps it was the bravado with which Pula said this, perhaps it was a simple call to duty, which made Sergeant Molefe choose this moment to act. Perhaps he saw Pula's challenge as sufficient diversion, as an opening for his own attack. Perhaps he really thought he could arrest the murderer.

Sergeant Molefe leapt on Potlako Lereng and tried to take his rifle from him. Potlako fell to the floor from the ferocious charge of the big man. Dr Pinto and Pula sprang together and Dr Pinto tried to grab the barrel of the rifle as the man fell. A shot went off, muffled by the big body of Sergeant Molefe.

The engineer and I made for the two armed men at the door just as both of them fired from the hip, aiming at the tangle of men attacking their leader. They then turned their rifles to us and both the engineer and I stopped where we were, held up our hands at once in traditional surrender in the face of madmen. The distance between us and the door was such that the two with the rifles could have taken their time about bringing us down. Nobody closer to them seemed inclined to act. This was the end then, the terrorist success, the complexity simplified, many lives lost, this was the sudden tragedy.

The passengers were in fact very still, frozen in their places, hushed after the explosions in the confined space. One hijacker still covered us, the other went to the knot of bodies on the floor.

Potlako and Pula rose together from the floor. Pula still held his small knife and Potlako still had the weapon with which he had killed Sergeant Molefe.

Slowly Dr Pinto also struggled to rise, his one arm hanging. There was blood pouring from his hand. He held a thumb to a pressure point on the injured arm, moved to find his own doctor's bag.

Potlako Lereng shook the familiar AK47 in a quivering hand, lifted it like a prize, kicked the bleeding body of Sergeant Molefe. He stepped to Pula and jabbed the barrel of the weapon into his stomach once more, then hit him with his own carving.

'You die and your girlfriend dies!' he shouted, 'I will collect some *diretlo*.'

The threat to Julia, the very melodrama of the man's words, the open violence, chilled me to paralysis. I heard, I understood but I could not move. This man lived in the shadow of ritual, he understood very deeply the role of violence in Africa and the fear which rendered it powerful. All those from the Mountain of Night, where light is the enemy, must preach violence to ensure that light does not destroy them. It has ever been so. Who, seeking power over the spirit of man, has not resorted to violence? Who in history, believing, has not threatened the disbeliever with violence? In the murky darkness of fearful spirits, violence is the final discipline. Until the individual spirit can come out into the light, can live without fear of others who wish to control it, violence will win.

13

Potlako Lereng took great pleasure in ordering me to drag the big body of Sergeant Molefe to the door. The engineer was told to help me throw the body out and into the water. Potlako and his men covered the operation as I took the sergeant's arms, the engineer his legs. We shuffled together with the heavy body towards the door. It dragged on the floor and we were told to lift him higher, to throw him far. Some women began to chant, a funeral chant.

Potlako Lereng shouted out that the chanting must stop and it did. We also stopped near the door with our burden. Potlako Lereng called to his two comrades, told them to stand next to him, like armed guards, to face the cortege. He then addressed us in a voice of heavy scorn.

'What is an Mbukushu?' Potlako asked. 'It is only a grape which grows along the banks of a river! You are only wild grapes for others to eat, that is what you are. You are little people, useless people, with no power.'

This they all knew, they had no power, but what was the mad man about to do now? His voice altered, became one of heavy authority, as if, having dismissed the Hambukushu, he would address the rest, including me.

'But Africa has the power, not you! It also has many people many cattle and many diamonds! That is what! Diamonds for Africa! Here in Botswana, at my home in Lesotho, in Angola, in Namibia. Do you know these places, you stupid people? Do you know about the diamond mines? Soon we will have them all! From Angola to Moçambique, from the Cunene right along the Okavango, the Zambezi, down to the sea on the other coast, we will occupy all Africa, own all the cattle and all the diamonds!'

'Amandla!' his colleagues called in unison.

'And listen, when I have finished what I have to do, I will take the *diretlo* back to the Mountain of Night and I will rule from there. You will then truly see the power that is in my hands.'

He raised the carving once again, the lizard and the chameleon, the young man and the old man. He waved it above the listening people who eyes watched the wand as it moved.

I felt the dead hand move in mine, felt it respond to the man's madness, as if in reflex. It was as if Sergeant Molefe had heard the word 'amandla', was reminding me of it. Power was the difference, power to fly, power for the Hambukushu to survive the flood, power to remain free of the barbarians. Power for each to define his own space, power over the land and the sky, power to make rain, power to stay alive. That became paramount for all of those under the reality of this immediate terror. It was a very simple need, a universal need. We needed to mobilise the power of living men, the power of a conviction which would lead to action against this madness. We needed the power of those rifles, we needed our own soldiers, we needed the restored power of Sergeant Molefe, we needed the symbol of his baton. We wanted to live.

On Potlako Lereng's command we lifted the sergeant's body again. I returned the pressure of the dead hand as if I might persuade the flesh to revive. We had no power and we had been told to throw a body into the water. This body was not needed, only the bodies of Pula and Julia, they were still needed.

The engineer had no power, the navigator, the doctor, the priest, the pilot, we all had no power and that was the root of our terror, the root of all terror for the future. Only these men with the guns had the power, three bandits, three savages led by a maniac. The judge, where is the judge?

There was a commotion amongst the people, a tentative

ululation began again and grew stronger as an apparition moved along the aisle. With a skin cloak covering her like a carapace, Bubi moved past the people huddled on the floor, came forward towards Potlako and his troops at attention. She mumbled in Sotho, repeating a phrase:

'Thaba Bosiu, Thaba Bosiu. Mountain of Night, Mountain of Night.'

Potlako Lereng must have heard it too, because he smiled as the apparition approached.

Bubi shuffled forward, draped in the well-worn skin of a sitatunga. She moved like some ground animal seeking its hole, moaning, rolling her shoulders as she crept, as if suffering beneath her carapace, on her knees in some urgent supplication. She crawled along the aisle like some lowly creature, scratching her way forward towards the new power, the new chief, the new god. She grovelled at the feet of the armed men, who seemed to welcome the new apparition and its purpose. The ululation swelled up as she shuffled closer to slump at Potlako's feet.

'It is Bubi, from the Mountain of Night,' Potlako said, reaching down to touch the mound of animal skin with his baton, as if in honour. The men beside him knelt to touch the hem of her skin cloak. The ululation grew to crescendo.

I slowly lowered the dead arms once again, the engineer lowered the legs so that Sergeant Molefe was an offering of some kind, a spread-eagled sacrifice for Bubi.

At that awesome moment the priest, the one from Calai, the man with the book, came defiantly from amongst his people to stand above Julia's bed, stand next to Pula. He held both hands out as if he were blessing his congregation. He spoke in his missionary English and even the bandits seemed to listen for a moment. They looked towards him from their position of homage to Bubi, heard his blessing.

The priest droned on above the limp body of Julia Pinto, his arms held out in blessing. I stood near a dead man's head, the engineer stood at the feet. Potlako Lereng and his comrades were in awe of Bubi from the Mountain of Night. The macabre tableau was held for a moment as if the players were frozen in their awful roles. I saw Dr Pinto move closer to Julia, closer to his doctor's bag, saw him touch Pula with his good hand, as if passing on some message. The ululating reached a peak of intensity as Bubi writhed like an animal, holding the attention of all who were witnesses to the moment.

Dr Pinto opened his bag with his good hand, took out a bandage as well as a small canister. He nodded to Pula who also reached for something in the bag.

The bundle of skin which was Bubi then burst from her hunched position of supplication like an explosion; fires and sparks flared beneath her cloak. Her sudden scream joined the ululation at full pitch, it filled the cabin with savage sound, a terrible siren. She flapped at the startled men who seemed to forget their rifles. She rose like a fighting cock and the women's noise behind her was like a strong wind, as they massed to support her, a tide of moving shapes following her lead. Bubi leapt in one final frenzy, another flash of fire rose from her.

Potlako raised his rifle to waist height as the mob poured towards him behind their protective animal, the fighting cock. He pulled the trigger just before Dr Pinto and Pula got to him. The doctor had a cannister in his hand, squirting a foul spray. Pula attacked Potlako Lereng with a scalpel. He slashed with the knife before Potlako could raise his arms to protect his eyes from the stinging spray. Potlako dropped the stolen baton, his staring eyes were opened, the thin blade cut a neat line across his face and then Pula brought him down, ripped the rifle from his hands. Without his weapon, Potlako rolled away from Pula and ran like a wounded crab, scrambling over the frightened people with sudden agility. He did not stop at the door but leapt down to the water.

The doctor was still attacking with his awful-smelling stuff, going for the eyes of these raiding comrades as if he were destroying vermin. The engineer had his man, had the rifle. The fighting cock subsided in a heap of animal skins.

The Hambukushu rose then, like a tide, and covered the blinded bandits who had seen their leader run. That was the last thing they saw.

Pula ran to the door of the aircraft. He still held the rifle which he had taken from Potlako, blood up like a hunter. He raised the unfamiliar weapon to shoot the man in the water. His hand shook but he pulled the trigger. Bullets spattered the surface of the water below, a sudden misdirected burst. From the height of the aircraft door Pula saw Potlako Lereng rise from the water to grope for the low gunwale of a *mokoro*. As the murderer lifted himself aboard in hurried escape, the *mokoro* rolled and the wounded comrade who had been lying there was tipped into the water. Pula saw Lereng try again, twist awkwardly into the *mokoro*, which then took in more water and lay low, flat and flooded.

Pula had time enough, position enough, to pick out his target before it floated away under the big wing of the crippled aircraft. Again he raised the rifle to shoot, again he pulled the trigger, but the magazine was spent. His finger remained on the trigger. He looked along the length of the weapon and, partly through the sights, saw a crocodile rise to pluck Potlako's wounded comrade from the water. He saw Potlako himself swim strongly away from the slaughter, thrashing his strong arms in a desperate effort to escape. He was also pulled down near the stricken *mokoro*, but he rose again, fighting. He was awkward in the water, one arm trapped by something, but then he appeared to free himself. He swam unevenly away, another victim of the flood.

There would be bodies in the mud when the waters finally subsided. The bodies of men and cattle and wild animals. The ancient gods, the feeding crocodiles, might be able to offer some answers to the eternal cycle of violence. Man lived always in awe of the gods, sensing the ritual power of flesh and blood.

Deeply disturbed by the sudden violence, Pula turned away from the door, only to witness the final dispatch of Potlako's comrades. The Hambukushu threw their remains out to the flood waters.

Bubi had risen unharmed from beneath her cloak. She now stood over Julia, stroked her prostrate body with the carving which had been abandoned by Potlako. She lifted the blanket, laid the figurine at Julia's side so that she could embrace it with limp arms.

'You hold on to this thing which Pula has made for you,' Bubi instructed. 'In it is all the strength of the Hambukushu.'

O GODS — I

14

I was still meant to be in control of this disintegrating society, but I watched as things steadily worsened. Dr Pinto had treated his own hand and he still treated his daughter. When he told me that his daughter might be going blind, I did not wish to hear it. She complained, he told me, of a dark haze in front of her left eye, an opaque film of blindness. Her eyelids were very puffy. Her father felt below her ears with his good hand. Her lymph glands were badly swollen, he told us.

Dr Pinto tried to make Julia eat. She would take a little, then fade away. She appeared to be paralysed for long moments, the depth of her fatigue was profound. Dr Pinto was also fatigued. He had washed his wounded hand free of his own blood, as he had washed his hands of other blood on so many occasions, but he could not wash away the infectious detritus around him. The vivid memory of the big man's death, of the bullet which had passed through the big body to shatter his own hand, had unsettled him deeply. He had done what he could, but he knew well enough that he needed treatment himself. He knew the complexity of any hand, the danger from ripped sinews, shattered bone, let alone from infection.

Pula and I together changed the doctor's dressings, following his instructions. The wound looked awful to me and Pula asked Bubi to examine it. She brought some fine powder and dried herbs and wanted to dress the wound with her own materials. Dr Pinto politely refused, pointed to a phial containing his own kind of powder. He did not really know the extent of his own disability, and now he examined the body of his daughter with a dangerous mix of fear and profession. Her eyes were going. He had to accept the Hambukushu diagnosis and then he confirmed for himself Winterbottom's sign. He was looking for proof, not wanting to find it. Enlargement of lymph nodes in the posterior cervical triangle. He considered error, some other cause, some other site on her body. He stood up, away from his beloved patient, away from his searching for that which he did not wish to find. He finally confirmed what Pula already knew. It was the sleeping sickness, she could fade away within days.

I had given Dr Pinto all the first-aid boxes and drugs on board, gave him the full medical inventory. There was not much, but Dr Pinto, despite his own disability, was thorough and professional in his effort to ameliorate the worsening condition of the passengers. He expanded his sick-bay, moved the crêpe bandage barrier to include more space. The people now came to him with their complaints, many of which he could not understand. He asked Pula to stay with his daughter, regularly checked her condition himself. He treated his own wound as best he could with our inept help and I shuddered when I saw the open and ugly mess of what had previously been a precious healing hand.

There was now growing disorder. The passengers became a huge burden to me, refugees who disturbed my spirit. Even in the aircraft which could not fly, there was continuing responsibility for me, but I also felt weak, wanted someone else to take over. Some one else must heal Dr Pinto's hand, help him heal all those sickening people. Now I knew how remote my mercy missions had previously been. I had flown in with the rescue equipment of the first world, arrogant, sure of my next take-off back to base. I had been quite unaware of the true conditions on the ground. Like a rich man in a cloak amongst the unclean, I had wrapped myself in the soft silk of superiority, knowing that I could spread my cloak any time I wished, fly away from it all. Now I could not fly away.

Pula and the doctor tried to bring some kind of order to the rapidly deteriorating society. John Barotse suggested the appointment of a Kalanga policeman to take Sergeant Molefe's place and he in turn appointed two Kalanga to be his constables, men he could trust. We fell at once under Kalanga control.

Even in that closed capsule the order of this mixed society was established by rows. They became groups, small societies within one society. They created around themselves conditions as near as possible to home. There was little water, inside, for the Hambukushu women, but they made themselves a small kraal in the back and continuously fetched water for the kraal. They washed their babies in flood water, wrapped them in dry skins, let them sleep in primitive cradles hitched to freight webbing.

The Ovimbundu, somewhat aloof, found a place a few metres away from the main body of Hambukushu. They appointed one of their women to negotiate space and facilities with the Kalanga policemen. A woman, through whom life was inherited, could be as powerful as any man through whom only land was inherited. She asked the new policemen what power they now had over land, insisted on separate cooking facilities for Ovimbundu food and demanded priority in the matter of water collection.

The Hambukushu thereupon tried to stop the Ovimbundu women fetching water for themselves and blocked the path to the door. They said they would control all water. The swamp was theirs, they insisted, the gods had bequeathed it to them. Once, it now seemed so long ago, I had trivialised such things, but now I was beginning to understand.

Julia's temperature became truly alarming. Pula sponged her down, treated her with great tenderness. Even in his own distress her father knew that Pula was in love with her, and he seemed to sense the poignancy and the futility of it.

The navigator told me that he had been able to contact the private tower at Orapa. He had asked them to contact the South African military to send a chopper with floats. The response was vague; further diplomatic difficulties had arisen, there were other stranded communities seeking help. Besides, Orapa told him, further heavy weather was approaching Ngamiland.

I did not discuss this contact with anyone else until a small plane approached us in the evening sky, flying quite low. The navigator spoke to him by radio, suggested supply drops. I called Dr Pinto and he immediately took the microphone with his good hand and explained his desperate need for medical supplies. He seemed to ramble on about disease, about antibiotics, mentioned specific drugs and was obviously becoming incoherent.

'Say again,' a voice suggested.

The light aircraft buzzed the Hercules once more, waved wings in departure.

'They have our exact position,' I said to Dr Pinto as if that might be some comfort to him.

I looked with some envy at the disappearing aircraft and then at my pathetic load. I had nearly made it, nearly lifted the lot off as I was supposed to do, but it now seemed to be so long ago. There was such power in my machine, if only I had been able to use that power in time, lift off. Perhaps that was the origin of my mercy missions: I had once seen myself above the suffering on the ground, using my power to rise away, to remain aloof from it all. This time I had failed. Pula told me that my aircraft was like a fish-eagle brought down, struggling with a load it could not carry.

After the departure of the small plane there was some excitement amongst the people. Pula spoke to them, told them that they should settle down for the night. In the morning he and the rainmaker would go out on to the waters and they would see what had happened out there. They would take a good *mokoro* and they would go to the Fishing Camp. Then they would come back and help them all decide what to do.

There was a moment's silence in the cabin, a moment before the dark descended outside, a moment when everyone heard something unusual and all listened together. They felt something move the aircraft, shake it.

The grounded Hercules, which had been the stage for such violent theatre, began to shudder as if it had hit some clear-air turbulence in high-altitude flight. The Hambukushu, now settled in their places, were shaken about like light dolls. Babies began to cry again and a low tremulous wail rose from frightened mothers. It was a sinister sound this time and some of the men called to their women to stop their noise. Their wailing was cut off for a moment, but the rumbling outside continued as the cabin was shaken by the elements.

The tremor continued like an apocalypse of time, some elemental shaking of an unstable world, a severe jolt to the cocoon of our confinement. It shook us all, as if to jolt us into the reality of our terrible predicament.

Outside there were flashes of lightning. It began to rain very hard. We could all hear the drumming of it on the fuselage, a low drone above the rumble of the moving earth. A woman called urgently for John Barotse, for the rainmaker.

The rainmaker rose from the place where he had been sitting next to his son. He seemed to be much older now, as if the recent crisis had drained him, sucked away his spirit. His son helped him to his feet. He held his father's upper arm as the rainmaker stood to talk to his people. It was only a storm in time, a settling of the earth, a groaning of the great rift valley, the rainmaker told them. They had lived between the water and the land since the beginning of time, they had lived at the mouth of a river, and soon they would be able to leave this unnatural place and ride on the river once again. In the morning they would go out to look, just as Pula had said.

The rumbling beneath them faded away after a while, the people settled too after John Barotse's assurance. Pula went to Julia and her father was at her side. Dr Pinto raised his good hand in greeting and smiled, tried to be lighthearted.

'I need my clinic!' he said to Pula.

'And Julia? The sleeping sickness?'

'You were right. I have confirmed Winterbottom's sign.'

He lifted his good hand to his eyes as if to blot out the fact of his words, his senseless use of an awkward English name, the distant clinical formality towards this strong young man who was so concerned about the girl he had saved from the flood.

'She asks for you,' he said.

Julia complained in a weak voice that she could not see properly. Pula moved closer, sat on the lowered back of the seat nearest Julia's head and he strained to hear her, still feeling the rumble of a disturbed world. He began to talk quietly to her, in a gentle voice. He touched her hot forehead.

I was in the cockpit, the door was open, I was sitting at the navigator's little desk. I looked up to see an angry sky through a framed windscreen. The familiar frames had shuddered as if we were flying. I turned to look back at Julia. I was now flying her through a new turbulence of some kind. I so wanted to be in Pula's place, to comfort her myself. I was as close as I could be to her, but never close enough. I knew that my desire was ridiculous, even obscene, but above all I needed to see her survive. The wish for her salvation was now a central issue in my own dilemma. Somehow Julia had to be saved from the malevolent and bitter violence which she had so recently witnessed. I wanted to free her from the anarchy which threatened to corrupt her so utterly.

She only wanted Pula to talk to her. He talked of anything that came into his mind, told her old stories about hottentot-gods, about lizards and chameleons. He talked to her about life, told her that God had said to the chameleon that he must go and tell the people that man would not die. When the chameleon delayed on the way to eat some mulberries in a big tree, God sent the lizard to give the people the opposite message. Man would die. Lizard hurried along with his particular message. When chameleon finally got to the people with the original and correct message, no one would believe him. That is why people die in one sense but live in another, they live in a cycle. The real God did not mean them to die.

Beneath the blanket Julia held the carving which Pula had given her. With her fingers she followed the lines of the lizard which wound itself around the body of the changing man. The other wand which Bubi had wielded, the one with the bladder attached to the end of it, had also had its power over her. Bubi had removed the bladder, touched Julia's eyelids with some powder from it.

Now, lying in her sickbed, Julia turned the created thing in her hand. She could see the hazy shape through a lifting shadow. She could see that the carving depicted the story which Pula had told her. The chameleon and the lizard, one slow, the other fast, twisted round the stick, writhing upwards towards the flat head. The lizard was smiling, a wicked smile, the chameleon was slow and serious, his head just below that of his competitor. It was a race, a race between two messengers who twisted around the body of a man who grew old in a single turn.

'Tell me about the hottentot-god,' Julia asked him. She could now see his face more clearly. The film which had earlier covered her eyes appeared to be lifting. Thankfully, she closed them to listen to his voice.

Pula spoke to her as if he was sharing secrets with her as he would with no one else in the world. There was some mystery in his words and yet some fun and cheerfulness as if this particular god had a human face, understood human frailty.

'He came from a pile of stones,' Pula told Julia, 'like some other gods the world knows about. He stole cattle, he loved music. Did we not learn about some Greek god who made a lyre out of three strands of gut and a tortoise shell? He could make fire by rubbing two sticks of laurel together. Hottentot-god made music too, he stole his fire from ostrich. That other god was a god of fertility, so was hottentot-god. All the children that were ever born, even you and I, received a little pinch from those sharp claws to make us scream when we came into the world. He is like that, he knows where to pinch so that it hurts, where to tickle so that one laughs.'

Pula's hand on Julia's shoulder moved just a fraction towards her armpit, a finger touched her lightly there, as if to tickle. Julia smiled. Pula continued, his heart lifting with her smile.

I saw the smile too, was thrilled to hear that her voice was now much stronger.

'That was Hermes,' Julia said gruffly in a firm voice, and Pula was encouraged by her response. He continued to tell her about his gods. She closed her eyes to listen.

'The world was water, first there was water and then there was the world, that is how all the Barotse tell it, and it is so. All the elements of woman are of water and hottentot-god knows this, he knows that women will survive. You are all the fluid of life. Everyone tries to suck it away from you, even man. That is why man has been so afraid of you, because you are water and life, and he can drown in you. If he breaks the dams which he has built up around your spirit, he will drown. So for all the years of your history he has dammed you up, limited you so that he would not drown. The Queen of the Barotse knows that, so do the Hambukushu. Unlike your people, we do not follow the man's line, we follow that of the woman.'

'Is the earthquake a man or a woman?' Julia asked, now in a hoarse whisper.

'A woman, she opens up the valleys.'

Julia opened her eyes then, looked up at Pula, smiled again.

'To me that sounded like a man. I think he is an angry man, demanding.'

'We have yet to hear his final warning.'

Just then there was a huge flash of lightning outside, the crack of final thunder. The aircraft was shaken like a basket on the water, the people were tossed about one final time and the plane seemed to lift then drop again as if bumping through clouds. The people screamed, Julia shouted out to Pula to save her. Pula wrapped Julia in his strong protective arms, whispered that the storm would soon pass. 'We will be saved, the water will now begin to flow away, into the caverns beneath the desert.'

The next morning John Barotse reported that the wheels had somehow moved in the night, the plane had been lifted and put down again. The level of the water was now dropping fast, he reported, there was a definite mud-line on the metal struts of the undercarriage showing the height of the flood. He told me first, then Pula, then Julia, then Dr Pinto. Then he told the Kalanga policeman, who was still asleep on the two seats which he had commandeered for himself near the door.

On the same morning Julia's recovery did begin. Once the storm had passed, the movement of the earth had subsided, she had slept with her carving by her side. She brought it out from the blanket covering her and waved it in the air above her head, watching it with clear eyes. She called for Bubi.

Pula went to fetch Bubi, led her to the bedside. Julia tapped Bubi's shoulder with her carving and Bubi reached up and took it from her. She held the carving to her breasts for a moment, tapped its head lightly with her own stick, her own wand, then returned the carving to Julia. She removed a piece of skin from a pouch which hung at her throat. She puffed into the skin bladder, quickly squeezed it, allowing a wisp of fine white powder to escape. She then blew up the bladder like a balloon and carefully attached the new balloon to her wand by means of a thin sinew. She wound the sinew around the mouth of the bladder and around the stick. When the bladder was secure she twirled the re-created wand above her head. She let out a banshee screech, a witch's call, and the women in the aircraft followed her in shrill imitation.

Then Bubi rose to beat Pula with the bladder on the stick, she beat Dr Pinto on the head, gently touched his wounded hand with the bladder. She came to me, fluttered the thing in front of my eyes and tapped my nose lightly with it. She walked through the door into the cockpit and she tapped the instrument panel with the bladder on a stick. She moved purposefully around the cockpit, tapping at any dial or switch or control that she could see around her or above her. She cackled all the time, a wicked laugh at all this useless equipment. She returned to Julia and tapped her forehead with the bladder on a stick, telling her to hold it very firmly. Then she grabbed Pula's fingers, made him wrap them around the hand which held the stick. She covered the holding hands with her own, spat on them once and then raised both arms in a wild gesture so that the ululation stopped at once.

'The flood is over!' she cried.

Some of the Hambukushu began to dance in a circle on the ramp by the tail-gate, making explosive noises, kicking against the fuselage as if they might break out at once. Some sang.

The priest called for order, said that his congregation should all kneel before the power of the One God. Some settled, most shuffled more slowly as the priest read with great fervour from his Bible. He held his little black book in front of him, his arm very straight, but his hands shaking. Perhaps he thought the flood had just begun.

> 'And God looked upon the earth, and, behold, it was corrupt; for all flesh had corrupted his way upon the earth.
>
> 'And God said unto Noah, The end of all flesh is come before me; for the earth is filled with violence through them; and, behold, I will destroy the earth.
>
> 'Make thee an ark of gopher wood; rooms shalt thou make in the ark, and shall pitch it within and without with pitch.
>
> 'And this is the fashion which thou shalt make it of: The length of the ark shall be three hundred cubits, the breadth of it fifty cubits, and the height of it thirty cubits.
>
> 'And behold, I, even I, do bring a flood of waters upon the earth, to destroy all flesh, wherein is the breath of life, from under heaven; and everything in the earth shall die.
>
> 'And the flood was forty days upon the earth; and the waters increased greatly upon the earth; and the ark went upon the face of the waters.
>
> 'And all flesh died that moved upon the earth, both of fowl and of cattle and of beast, and of every creeping thing that creepeth upon the earth and every man ...'

Above the drone of his voice came a strident female sound, not quite a scream. It was Bubi calling in a shrill voice to all the women to behold the miracle.

The priest closed the good book and looked up at his congregation, disappointed that they seemed to be uninspired by the sound of his words and his voice. He now saw that they were all facing away from him, that even those few on their knees had turned to look towards Bubi and Julia.

Julia now sat up in the stretcher which had been her sickbed. In one hand she waved the carving in the air, joyfully, miraculously recovered. They all knew about the sleeping sickness, now they all knew why Bubi had saved her. She now sat close to Pula Barotse, who was destined to be the next rainmaker. The white girl was destined to be the new *mugrodi*.

This was the girl who would become the next rain-mother and who would therefore need to carry out all the mysterious duties of her calling. Bubi had called upon the gods in the diamond sands, she had commanded the earthquake, and now the flood would subside and a new season would begin. This was the miracle which Bubi had performed. Such was the power of Bubi and the gods.

I saw the white girl lean on Pula beside her, saw Bubi remove her skin cloak to place it on the floor next to the stretcher. She told Pula to help Julia to her feet, to make her swing her legs away from her bed and stand on the skin cloak. I then saw Pula stand next to Julia on Bubi's command. They stood there like a bridal couple. Julia was pale, almost as pale as she had been on that first fateful day. My heart went out to her as Bubi lifted her left hand and ceremonially slipped a copper bangle over it. The bangle depicted a crocodile devouring its own tail.

Julia saw the terrifying thing on her wrist and she shuddered as she struggled to remove it with her other hand. She pulled it at an angle to her wrist and could not release it. I ran to her, held her hand firmly, removed the bangle. It moved in my hand.

Something terrible was happening, it was as if Potlako Lereng had returned to our midst. I could not let go of the bangle, I could not throw it away. I looked at the awful thing, seeing only the crocodile linked in a ring. I tried to convince myself that there had been no movement. It was a ring of copper, nothing more. I did not resist when Bubi plucked the bangle from my fingers and gave it to Pula.

'You must put the ring on her hand,' Bubi said to him.

I was as useless as my stricken aircraft, I could not take off, I could not help this girl. I wanted her to escape from Bubi, I wanted to rescue Julia from the clicking crocodiles, I wanted to fly away with her.

There was further evidence that the level of water was falling fast. Perhaps the water was draining away into caverns beneath the desert. There was still some water around the plane, as around a stranded ark, but the horizon appeared to be coming closer.

The Hambukushu offered Pula and John Barotse the best of the craft. Both men chose good strong paddles. Pula sat in front of the very long *mokoro*. It was also wider than most. It must have been cut further north out of a very old tree, somewhere in the Caprivi perhaps. It was made of a dark wood, the colour of dried blood, and it had intricate carvings along the gunwales. As he dipped his paddle, Pula ran his curled finger across the patterns at his side, admiring them.

They moved away from the aircraft, slid quietly beneath the monstrous wing, out of its shadow towards the distant glint of the tin roof in the sun. Pula looked again at the pattern of the *mokoro* in which he was now obliged to move away from Julia. The shapes on the gunwale were of fish and animals and crops, sheaves of mealies entwined with the bodies of eels. The owner would be one of those who moved with the seasons to till the lands made rich by floodwaters. Pula admired the intricate carvings once again, recalled for an anxious moment his own *mokoro* which had floated away.

Father and son paddled first to the roof of the police station. They both saw the dark line on the wall of the building which marked the height of the flood. The top of an open window was revealed and they both peered through it to see a wooden bench floating on still water. There was a table too, its flat top at the level of the lintel, floating. They moved on to check whether other houses were still standing on the river bank.

First they passed the small colony of forlorn vehicles which had been standing at the end of the landing strip. The water was still well above these windows, but the top of each cab was a resting place for cormorants. They had begun their own colony. John and Pula Barotse looked back at the aircraft which they had left and there, sure enough, making a line of black figures on the high tail, were more big birds, vultures waiting.

'After the flood comes the cleaning up,' John Barotse said to his son.

The vultures did not move, but the cormorants left the cabs of the sunken vehicles, ran for a few yards along the surface and rose into the air.

'We will check the other houses on our way back,' John Barotse said, as they moved away from the stranded vehicles, past the limp wind-sock on a pole, past the collapsed hut. They made for a distant line of tree tops, the Fishing Camp at Namaseri.

Below them would be old roads in the sand. John Barotse could tell from the position of the tops of trees that they were somewhere near the drift which marked the beginning of the river. Then he saw an illusion on the water, a magical thing, a walking tree. It danced across the water, waving its branches in the air, its roots held to a moving hole in the river. Above it, birds circled as if waiting for it to settle so that they could do the same. It moved along in the direction of the Fishing Camp, dancing in crazy circles on a carpet of papyrus. John Barotse had never seen anything like it before and Pula was sure that it was coming to meet them.

They turned away from the direct route to the tall trees at the Fishing Camp. Those trees remained in the same place, they did not move, but the dancing menace came closer. Pula saw what it was. He had seen the same movement of the water above other rapids, the same crazy circles in the flood, the same behaviour of the river, but never a dancing tree. It was like the movement of dust in the wind, a twisting upwards or sucking downwards. In the dust the twist rose to the sky, here the suck pulled down to the diamond sand. This whirlpool could lift a tree by sucking it into its curling vortex, the tree itself would not go under, it only danced on the surface, resisting the deep tug of the diamond sand. Other things, smaller things, reeds, logs and papyrus, even a *mokoro*, could be sucked under.

'We are in the river!' Pula shouted.

'The tunnels beneath the sand are open!' his father called.

Other pieces of debris slipped towards them, seemed to pick them up, curl them away to enter the trap of the dancing tree. The *mokoro* was drawn slowly towards the moving whirlpool. Both John Barotse and his son Pula paddled hard against the rip, both on the same side, trying to turn the head of their own hollow tree.

The centre of the whirlpool sucked away at that moment, veered away from them as if pulled by some greater power. It continued on a different path. The dancing tree also flicked away from them, its branches dipped low over the *mokoro* in a bow of farewell. Above, the birds still circled, following the big tree and the line of the river below.

Pula and his father sat quite still in their *mokoro*, their paddles resting across its carved gunwales. They watched the dancing tree and the swirling water move towards the other trees at the Fishing Camp at Namaseri.

The water beneath them was also moving now and they both paddled again, keeping a respectful distance behind the dancing tree. They watched in wonder as the whirlpool hit the bend in the river beneath the tall trees of the Fishing Camp, where the high bank used to be. The dancing tree hit the rigid trees, reluctant partners, there was a crashing and breaking of branches, a cloud of birds rose to join the others, like the dust of an explosion. Then the whirlpool was only a hole in the water moving fast, into the delta.

After the whirlpool had passed, the river was almost calm again, its moving line was only defined by eddies at the edge, by floating slicks sliding into the growing current.

As they came closer to the tall trees John Barotse saw the hanging rope, the one he had tied so carefully, and then he saw his boat. It was in the bare branches of the tree, upside down. There was no red engine at the back and through the timbers of its hull John Barotse could see the sky above the tree and the disturbed clouds of birds without a perch. His boat, his new engine! He looked beyond the tree to the flat bank where the Fishing Camp used to be. All the tents had gone.

There was something else in the tree above him, dark and twisting. It was a dead sitatunga, its legs hanging above the water, its horns caught in bare branches.

'We must get back! Report back,' John Barotse said.

Looking at their broken boat, seeing the carcass of the dead sitatunga hanging above the memory of the Fishing Camp, neither father nor son saw the next but smaller whirlpool. There was no twisting tree caught in it, only mats of papyrus, reeds and broken branches. It whipped round the deep corner, shook the trees again, sucked the *mokoro* into the mainstream. The *mokoro* turned in a full circle on the edge of the whirlpool, the inside gunwale dipped low into the water. Then it was flicked out along the lip of the vortex and carried away downstream. Both father and son held on firmly to the carved gunwales, their knees braced against the sides of their flooded *mokoro*, becoming part of the river.

They floated that way towards a calmer stretch of water, away from Gowa towards Samochima and more trees. John Barotse guessed that these would be the trees above the Red Hills. He saw a papyrus island nearby, moving only slowly in an eddy of some kind. The second whirlpool had also gone, had followed the earlier one.

'They are sucked by the caverns that reach to Magkadikgadi,' John Barotse said to his son, looking back to see whether yet another menace approached.

'It all goes into the diamond sand.'

Paddling awkwardly in their flooded craft they made for the moving papyrus island. It too had held up a raft of debris. Pula in the bows moved away the reeds and muck until he could grab a tuft of papyrus and pull the *mokoro* closer to the matted base of the floating island. Then both men paddled hard, forcing the flooded bow to rise slightly on to the island. Pula sloshed through the water along the length of the boat, back to the stern to sit near his father. They both paddled again as the water ran down from the bow, sank them deeper. At the critical moment, when the bow was highest and the hollow of it could be seen above the water, Pula hurried back to his place. His weight levelled the *mokoro* which slipped back to the water. Now there was a freeboard of an inch or so along the whole length of the *mokoro*. With their paddles, floating slowly with the papyrus island, they flicked water out of the long *mokoro*, which gradually began to float higher.

There were no more whirlpools now as they moved with their island. Other creatures also stayed with the island, some water birds, gallinules, jacanas, pecked around the edges, egrets and herons fluttered in the papyrus. Pula saw a coiled puff-adder on the water float towards them. It was brown, with a rough, ridged back, the coils symmetrical, like a thick cow-pat on the surface. Pula could see the eyes of the small head in the middle. The curled traveller touched the floating mat of reeds, sprang to life and slithered to safety on the island.

'There will be many snakes in there,' he said to his father.

'Rats too, baby crocodiles.'

'Mambas too.'

'The next trees could be Chief's Island.'

Once they saw the next set of trees in the distance they left the papyrus island and paddled towards them. They could find a place to stop on Chief's Island; there would surely still be people and huts on Chief's Island. Who had ever heard of Chief's Island being covered by water?

They had not gone far when they also saw in the distance a white boat approaching, against the current. The boat made a big bow wave as it forced its way against the receding floodwaters. They stopped paddling, waited, drifting.

It was a beautiful boat, John Barotse thought, white hull, double chine which could be clearly seen as it travelled with its nose in the air. No engines at the back, so the engines would be inside, the shaft deep in the keel. On top, it had a heavy house with a platform on which a man sat behind a wheel. He was protected from the sun by a coloured umbrella, or a roof of blue and yellow cloth. Shining rails adorned the sleek line of the high bows. A tremendous voice boomed out to them.

'Ahoy there!' it said.

The bow wave sank as the boat slowed down on its approach, and a man with a machine held to his mouth called again.

'Ahoy!'

John Barotse looked at his son, nodded to him to stand and say something. Pula stood up, raided his paddle.

'Are you all right?' the voice asked.

John Barotse nodded again.

'We were taken from the Fishing Camp by the river.'

'From where?'

'The Fishing Camp. It has gone.'

'Have you seen the big aeroplane?'

'Yes. We came from there.'

By now the gleaming boat was very close and its painted hull loomed alongside. A white man came to the shining railings. He had a small canvas bag in one hand.

'Is there anything you need?' the man asked.

Pula was silent. Was there anything they needed! Some food, some dry land, some dry clothes, some protection from the sun like a big blue umbrella, an engine even, a small Yamaha, some respite from the flood, some hope.

'Hooks and line. For fishing,' John Barotse answered.

'Are you Hambukushu, water people?' the man asked when he was close to them. He stood at the railings, held out the canvas bag as if offering a gift to a creature in a cave.

Another man, struggling with a large video camera on his shoulder, leaned out from beneath the big umbrella and shouted at his production colleague. Pula had his hand up to take the proffered canvas bag, but the bag was pulled away. It hung there for a while in the man's hand as the boats drifted apart. The man with the camera called again. He was swaying awkwardly under the blue and yellow umbrella, but he kept his one eye clamped to a black tube. John Barotse touched the water with his paddle, brought Pula close again to reach the canvas bag. He now wanted it, whatever might be in it.

The man with the canvas bag leaned out again. The railing made a deep line on his khaki trousers as he pressed against it. He offered the bag again, turning to smile at his colleague with the big camera. Pula took the bag the second time. The camera remained on him.

The big voice boomed out.

'We have to take the people off the plane.'

'You will fetch only the white people!' Pula accused in sudden annoyance. His voice was very loud, very angry. He thought of Julia in the aeroplane, of the size of the white boat. The pilot would be taken away, the crew, Dr Pinto and his daughter. Everyone else would be left in the swamp because they were water people.

'Make for the trees on Chief's Island!' the voice called, moving away.

The beautiful boat swung away, opened its inboard engines bedded deep, roared away against the weakening main stream. The exhaust spat at them from the stern, farted at them, left them.

Pula opened the canvas bag, pulled out each item in the order in which it had been so neatly packed in there. On top was a packet of chips, then a slab of chocolate, a little box of tea-bags. Under these were six small boxes of Post Toasties, wrapped together, a cardboard box of Pronutro, a carton of Ever Fresh milk, then some tins. Two Botswana bully-beef, one Nestlé sweetened condensed milk, one yellow cling peaches, one meat balls. No line, no hooks, no knife.

Pula watched the boat disappear across the expanse of moving waters. He ripped open the packet of chips in continuing anger, thought in mean terms of the girl he had rescued from the flood, thought of her whiteness, of the food in her house.

The *mokoro* drifted further towards Chief's Island but it was the power of the other boat against the current which made the distance grow so quickly. They watched the boat disappear to pick up the white people from the aeroplane.

'They behave that way because of the engines,' John Barotse said. 'With strong engines you can beat any flood.'

'But their aeroplane stuck in the mud. That white boat too, it can get stuck in the mud.'

Pula picked up a paddle, began to turn the head of the *mokoro* to return the way they had come, to follow the powerful white boat.

'We'll take longer but we'll get there, even against the current,' Pula said.

His father also began to work his paddle.

16

Before nightfall father and son shared the slab of chocolate. Pula opened one tin of Botswana bully-beef for an evening meal. One paddle was always at work to maintain forward momentum. When Pula stopped to dip his finger into the tin of bully-beef, scoop up some food, his father paddled. Then Pula would paddle, both would work for a while. Pula would look ahead, work at his paddle while his father ate. Slowly they made their way back to the aeroplane.

When it was dark the floating logs and debris seemed to bump more often against the hull, but it was only the surprise, the lack of light to see what was coming in the water, which made the difference. In reality there was less material in the flood around them, the current was not so strong, the main thrust was lost. The water now moved slowly away from the land, sliding back to its original order, leaving mud and low-lying lakes.

The moon came up after a few hours of darkness. It was not a full moon but it was at first huge above the horizon. It was red too, shining through someone else's dust far away. Then it rose clear and serene above them, more than half of it, enough light to reflect on moving water.

'Would a white boat travel by moonlight?' John Barotse asked, but Pula did not reply. He was thinking of Julia, of her illness, of her recovery. Although he was on water, surrounded by water, he thought of the dry paths on which he had walked with her in the bush below. Dry paths, African paths of sand and dust, ant-hills, carmine bee-eaters nesting in dry river banks. Which was the illness and which was the recovery? Which required the sacrifice, the drought or the flood? He looked up at the moon, kept paddling. His left shoulder ached.

The flood was the recovery, he decided, the fluids were life, not the drought. All this water only proved the cycle, the swamp would grow huge and become small in its own time, maybe one day it would disappear for ever into the caverns beneath the desert. If he could choose to be a bushman of the desert or a bushman of the water, he would choose the water. The desert bushman carried water in ostrich shells, or in the stomach of an oryx. To that bushman the water was something crystal, like diamonds from the sand. To the water bushman, at the time of the flood, dry sand itself could be something crystal.

'We used to set traps by moonlight,' Pula's father said.

They both saw a light moving in the distance, it looked like a window of a house on the water, but it was moving.

'They have picked up the white people,' John Barotse said.

'Julia!' Pula called from his working position, turning towards the lights. It was an involuntary shout of her name, one word, foreign in their talking, but full of personal meaning. Like the shout of Pula! in his country. Pula! Julia!

'You saved her from the flood,' John Barotse said very quietly, from the darkness behind, still paddling.

Pula was embarrassed by his sudden shout, embarrassed that he should reveal so clearly to his father how constantly he thought about Julia. He had not mentioned her since they had left the aeroplane together, and now it would be clear to his father that she had been with him all the time, in his mind. With that clarity of something hidden suddenly revealed, he was struck by the thought of what it would mean if he was never to see Julia again. What if she had been taken away by the white boat, with the other white people?

'She was very sick,' he said.

'So was the doctor. His hand was bad.'

'I knew it was the sleeping sickness.'

'You looked after her well. Bubi helped her recover. She should now go and live amongst her own people.'

The lights were still far away, and now on the land, it seemed; but of course there was now no land for roads. If it had lights, a white boat could travel where it wished in the night, with Julia. Or could it? The water was now moving to the Makgadikgadi and soon some high ground must show itself. Maybe they would see the high ground of the Fishing Camp, the land at the bend in the river which had sucked away the whirlpool. Or a fence pole might rise up, or the fence it carried. How would those fast propellers deal with wire? Even the cords of a fishing net can foul a propeller, while a *mokoro* moves quietly across the surface. Perhaps the white boat would run out of water, be stopped by the bush.

'They seem to be on the land,' John Barotse said.

'Soon it will not be deep enough for a boat like that,' Pula added as the *mokoro* scraped the edge of a papyrus island. Pula pushed it away with his paddle. The island was alive with birds, some shuffled on their crowded perches, others dropped, struggled in the dark. The island was not moving very fast. As they passed under papyrus fronds, under the birds, something fell into the bottom of the *mokoro*, a big nut or a fruit dislodged, an animal, a bird? The island slipped away and the two men kept working against the current.

What else was on that island for the night? A living sitatunga maybe, a letchwe, certainly more snakes, rats risen above the water. All those creatures waited for the dawn and when it came, where would they be? In the swamp somewhere. There would be other tall trees, other floating islands, other chances.

The sound of their paddles dipping rhythmically into the water soothed the two men into the presence of other life on the water. The flood was part of life, a disturbance in the cycle maybe, but very much part of life, like so many other extremes. If it is possible for two people to think the same way just as they paddled the same way, then father and son did think together for a while in the darkness. They both thought of the boat which had been destroyed, and of the home which had gone. They both thought of the future and they both thought of Julia. Pula considered her life and her people, his life and his people, John Barotse considered the same things. They both knew that doctors and fishermen were very different, they both wondered whether there was anything which might help bridge the wide gap, bring about the impossible. The impossible was not meant to be brought about, stones were rounded by the sea or by a river going somewhere, their shape could change but they were still stones. In the river they were tumbled along, taken to another place by the flood, where man might marvel at the colours and their shapes in the sand, but they were still stones. The core was still a stone. Unless, unless the stone was consumed by a crocodile somehow, along with its rotting food; unless it became a different stone, with spiritual properties. How strong was the spirit when all other things were destroyed?

Was there a core hard enough in any woman to be a stone? Was there anything as strong as the river to shape man, to make him as honest and pure as those first stones from which man arose? Make of him a diamond in the sand; still a stone, but a diamond in the sand. Rock of the Tsodilo Hills, thrust up out of the very guts of the earth, original rock, desert worn from you, who can change our nature?

The gods, they both thought, John Barotse for an anxious moment, Pula in a plea for Julia and her safety. Then their minds diverged: Pula considered the beauty of a girl, he looked at the moon and dreamed. His father thought of his own age, of the carving which was lost the day he fell into the swamp, yet found again. The young man brought so quickly, with the twist of a wrist, to old age. He thought of Pula's mother, of all those sacrificial children offered for the rain. Until this one, her very last, this one who was destined to survive just as she was destined to die in producing him. Those impossible dreams, they were so fragile. Even the dreams of the Tsodilo Hills could break, even the dream which was the Hambukushu diamond, the pear-shaped gem, the richness of his people. Even the dream of an abandoned duty, a sacrifice refused.

They heard something splash in the water which lay in the bottom of the *mokoro*. It splashed somewhere near the middle of the boat, where the usual low platform on which to make a fire had been cut by the *mokoro* maker. Something was moving through the water to the sand of the fireplace. Pula reached with his paddle, touched the patch of sand and weeds which was held in its carved position in the bottom of the boat. He could feel nothing unusual, only the grating of sand.

Towards dawn Pula opened the other tin of bully-beef with a small metal key that was attached to the bottom of it. He removed the lid, cut away a piece of meat for himself and handed the tin to his father. After he had eaten, Pula dipped his hand into the water, drank. After he had tasted the flood water, he left his hand dangling there for a while to cool it, moving his tired fingers below the surface. He heard the splashing sound again, near the fire place.

By first light they could both see that they were not on the river but above the land. They had somehow avoided the mainstream and had left the trees of the Fishing Camp at Namaseri well to their right. They were approaching Shakawe from the land, not the river. Either they were above the road which ran beneath them from Sepopa and Dichaube, or they were somewhere near Gauxa Lagoon. The white boat may have returned this way, with the pilot and his crew, with Dr Pinto and his daughter.

'It is Gauxa Lagoon,' John Barotse said, knowing that they would soon see the windsock on a pole, the big machine in the mud, even the cormorants resting on the flat roofs of flooded vehicles.

In the dawn light Pula shifted his position so that he could throw out some of the papyrus heads which had fallen into the boat when they had scraped the island. His father smiled as he watched his son clean up for the new day, saw him pick up pieces of papyrus from the sand of the fire place, then lift a baby crocodile. He held it up, an unexpected passenger discovered. The crocodile's legs moved as if to walk away. The baby creature barked like a puppy as Pula held it tightly behind the head. John Barotse laughed.

'He complains, he wishes to go back, to grow old.'

'There are two babies!'

Pula picked up the second baby in his other hand, also holding it firmly behind the squirming head. It too barked, its mouth open, its tiny teeth exposed. Pula barked back, baring his teeth. He put the babies down together into the bottom of the boat, and they made for the only patch of sand and weeds. Pula moved bits of grass and some leaves to cover them.

'We will ask the priest to bless you,' he said to them.

'Stones,' his father said, 'no one can change stones.'

The roofs of the vehicles at the end of the airstrip now showed clearly above the surface of the water, more cormorants nested on the small flat islands. The water had drained away during the night. The long line of *mokoros* still floated behind the stranded aircraft. The steps were still down, above the water now, like guts dangling from a wound in the stomach. The exposed mechanics of the landing gear were now slimy, festooned with muck from the flood. What was very different was that the back of the aircraft was wide open, like a cloaca which had recently excreted into the water. A large flat platform lay level with the water, above it was a big gaping hole, a hole into the stomach.

The ugly sight of the hole in the huge beast, of his own people clinging like ticks to a tail, made the blood drain suddenly from Pula's body, made him shiver once in awful fear. Julia had been taken way by the white boat. She had gone with her father, with the pilot. She was a white person, she had been taken away by the white boat.

Cautiously the two men paddled closer to the platform to investigate. Some of the people waved. Some old women sat on the very edge of the metal platform, dangling their legs.

The Kalanga policeman was still there. He stood in the middle of the big hole as John Barotse and Pula approached. Eager hands tied up their *mokoro*. Father and son came to report back, with a canvas bag and two baby crocodiles.

'Why were you so long?' the policeman demanded, with new authority. He dismissed the offering of baby crocodiles with a gesture of annoyance. Next to him, looking over his shoulder from inside the body of his diminished church was the priest, the man from Angola. Pula offered a crocodile to him but the priest shook his head.

'It was a dove which returned,' the priest said.

At that moment Bubi appeared and she was leading Julia by the hand. Julia followed dutifully, as pale as a ghost, with a bandage wrapped around her head, blindfolded. She could not see Pula in the *mokoro*. She stopped when Bubi stopped.

Pula scrambled out of the *mokoro* and hurried past the priest. The older women laughed as he went to Julia. Pula recognised the bandage as part of the barrier which Dr Pinto had used to define his clinical territory.

The priest held out a hand to help John Barotse out of the *mokoro*. Some of the men also came to help the exhausted old man back into the aircraft.

In low and urgent tones Pula asked Julia what had happened, why had she not gone on the white boat? And her father, did the boat take him to hospital? Had the pilot gone in the boat, even the pilot? What happened to the pilot? Can you hear me?

'All of them went. Even the pilot. It was all his fault, they took him away.' Bubi answered for her.

'And her father? Leaving his daughter here?'

'Her father's hand was very bad. There was awful swelling, right up to his shoulder. He was very hot. I nursed him, just as I have nursed Julia. She is still very ill.'

'Her eyes! Why have you covered her eyes?'

Pula held Julia's arms, shook her to waken her.

'What have they done to you?' he shouted.

Bubi lifted Pula's hands from her patient's arms, turned her around to face the way she had come. She began to lead her away, but Pula followed, reached for a fold of the bandage to tear it away. Julia stopped and she herself began to unwind the cloth which covered her head. Bubi slapped at her hands, scolded her, but Pula stepped between them, helped Julia unwind the blindfold. The women surrounded Pula, urged him to move further into the aircraft to be with his father. He stayed close to Julia while Bubi fussed about them, saying that the light would hurt her eyes.

Julia removed the bandage, the strip of crêpe from her father's bag, and Pula saw at once that she had been weeping beneath the wretched device. Her eyes looked at him however, and she tried to smile, moved to embrace him at last.

John Barotse had heard the urgent questions from Pula and he could now feel the tension amongst his people. He was becoming a burden to them, so tired after a trip along the river with his son. He was also becoming very weak, a weak old man with water in his legs.

'I blessed them and they took a photograph of me,' the priest said to him with some importance. 'I stood at the back, at the bottom of the big door. I blessed them on their journey, prayed that they would find land. The mud churned from beneath the boat as they left.'

'What has Bubi done to her?' John Barotse asked in a whisper.

'She saved her. To be the new *mugrodi*.'

'She took Julia away from her father? How could the father get into the white boat without his daughter?'

'When they saw the white boat coming, the white men opened this back gate. They stood here waving. Bubi and two women carried Julia out of the other door, to a *mokoro*. They took her away, to hide her from the white boat. Bubi told us to say nothing to the doctor, she was taking the girl for your son.'

'I do not understand,' John Barotse said, moving away from the priest.

'She will be happy to be the new *mugrodi*,' the priest added and

John Barotse sensed a sinister wish in the words.

'Why do you say such things? What do you know about sacrifice, about the Hambukushu?'

'I was only telling you what Bubi told us. The girl was for your son.'

'But the father? He also loved her.'

'He was very sick. I think he had the idea that he was dying, that he was being taken away to die. We priests, we know these things.'

'I do not believe that he would leave her.'

'They put him on his daughter's stretcher and carried him away. The pilot helped to carry him. The pilot told us that he would return, in another aeroplane.'

In utter confusion John Barotse now saw Julia hold his son in her arms, saw Pula's arms about her, as if the two would never be parted.

'She will be happy to be the new *mugrodi*,' the priest added once again.

17

The Hambukushu all prepared to leave the aeroplane while there was still some water to float their *mokoros*. They ventured into the aftermath of the flood to find out where the water had stopped this time, to discover what limits now governed their renewed existence. Some found mud covering the places which they had left in a hurry, others found that a new course of the river had altered the landscape as they had known it, islands had been washed away, quiet lakes were now mud, oxbows had broken through.

The papyrus patterns were much changed too, and below Dichaube there was a huge mound of debris drying in the sun.

Pula was concerned that neither his father nor Julia really had enough strength to move away with the others. Bubi wanted to take Julia with her along with other Hambukushu women in one of the last *mokoros* but Pula would not let her go. He said that he would wait one more day, Julia and his father would eat the food from the canvas bag and if no one came to the plane they would follow.

'The pilot will come to look,' he told Bubi, 'he will come in another aeroplane and he will see us here.'

'And then what will he do? Stick in the mud again?'

Bubi then whispered to Pula in deep confidence, told him about a hidden cave which he had seen once before, when he was very small. It was like a beautiful fountain in the desert, a place where life began. He should take the very last *mokoro*, put Julia and John

Barotse into it, then follow to the Hills.

John Barotse grew more and more depressed. The sight of the *mokoros* moving away seemed to anger him further. He ripped the rainmaking necklace from his neck as if to get rid of it, then he gave it to Pula, not in ceremony as he should have done, but in surrender.

The abandoned aircraft became an awful place in which to wait for the morning. Inside, the remaining detritus of human living smelled of despair. Outside, the water slowly drained away and soon no *mokoro* would be able to begin any journey.

Pula, disturbed by his father's behaviour, wondered whether the meagre food from the canvas bag would offer strength enough to either Julia or his father to undertake the necessary journey to the Hills. The three of them might have to wade through thick mud just to reach the river and once on the river could they find their way to the Hills? Bubi talked of caves and fountains and the source of life.

In the morning Julia at first refused to go. She insisted that it would be safest for her in the aeroplane because her father would surely come to fetch her. Once he was better, when his hand was mended, he would come to fetch her. When the airstrip was dry again he would come in another aeroplane to take her home. She would wait on her own if necessary. If she was left some food, she would wait.

Pula showed her the empty last bag of mealie-meal, the meagre bits of manioc abandoned by the Hambukushu, the last tin of peaches from the canvas bag.

It was a very silent departure from the plane, in shallow water. Julia sat in the *mokoro* wrapped in the same blanket that her father had brought for her when he had first set out from the Fishing Camp with John Barotse. She touched her lips to the carving which she now held, she kissed the flat head, tried to smile bravely at Pula. Pula said that they would soon reach the river.

Before they reached the bend in the river where the Fishing Camp used to be, they could see that the shape of the river had changed. Where there was once an inlet to quiet pools, there was now a stark rip in the black earth of the mainland. Large slabs of the bank undercut by the new course of the river still fell heavily into the moving water. The familiar papyrus island which had been caught for many seasons before the corner, had now gone.

Also the channel leading to the corner at the Fishing Camp had been cut deeper and in the centre of the current big waves rose like the ridges on the back of a crocodile. Before the channel, in the wider stretch of mud on the inside of the turn in the river, they could all see the black hump of a dead hippopotamus, covered by huge maggots, eating it. Julia held her hands up to her eyes as they approached the swollen bulk and then she pressed fingers to her nostrils as a breath of wind brought with it the stench of rotting flesh. The bulk before her, the huge carcass on the mudflats brought back to her a childlike horror of crawling things, like worms on a dead bird. Her more controlled self knew that the process was necessary, the natural cleaning process of scavengers, the carrion carriers, but she stared like a child at the seething ugliness of the natural process. The crocodiles gathered around the body and on top of it, as black as the hippo itself, the same murky colour as the mud in which they feasted. The creatures ripped flesh from the bloated carcass and one of their number lay with its head hidden deep, working in the cavern of the belly.

'Where do they hide when the floods come?' Julia asked, awed by the presence of so many scavengers in one place.

'Deep in the mud, like *vundu*,' Pula answered, but John Barotse was not satisfied with that.

'Not like *vundu*. They go deeper than the *vundu*, they go into the tunnels below the desert.'

As the *mokoro* floated past the scene in the shallower water close to the mud, there was little movement amongst the feeding creatures, only the occasional lift of powerful jaws, revealing teeth and meat. The primeval cycle of the swamp disturbed both Pula and Julia. They saw differing but awful symbols in the death and devouring, some visions of hell so far removed from their mutual

0 GODS — K

hope. Pula's apprehensions over the future of the swamp, over his own future, disturbed him. At that moment he did not feel strong enough to accept the messages that were being sent to him. Julia took her hands from her eyes, tried to face reality.

John Barotse stumbled when he got out of the *mokoro*, on to the high bank that was once the landing place for the Fishing Camp. Pula caught his arm, high up, to steady him. He gripped firmly and he could feel the stringy toughness of the muscle but also the bone beneath. He held the skeleton of his father and reached out his other hand to help Julia out of the *mokoro* and on to the bank. Julia stood very close to John Barotse, also put an arm around him. She was deeply struck by his sudden ageing. When had it happened, that he had become so old? When the people rejected him on returning, or right now, when he saw the awful crocodiles?

Julia examined *feitiço*. Pula had told her that the carving had floated away downstream, before the flood, the young side facing the sun. The Zulu had found it somewhere in the swamp and he must have died with it by his side. Sergeant Molefe had used it as a baton of authority. He too had died. Perhaps she should throw it away, throw it back to the swamp. Perhaps it was itself *diretlo* of a kind. The image of a child buried, or of the ruthless cycle of life. What was she doing with such a thing? What would her father say of her worship of idols?

John Barotse now stood on the high bank and only now did Pula notice the smooth rock face which secured the ledge of earth. The rock was shining black, washed clean, with no green grass growing. It was the rock of the mainland, slippery rock, solid forever, protecting a slab of high land and the big trees. Beyond the trees was more mud. All the tents had gone, John Barotse's house too, even the fence. At the highest point they could still see one concrete slab, the biggest, where the restaurant and the kitchen had once been. On another concrete plinth stood the diesel engine and the generator. Long trails of mbukushu vine clung to the bolts of mountings.

John Barotse walked slowly through the mud towards a low and ragged wall which marked a hollow where his home had once been. He could not believe that all that work and all that living could be swept away so ruthlessly. He looked back towards the river to see if the roof beams or the roof itself had been caught by the trees, even some shreds of thatch. Or perhaps a few bits of furniture had been caught by the rock and the tree, his bed, his table, or the wooden cupboard in which he kept his clothes and the few things with which he lived. There was nothing, not a wisp of thatch grass caught in branches, not a floating piece of wood in a still pool.

He stepped over the low wall into the water of the hollow and sloshed about on the floor of his home while Pula and Julia watched him. He shuffled across the floor, sliding his feet forward as if walking in the dark. He held both arms out as if to reach for the absent wall which he should be approaching. As he slid his foot through the mud, it touched something hard. He dropped his hand into the shallow water to feel what it was, to lift it up. He knew at once when he touched the metal head that it was his axe. He turned to show the axe to Pula. John Barotse had always kept that axe under his bed, a heavy weapon, an axe for defence at night. He held the shaft of it in his right hand, raised the axe and cut into the mud of the low ledge which was once a wall. The axe cut deep, dislodging some mud and muck. He lifted the weapon again, moved out of the gap which used to be his door.

He stood with the axe at the spot where he had planned to build anther room for Pula, felt the remains of the pile of building sand beneath his feet. He called to Pula and Julia to join him, to stand where he was standing, on the remains of the sand.

'This was the place. It all went wrong.'

He collapsed again into the mud, still holding the axe. Pula quickly put his hands beneath his father's armpits to lift the ageing body out of its despair.

'Take me away,' his father said.

Pula and Julia together helped John Barotse back to the high bank and then into their waiting *mokoro*. Carefully, each taking a paddle, they edged away from the Fishing Camp, keeping to the inside curve of the river where sand had now settled and the current was weakest.

Julia had heard John Barotse say 'Take me away'. The words repeated in her mind like a prayer. The image of the pilot as something of a possible saviour joined the prayer. She saw him standing at the door to his cockpit addressing the Hambukushu. She also pleaded with him, her lips actually moving. Take me away, take me away.

'Why didn't you take me away?' she asked of the swirling puddle that her paddle made in dark water.

'Pilot error,' she imagined the pilot saying to her in jest. His voice was light and cheerful, like bubbles in the water. He was smiling at her as he had smiled before, reassuring her.

Then she heard Bubi laughing at her. She smelt smoke, her eyes stung. She felt a cloth cover them, and for a moment she could not see. She was blindfolded, and she did not know where she was going. The pilot did not know where he was going, Pula did not know where he was going! Could it be that these two men were only full of errors, that they had no direction, that they wandered around the sky and the water like eagles searching for prey? Maybe all men only did that; wandered through clouds in useless search of prey?

She pulled the paddle through the shallow water once again, glanced at Pula doing the same thing. They were approaching the crocodiles in the mud, but swinging away from them. The current was stronger in the deeper water and Pula dipped his paddle to return to the inside track. He too did not want to see the crocodiles again, so many of them, but he preferred the shallow water to the rip of the river.

John Barotse sat in front of the *mokoro* as it glided over the mud. He turned to watch the crocodiles on his right as they passed. Then he swung his head to the left to watch the current for a moment, see the angry rush of dark water.

When the water was finished with its task of reshaping, there would be new banks for the Okavango, a new course.

The water was deep on that bank away from the crocodiles and the stretch of mud. It was all floodwater from Angola, seasonal power. This was the water in which he and his ancestors had lived for so long, between the high and low marks of its movements, in the mouth of a river. This was his water, his swamp. It would last forever but his own days were numbered.

John Barotse stood up in the bow of the *mokoro* and Pula called urgently to him to sit down. Still holding the axe John Barotse stepped out of the moving *mokoro* into the mud. He sank into the sludge to his hips, lunged towards the crocodiles. Pula swung the *mokoro* towards the bank, tried to sweep his father away from the water.

John Barotse wallowed towards the hippopotamus and the crocodiles, his axe still in his hand. He lurched awkwardly through the mud, lifting each thigh in turn like a water bird, making slow progress towards the feeding creatures. Pula and Julia used paddles to scrape ahead over the soft mud but the length of the *mokoro* was soon sucked to a stop. Pula jumped out of the *mokoro* and he too sank into the mud. It held him in its awful suction grip as if it might drag him deeper. He struggled to pull the *mokoro* further into the mud to secure it. He saw that the crocodiles were not yet disturbed by the creature approaching them. They continued their slow devouring. It was not a man crawling so close, only some other animal from the river, come to join the feast.

John Barotse bent low, his chest touched the mud as he slithered along like a crab, one claw reaching forward as he moved to the creatures. When he reached the nearest crocodile he lifted his axe and chopped hard into the creature's back. The heavy head of the axe slid off the solid ridge of the slimy back, did not cut deep. The whole pile of creatures then became alive like disturbed vultures stuck in the mud. They slithered and sloshed away from their prize, making for water, moving in flat urgency, twisting like *vundu* through the muck. As Pula reached his father he also wallowed in the mud, becoming the colour of it, the consistency of it, becoming part of the muck left by the flood. He pulled at his father's arm, the one holding the axe, dragged him to the nearby *mokoro*. He then tried to raise the top half of his father's body on to the wooden craft so that he would be lifted out of the mud by it.

His father's legs dragged in the mud. Pula could not lift them because he was himself slipping, he had no firm footing. Then he saw one huge mouth clamp to the old man's thigh, pull him away from the *mokoro* then down. He saw the body of his father dragged away through the mud, disappear towards deeper water as if only a ripped piece of hippo meat, food for scavengers of the swamp.

Pula wallowed over the gunwales of the *mokoro*, felt Julia's hands assist him to swing his legs into the dugout.

He brought with him the black primordial mud and the stench of death.

Pula stood up and the mud oozed off his legs, gathered in globs at his feet. He simply stood there in the same spot in the *mokoro*, unable to take his eyes off the mud into which his father had disappeared.

Julia shuddered, bent to pick up *feitiço*. She hugged it to her breast as if it might offer some comfort. In shock she looked at *feitiço*'s older face and saw the face of John Barotse. She turned the carving slowly in her hands, saw the young man. The young man was now Pula. The lizard was laughing at her, so was the chameleon.

They both stared at the place where they had witnessed such horror. They saw other movement in the mud, other crocodiles slithering towards the water.

'We must return to the water,' Pula whispered to her.

'We must say a prayer.'

'To whose gods?'

'To the one God.'

'Say it to my father. He showed me the way. He is now a god.'

'What way did he show *you*? You don't know where you are going!'

'And you? Do you know where you are going?'

Pula did not look at Julia as he asked her this. He had stood there all the time, hearing Julia but still watching the place where his father had disappeared into the mud. Now his knees seemed to fold beneath him and he slumped down into the *mokoro*, sat in his own mud. Julia put the carving down and took up a paddle. From her place in the stern she first scooped mud with her paddle, then swung the *mokoro* towards the river.

'We should go back to the plane,' she said.

Pula heard her and he sat bolt upright, alert again. He scrambled the length of the *mokoro* to Julia, took the paddle from her and wrapped his muddy arms around her. They rocked together for a moment like that, Pula making strange noises of disquiet and grief. Julia was deeply disturbed. She held him, seeing the young man turn old, seeing herself drown in the river. Suddenly she found herself screaming in panic reaction.

'We must go back!' she screamed.

Pula sensed that the *mokoro* was being moved by the river and he took up a paddle himself.

'No! We go to the Tsodilo Hills,' he insisted.

Julia reached for the carving and held it like a weapon once again. She held the feet, hit the flat head against the muddy gunwale of the *mokoro*.

'What do we do there?' she asked.

'Find Bubi,' Pula answered.

'My father will come back to the plane. He will look for me.'

'We are finished with the aeroplane.'

'What can Bubi do?'

'She can say prayers for us.'

'The plane! We must go back to the plane! What will he do when he returns to it? For God's sake let us go back.'

'I must take you to the Hills. Bubi lives there in a deep cave where the water bubbles out.'

PART THREE

THE DARKNESS AND THE LIGHT

'You were given the kingship, such was your destiny, everlasting life was not your destiny. Because of this do not be sad at heart, do not be grieved or oppressed; he has given you power to bind and to loose, to be the darkness and the light of mankind.'
– THE EPIC OF GILGAMESH

18

When darkness fell over the swamp, Pula and Julia were still in their *mokoro*. *Feitiço* floated in the water sloshing in the bottom of the *mokoro*, forgotten for a moment. They were carried downstream as they had been once before, but this time Pula seemed unable to do anything to maintain control or to work against the current. Julia herself paddled to nearby papyrus, caught several hanging heads, held on to them. The *mokoro* swung into the papyrus and Pula also grabbed at hanging fronds as they swept past him. He too held on.

'Which way?' Julia asked.

The darkness seemed to have defeated Pula, as if it too carried the stench of death, like mud. He would not take up his paddle and he would not answer Julia. He only stared at the heads of papyrus which he held. He imagined insects in the rough fronds, he saw gods in the swamp.

He who was a survivor of the flood, he who was to live at the mouth of rivers, he should make for the mountain. He looked up beyond the thick papyrus around him but could not see the Tsodilo Hills. Was he to wander through the wilderness, like a poor hunter wearing the skins of animals? Did some god also condemn him there in the mud? Did not some god pass by, making his limbs numb with fear?

With his father gone, what was to be done? What could he offer his companion in the wilderness? The boat had gone, the engine too, even the house near the Fishing Camp. What could he offer of the spirit? He fingered the rainmaking necklace and thought again of Bubi. He must find her, tell her of the terror in the mud. He must tell her that the rainmaker is dead.

'We must find Bubi,' he finally said to Julia.

She still clung to the papyrus and she beat her feet on the bottom of the *mokoro*, stamped on *feitiço* in her anger and frustration.

'No, we must go back to Shakawe! Which way is Shakawe?'

Pula thought then of the ferryman who had been his father's friend. How he took people across even flooded rivers, to islands which he knew. He would know the channels beneath the sands, the way to the mountain. He would know the way to Bubi's place in the Hills. Where was the ferryman? What had happened to his daily journeys, his daily transit at the mouth of rivers, like the rising and the setting of the sun? Even the ferryman had failed him. Now he was alone, but with a woman. A man of the swamp and a woman of the city. But what city? Where did she really belong? Would she try to take him there, away from the swamp, away from the inlets he knew, the hidden islands?

Could there be such a thing in his future, a hidden island on which he could be happy? Would he ever have his own son holding his hand? Was that not also the lot of man, to cherish the little child that holds your hand?

'I can find that island,' he said to Julia. 'Do you remember it?'

'It was near Shakawe.'

'We were caught there, by the flood.'

'Find it then. Come, we can both paddle.'

There was no ferryman but they were crossing some divide together. Before nightfall Pula did find the inlet and the hidden island. This time he also cut papyrus, settled Julia alone in the shape of a hut. It was only a round mound where walls had once been. He gave her the tin of peaches, food from the white boat, food for a white woman.

That night, while Julia slept on papyrus in the shape of a hut, Pula sat for a long time beside the fire he had built. He saw other shapes in the flames of the fire, other places destroyed by the flood.

He also saw the faces of gods, saw flashes of their great deeds, heard them mourn the rainmaker. He moved logs deeper into the fire so that sparks scattered, the gods dispersed. Some flames were friendly, as the normal rains were friendly, but they too could rage out of control, like a flood. Fire could burn any image which he might make out of hardwood, even the carving which Julia loved so much. Fire and water could get out of hand, even the gods could get out of hand. They could bring chaos and destruction by storm and lightning.

Pula moved the last of a log deeper into the flames, picked up a short piece to take its place. He examined its form. This short log was not like a snake, nor like a chameleon, nor a lizard, certainly not a crocodile. It was flat, with a thin raised twig at one end. It was the shape of a crawling creature, a man-scorpion. As he laid it on the fire the heat of the coals lit the slender twig at the end of it. The flame rose up like a scorpion's sting. The sting thrust upwards in a bright flash, then was gone. Venom spent, the man-scorpion burnt.

In the morning Pula climbed the big tree, alone. He broke off dry branches as he climbed, let them drop to the ground as future firewood. From the bowl of the tree, from the slide-riders' platform, he could see the outline of the Tsodilo Hills. He could also see birds flying in the morning air. A lilac-breasted roller performed its evasive aerobatics above him, but was hit in mid-air by a swooping goshawk. It escaped, flapped feebly to the top of a tree, where it wobbled on a dry perch for a moment and opened its beak to screech.

'Kappi, Kappi, my wing, my wing.'

Pula returned the call, saw the bird's head tilt to one side, listening, one wing low. The cloud lifted from Pula's spirit and he made up his mind.

In some excitement at the beginning of a new day, he clambered down and went straight to the floor of the old hut where Julia still lay. She was in the same position on the reeds which he had prepared for her. She was fast asleep on her back. Her one arm was bent above her head, a slim white wrist touching her hair. She was a child again, in innocent sleep, a child of nature, not of the city. Pula watched her chest rise and fall with her breathing. He watched her breast rise beneath the crumpled blouse in which she had slept and he thought of her naked before him, lying on papyrus fronds.

He banished the thought at once, considered the white girl dressed in the skin of a sitatunga like Bubi. There was nothing beautiful in the image. The naked body reappeared so easily, the legs stretched out too, the flash memory of Julia on the grass, Potlako standing above her. He took one step backwards towards the opening of the hut, a level place where the door used to be. He tip-toed away from the sleeping woman and away from these hot and sudden images. Julia moved her head, opened her eyes with his movement.

'Good morning, Pula,' she said very simply, raising the one arm which was above her head, greeting him.

'We must go to the Hills.'

'Do we slide across to the other side?'

'We go by *mokoro*. I will find the channels which run beneath the sands.'

'They are underground channels. No boat can go there.'

'Come, we must try.'

'Shakawe would be easier. It is at least downstream from here!'

'Who is there in Shakawe to help us?'

'Who is in the Hills to help us?'

'Bubi. I must tell Bubi that the rainmaker is dead.'

He said this in such a soft voice that Julia could hardly hear him. But she sensed his anguish, at once understood. She looked into his eyes but saw there not only anguish but confusion and doubt. Pula still stood above her near the doorway to the hut. He stared at her in a disturbing way. Julia had had her own concerns about Pula's strange mood after the death of his father. Now she was drawn to comfort him, just as he had comforted her in the aeroplane. She was so much better now. Not fully recovered perhaps, anxious, but still able to help. She was much better in her body, and her spirit was very much alive on this new morning. She could even set out on her own, make her own way to Shakawe.

'First we go to Shakawe. Then to the Hills to tell Bubi,' she said.

'You will leave me alone? Now, in the swamp alone?'

His voice seemed so much older, almost his father's voice. It was a man's voice and Julia was touched by the plea in it. He was pleading with her! He who was so well equipped to make his own way in the swamp, was asking her not to leave him.

'At Shakawe we can ask the foreman to take us to the Hills in a truck,' she said, but Pula did not seem to hear. He left the hut, hurried away from the place while she rose to her feet.

She followed him to the water's edge and reminded him of the path he had shown her from high up in the tree.

'You told me that the path led to the road,' she insisted.

'Come, I will show you again,' Pula said as he walked away, back along the path which led past the big tree to the other side of the island. She followed reluctantly but he soon stopped in front of her, thrust back an arm to stop her behind him on the narrow path. She took the outstretched hand in her own. He turned at once and pulled her body to his, he hugged her with both arms, touched his lips to her forehead. Julia did not move away, but she gently eased herself from his embrace, open hands on his chest.

'What was it Pula? What did you see?'

Pula released her, pointed to a dry snakeskin hanging from a branch across the path. The sloughed off rind was dry, transparent, the patterns of the previously living skin of a green mamba. It decorated the bush like a sign left for travellers, a symbol.

'Perhaps he also survived the flood,' Julia said.

'He has been reborn.'

Pula carefully picked the skin from the branch, wrapped it around his hand to make a soft ball of it.

'I will take it to Bubi,' he said.

'And if she is not there?'

'She will be there. She is a doctor like your father. She does not send away patients who come to her.'

'You are her patient?'

'I am hurt. In spirit I am hurt. We must go by water.'

There was no breakfast of duck's eggs and bream this time and Pula hurried her into the *mokoro*, eager to be away from the place. He placed a flat hand on the gunwale, patted the carved patterns there, then picked up his carving from the muck. He washed it in the river and handed it to Julia as she stepped into the *mokoro* to join him.

'You left it in the mud all night,' he accused.

Julia considered how much the spirit might be hurt. She had been hurt that way. An image of Potlako Lereng in the bush, a feel of honey on her hair returned to hurt her again. She raised a hand to touch her hair, a finger stroked her forehead. She considered how vulnerable the spirit might be, and the flesh. She recalled Bubi in her hut, telling them of sacrifice. Pula's father, her own father, she herself, sacrificed?

The image of Potlako would not go away, it lingered ruthlessly and she knew with awful certainty that she would see him again. He was still somewhere in the bush, he had not died in the swamp. He too was a survivor of the flood.

Pula did not find the channels beneath the sand and he stopped again not far from the island. He asked Julia to walk along another game path with him so that he could see the shape of the recovering land, how it might have changed after the flood, even as their island had changed. They left the *mokoro* tied to papyrus.

'You must help me find what I am looking for,' Pula said and Julia followed, still confused. What did anyone look for in this waste after the flood? The shapes of old huts, the beginnings of familiar paths, the signs of life reviving? Or signs that would confirm her fear? Potlako had also survived.

Not only was he a survivor but he could be nearby, Julia reasoned. He might even be with Bubi. She considered this possibility with even more concern about their difficult journey.

Earlier, immediately after the crisis in the aeroplane, when he and his comrades had been defeated by the Hambukushu, another patient had made his own difficult journey. He had sought refuge in Bubi's cave. This one knew the water-way to the mountain. He had hauled himself back into a *mokoro* after his ordeal in the water. He escaped death but one young and eager crocodile had held him for long enough to do great damage to his right hand. The feeding creature did not rip his bangles from his wrist, but strong young teeth stripped the hand, severing three fingers.

Potlako Lereng was lying there in Bubi's cave when she first returned to it. He was lying in the cave, dying in the cave, and she had at once cleaned him up and dressed his wounds. She eased the bangles from his right hand, strapped the remaining two fingers together and treated the torn hand with her own powders. She hid the bangles in a safe place.

Bubi cut small strings of loose flesh from his hand, buried them outside the cave in the soil of a drying field. The field was already rich from the flood and this flesh would make it richer.

Bubi washed Potlako in the water that flowed through her cave, her one hand pecking at the remains of the ash dressing with which he had tried to stem the flow of blood. Her fingers spread over the wet ugliness of his torn hand, and she knew that if it mended, only a grotesque hook would remain.

He suffered and she did not mind hurting him. She also did not mind patching him up, treating him with her own medicines, saving a hook of a hand. She fed him, tended him, satisfied herself that he would survive.

When his suffering eased a little, he began to ask questions of her, he began to ask about his bangles, about the Hambukushu diamond. She told him to return to his own people.

She removed the sacred Hambukushu diamond from its place lying on desert sand in a child's skull. She hid the diamond from Potlako's now eager eyes. She offered only a calabash of ointment.

'You must take this ointment with you. Ask some woman to dress it as I have done.'

'There are no others from the Mountain of Night.'

'Any woman will do it.'

'What happened to my men?'

'They all died. The Hambukushu killed them.'

'Yet you help me?'

'You crept here like a wounded animal. You came to a doctor.'

'What happened to the rainmaker?'

'He is in the swamp somewhere, with his son. They will come to me, in time. Everyone needs time to recover after the flood.'

'What happened to the other doctor?'

'He was taken away in a boat. He was very sick.'

'And his daughter? What happened to Julia?'

Potlako raised his hook of a hand in awful effort, like a scorpion with a broken claw. He moved it slowly in an arc as if there were still sharp nippers at the end of it, scratching claws. He turned his face to Bubi so that she might clearly see the damage which Pula had done with his knife. The still-vivid wound was cleaner than his hand. He tried to smile and Bubi thrust the calabash of ointment at him once again.

'Take it and go.'

'Who looks after the diamond?'

'The rainmaker looks after the diamond.'

'And not you? It is here somewhere in your cave.'

'It has disappeared, like so many things in the flood.'

Bubi still held out the calabash of ointment for his injured hand, but he would not take it. 'Pula tried to kill me!' he said.

'You tried to kill us all.'

'When I am strong again I will come back.'

Bubi did not return the copper bangles to their owner. She had other similar items amongst the ornaments of her profession, but these two now had special significance. She pressed one bangle into the sand, placed the big diamond in the middle of the ring. She was pleased with her new design, with the jewel in its frame. She would show it to Pula and to Julia when they came to her, but she would not tell them about Potlako.

19

Pula's spirit lifted when he saw smoke rising from the direction of the Tsodilo Hills, but Julia followed only in weariness. She knew that she would be lost without him, and that she had to succumb to his insistence and his single purpose. She understood that he in turn had to go back to Bubi to consult with her after the tragedy in the mud.

Pula told Julia that it would not be too long now before they could eat in Bubi's cave, rest in Bubi's cave. Then he would show her why the Hills were known as the 'slippery slopes'. He would climb with her to the very peak. First they would eat and rest, then he would take her to the top of the Hills, to a place his father knew. Bubi knew it too. From there she would see right across the desert to the swamp. She could even see Shakawe.

Julia could not feel the same way about finding Bubi, nor did she long for the hills, but she too revived when the path led them between high rocks towards a cool and shadowed passage. Her legs were aching, she felt the heat more acutely than her companion. She stopped in the shade of the big rocks.

Pula came back to her, took her hand to lead her on. She held back and Pula felt that her palm was hot and clammy. In sudden alarm he took her in his arms again. He pressed her head to his shoulder, kissed her hair.

'It is not far now,' he told her. 'Look up there!'

They were in the shadow of caves, and from the shadow rose wisps of smoke. Above them on the flat rock surfaces were

Bushman paintings of hunting scenes, animals of all kinds, tsessebe, sable, even hippos, buffalo, but no crocodiles.

'They never painted crocodiles,' Pula told her, releasing her from his embrace and pointing to the paintings.

On the rock face above them was a drawing of two people together in a *mokoro*, the man was standing with a pole, the woman had a baby on her back. Above this painting, bigger, out of proportion, was the figure of a buffalo and above the neck of the buffalo was a praying mantis. It was also too big, out of proportion, but it was clearly a mantis.

'There he is!' Pula said, pointing to the mantis painted on the rock. 'That is our god of fertility. He loves abundance. He knows that many of those powerful creatures have died in the flood. Buffalo have died, elephant, giraffe, wildebeest. He also knows that they must all breed again, and he can sense the seasons of breeding. That is why he prays. Like my father who brought too much rain, maybe he thinks he may bring too much fertility. We will cover the earth, that will be the new flood.'

Julia looked up at Pula standing near the painted image of a buffalo and she was concerned that he should talk this way, after their experiences together, their journey together to find Bubi. She accepted completely that Bubi had to be told about the death of the rainmaker, that Pula already felt the weight of his new role in the tribe, that he had been deeply disturbed by the crocodiles, but now he talked in tribal riddles.

Pula did not seem to be talking directly to her. He was talking to the rock. Just as he sometimes spoke to crocodiles, or eagles. He was talking to the rock! Yet he was telling her stories, just as he had done when she was so ill. Sometimes she did not know which was story and which was reality. Up here amongst the rocks of Tsodilo, or down there in the swamp, which was reality? Pula still talked to the rock.

'Our god of fertility is eaten by his mate. She knows that he only has that purpose, that all the fluids and all the futures are in the female and her line. The female can feed on the male.'

Pula took Julia's hand again, to lead her yet higher.

'Our Queen knows all about it. The *maoma*, the royal drums, will first call the people to congregate to hear the truth. The big barge, the *Nalikwanda*, paddled by twenty men, ten on each side, will carry the Queen away from the flood. The men will sing about women, they will sing about their boat. The words of the song will tell of the manner of the making of the royal craft, what such a beautiful thing means to the people. They will tell how the timber is cut with great skill, the logs are shaped, the fibres to bind the logs are treated, shapes are formed by axe, how the whole thing is made by the tribe, with much reverence and ritual. Maybe one day you will ride with the Queen who is responsible for the floating of the tribe, for its well-being. *Nalikwanda* is kept on the water by a cycle of the powers of nature and the gods, the real things and the symbols.'

'Pula, let us rest a moment.'

'There will be many other barges, followed by hundreds of *mokoros*, by more singing people. The river will be a celebration for you. We are a matriarchal people, we worship fertility and we will welcome you among us. All the future is in a woman's hands.'

Pula had been talking to the rocks. Now he seemed to be talking in old riddles, in symbols, and he was talking to her. She wanted to rest but she also wanted him to know that she did not really like his talk of women and fertility.

'I do not like Bubi,' she managed to say.

'You may get sick again. Bubi knows about these things.'

'She only tells you to sacrifice.'

'That was done. I must tell her that. My father was the sacrifice. But *your* father is still alive. He will come to look for you.'

'Pula! You just say these things! As if you are receiving messages! You talk to the rock and you hear voices!'

'Don't you ever hear voices?'

Pula took her further along the passage between rocks until they came out into the sun again and could see across the plain below them towards the vast stretches of the Kalahari desert. Julia followed his gaze and saw heat-haze shimmer like a lake. Above the lake a cloud was forming, a dark cloud in the late afternoon. Outside the line of the shade where they sat, lizards lay still, a few dassies played near a ledge of rock. Directly below the rock was a small field of cassava, thin stems raising green heads. There was more green beyond, also patches of yellow against the brown grass, young leaves of mopani bushes. Above was a clear blue sky but in the distance was a black cloud approaching.

They saw a tiny aircraft flying away from the cloud towards the hills. Pula pointed to it, wondered why he could not yet hear it. They saw that it was flying directly towards them, gliding lower.

'I will fly one day,' Pula said, watching the craft approach.

Behind the aircraft the black cloud grew rapidly. It cut off the shimmering lake, wiped away the heat-haze, even blocked out the sun. The microlight was flying ahead of the black cloud and now they could hear the sound of it.

'Locusts!' Pula shouted. He clambered away from Julia up the last narrow chimney between dark slabs, to the very top. He called out once again and then returned rapidly to help Julia move up the same route to the peak. He pulled on her arm, hurried her for the last few metres to the top.

They stood together in the sun, a huge shadow approaching. The microlight reached the peak before the cloud of locusts, it was suddenly there, then it was gone. It turned away from the shadow, fled from the dark cloud, disappeared. Julia shouted out to the strange aircraft flying so close to the mountain, as she might shout out from an island to a floating thing that would pass her by. For a vivid moment she could see the lone pilot sitting there so close to her, his feet on a metal rung, the wind flapping his shirt, He seemed to be playing with the machine, playing in the air.

'Here we are!' she shouted, 'up here on the hill!'

They now saw birds gather, coming from all directions, from the land and from the swamp. For a moment Pula thought that the cloud might not be locusts but birds, birds on some unusual migration, some natural phenomenon of the desert, like a sudden surfeit of life, like flying ants in profusion after rain.

The sky grew darker and Julia now clung to Pula's arm as they stood on the peak of the Tsodilo Hills. Below them people lived amongst the rocks of the foothills, and now they saw women and children running out like ants to collect from heaven.

'It was the pilot!' Julia shouted, but Pula wrapped his arms around her, pressed her head down to his chest. He held Julia to him as the huge cloud approached. He watched the shadow of it close in on the hills. He saw the birds fly up to the edges of the living shadow, flutter and dive, snap insects from the air. Then the earliest of the locusts settled on the mopani bushes on the flats below, on to the meagre shoots of the cassava in a field. They quickly covered the cassava, a shimmering blanket of them.

The locusts hit the hill itself, blocking out the sun. Pula turned his back to them, hugged Julia to his body as the chattering darkness of millions covered them both. He could feel the bulge of Julia's thigh between his legs and he trapped it there, holding her. The locusts beat against her back, landed in her hair. She could feel them hit her legs, her ankles. She could also feel Pula's embrace, another demanding pressure against her body.

The locusts settled on the rocks around them as if they might cover the two people too, like a blanket of maggots. The creatures would smother the land, would smother them. The scraping jaws would eat away all the mopani of the Kalahari, all the grass and the mealies, like millions of tiny gods they would devour. Like a flood, they would cover their separate efforts, end their struggle. Pula stamped his feet as the bodies built up on them, like flood mud. He heard the bodies pop beneath his feet, felt the mulch move. He held Julia still, his big arms around her body, his one hand holding her head to his protective chest. One locust clawed at his neck, tried to penetrate his skin. He ripped it away, feeling the scratch of spiny legs.

'The swarm will pass,' he managed to say to Julia, 'stay still.'

The locusts settled on Pula's back as if he were something to eat, and Pula could feel their jaws working on his skin. He could feel other creatures on his neck. He did not move a hand to wipe them away this time but held on to Julia in some desperation, keeping the creatures away from her face. Like hottentot-gods they would eat him, devour him and his will, his young volition, his hope. He would be left to dry, headless.

'They only eat green things,' he said into Julia's ear, breathlessly, as if not quite believing it himself, as if they might rob him of air to breathe. They were a pressure about him, a mood, an omen of dry time to come, harbingers of drought after the flood, a multitude, a surfeit, a plague.

They kept coming, the swarm did not pass by quickly. It was as if the locusts had chosen to settle for the night on the Tsodilo Hills, to settle on the sacred rock and stay, covering the bodies which they found there. They would stay, they would smother all life as effectively as any flood; they were the multipliers, the endless fertility. They would eat and they would be eaten.

Suddenly the sun came out, the cloud passed and only shimmering millions remained in the hills, devouring what leaves were left on meagre bushes. Julia raised her head and looked out from the protection of Pula's arms, saw bodies about his feet, some crushed, some crawling. A yellow ooze marked the rock where they stood, but the swarm had passed. She shuddered, but Pula gently kissed her eyes, comforted her.

'Hambukushu will collect them, grill them on the coals, then eat them. There will be talk of dry times to come, of sacrifice that will be necessary to avoid famine.'

'More sacrifice?' Julia asked in a whisper, burrowing her head against his protective chest once again, closing her eyes to shut out the image of crushed bodies, the continuing rustle of their bloated presence, crawling creatures from another world, now helpless, with useless wings.

Those wings above the pilot, those strange and awkward wings, they were not useless. Surely the pilot had come to look for her. He had probably seen her on the hill, with Pula. He would tell the others and he would tell her father and they would all return to rescue her. Was he not always on rescue missions, the pilot, or was he not a ferryman, who would come to take her across the waters. He was the very ferryman who did not need a long *mokoro*, even for crossings of the sea. Go now, banished from the shore, you can even glide through the sky like an eagle. You do not need to walk through the bush, to struggle through the mud, to paddle any *mokoro*, to use any pole, you can fly. What eagle would be held back by locusts?

When the cloud had lifted they could clearly see the rising smoke once again and it now seemed to be much closer. Julia was encouraged by her thoughts of the pilot and his possible return, and she began to make for the smoke, treading ahead of Pula along the rocky path. Pula followed her gladly enough, heartened by her wilful action, knowing that they would soon find Bubi.

'Bubi will be feasting on locusts,' Pula said as he hurried after her.

'The pilot will come back,' Julia added, turning her head to smile at him over her shoulder.

20

The pilot, sitting under flimsy wings, had in fact seen Pula and Julia on the mountain. The couple were a vision from the past which brought back all the anguish of his failure. His besotted distance from the beautiful girl, his failed missions. He had been unable to get close to her, unable to work his way through the confusion she created in him, he had no direction, like a fool lost in the bush. His missions had always failed. He had not been able to rescue the people from the flood, he had sat with useless wings, an ark stranded in the swamp. Now he flitted around the swamp like an insect searching for a mate.

He had returned to the place of his failure. He was no criminal returning to the place of his crime. He was only a pilot with something of the frustrated ferryman about him. He ferried medical supplies, any supplies, to people in distress. He might also be something of a guilty conscience with wings. He observed the suffering below him, conscientiously wished to alleviate it, but usually ended up flying away from it.

When he saw the vision of Pula and Julia on a mountain he thought at once of the fight in the Hercules, of Pula Barotse with an AK47. The boy who carved such beautiful things from *moselesele*, who so gently cared for the sick white girl, had picked up a rifle. What could Pula Barotse do with that kind of power? Where did such a man of peace stand in the scheme of things? Where was the ferryman supposed to take him, from what point to what point? The place and the passage are difficult, and the waters of death are deep which flow between.

Even in this improbable creation of a flying machine, the pilot was a disappointed ferryman. He did not have much range or much fuel in his microlight and he circled Tsodilo only once because of the locusts. He flew through the edge of the swarm and the creatures splashed against his big propeller and were thrown back in a yellow mess. He lost lift and swung away, straight back to Shakawe.

At Shakawe he landed on the deserted road that ran past the garage and he removed locust bodies from the air-cooling system, scraped the muck from leading edges.

He performed these tasks with affection, recalling the eagerness of the foreman who had built the aircraft so well. He had fashioned it, protected it, given it a special place in his workshop, even in his heart. He had designed a dual fuel-pumping arrangement, a cooling system from an old radiator. The radiator conversion formed the nose of the bush aircraft. It was a remarkable machine, so light, so easy to handle. He patted the warm Yamaha which gave it power and as a last touch he fingered the feathered frills with which the foreman had adorned the wing-tips.

Early the next morning the pilot sat suspended just above the surface of the road, strapped to the bird-like contraption with high wings. His feet on aluminium pedals touched thin green blades of new grass as two willing youths from Shakawe village pushed the light aircraft along the road. The small pram wheels rumbled on the uneven surface, the wings of the microlight flapped as if in anticipation of lift-off, the feather frills flicking. The framework which held the pilot swayed when the men stopped pushing.

The pilot went through his simple routine, touched the limited instruments one by one with a checking finger. Then he started the fan by pulling down on the wooden toggle which hung above his head. The finely-tuned Yamaha burst into life.

The men watched anxiously as the light aircraft moved away along the dirt road, the pilot in solo control. The secret of solo control was to balance the number of take-offs with the number of landings. The automatic stuff in between was tedious.

As part of his first flight to the Hills the pilot had tested the aircraft well. He had cut power at the moment of stall, used more rudder in the first spin, forced one abort on take-off, looked for blind flying conditions in low cloud. The aircraft had taken such treatment with few strains, like a well-built *mokoro* in a flood.

This time he took the aircraft straight up, hanging on the high wing like a glider, right up to stall at about a thousand feet. There was no stall-warning on the microlight, but he felt the buoyancy of the morning air and sensed his relative speed as if he were in some other current in some other medium. He was really flying the flimsy thing, feeling the lift of its wings.

He set his course towards Tsodilo Hills. The microlight floated fast in the cool air. He let the nose dip just a fraction. Then, with a flick of a single black switch, he cut the fan. He would glide for a while, conserve fuel and sense the flying of a bird.

On the ground, the men who had helped him launch his aircraft had turned away shaking their heads in mirth. They were reluctant to return to their work of salvaging their homes in the village. They could still hear the sound of the engine, and they waved to the crazy pilot as he made for the Hills. Then the sound was cut off. The two men looked up in sudden alarm. The dreadful silence after the urgent beat of power taunted them, as if they should not have laughed at the white man and his machine.

In the same sudden silence the pilot sat alone over the swamp. He could hear the hiss of air through wing struts of wire. The soft throb of the idling fan was like a resting heart-beat. He took a deep breath. He drew in the fresh air with a hiss like the very hiss of free flying. It was to the pilot the hiss of freedom, the sound of wings. He shouted out to the sky, to the wisps of cloud above, to the hot and humid air of his swamp. Juuuulia! he shouted.

The pilot looked down at the swamp below, at Africa. He saw the familiar physical images, was exhilarated by his birdlike view of them. The twisting river, the stem of the pear, the clear line of the

Okavango as it flowed to its own delta, into the desert. Not into the sea, but into the desert. The earth which it had brought down from the mountains in so many floods over so many years had filled a huge valley.

As he glided for a moment in the supporting thermal, losing height, but holding there for as long as possible without power, he still made good ground speed. Like a glider, he floated towards the Tsodilo Hills. He could see crocodiles basking on sand spits, hippos in a pool. Hundreds of birds rose from the papyrus.

The pilot looked up to the sky above, saw vultures above him using the thermals just as he was doing. He flicked the ignition switch once again, but did not need to pull on the toggle which swung near his head. The throbbing fan brought the warm Yamaha to noisy life once again. He opened up the power and climbed higher, to join the vultures. He held his course towards the Tsodilo Hills. There was trained power in his hands, a miraculous blessing, but nothing like the power of the thermals above the desert.

Amongst the soaring vultures he saw a fish-eagle. He leaned back in his flimsy chair and waved to the eagle.

Using the same thermal, the pilot flew to the eagle, rose beneath it. The eagle swooped down to the intruder, feigned an attack, hovered near. The pilot saw a flash of anger in the eagle's eyes. He switched off again, hoping that the hot air would provide sufficient lift to allow both eagle and microlight to stay quietly together in the thermal. He preferred the hissing sound of free flight to the constant roar of the fan. The eagle's head move inquisitively from side to side, then it soared away.

It twisted higher in a graceful dance, the rhythm of the rising thermal. The pilot wished that Julia could witness such free flight. He would like to take Julia with him to join all soaring things, free, self-willed, independent, even powerful at last.

The pilot flicked the isolator switch again to regain power but this time there was no response. The soft throb mocked him, it did not bring the Yamaha to life. Power was meant to be there at a flick of a switch! That was how it worked in the real world. These things worked because they had been made to work. That was the flying rule. He pulled twice on the toggle and recalled other floating times on the river when an engine would not start. A tiny panic began to build in his stomach, he began to sweat.

Now there was only betrayal. Betrayal of an innocent. How could such a thing happen to him? Power was power, at the flick of a switch. Why had he been playing in the air, why had he forgotten his purpose?

He felt the searing void in the pit of his stomach more acutely now, a sudden fear of his fragile wings. Useless wings, useless hands, absence of power, a void as huge as a hold in the desert.

The hiss of the hot air over the wings was this time like a hiss of derision, some snake from the diamond sands hissed at him, threatened him. In a flush of near panic he thought he heard a woman scream. It was Bubi screaming as she had screamed in another aircraft. It was an awful sound above the hiss of the air. He shook his head briskly, shut his eyes for a moment, then looked up again. It was only the fish-eagle crying, high above.

The pilot checked all instruments, flicked the switch again and again. He went through his forced-landing routine: above all stay calm, remember NATURAL:

Not too fast!

Analyse your situation.

Tanks.

Upwind.

Rich mixture.

Altitude, airspeed.

Land, lines.

NATURAL.

He could see the Tsodilo Hills ahead. He had an upwind approach. There were no power lines. He tapped the second fuel gauge, a primitive one. It showed a tiny needle E to F, stuck on F. He flicked the isolator switch on and off, turned the fuel cocks below both tanks, off then on again. He repeatedly pulled on the toggle to help the slowly revolving fan start the engine. He grasped the small brass handle of the unused auxiliary fuel pump. His hands were still in control, they were acting as they had been trained to do, his mind tried to direct them, take hold of the crisis, naturally.

There was still this awful hole in his soul, a void in his volition, he was powerless.

Frantically the pilot worked on the little brass handle of the auxiliary pump, thrusting powerfully with his right hand. His hand slipped off the handle as he forced it down. He cut his knuckles on the flange at the base of it, but still the fuel was not forced through.

The pilot lifted his hand from the pump, flexed his controlling fingers. He placed his hands together, raised them to his lips with a reverent nod of his head, praying like a mantis. Blood from his knuckles oozed slowly down the back of his right hand, down his arm.

He looked at the hand which was bleeding and considered how it had failed him. Now it was powerless. He could not make the contraption fly, he was without power, with useless wings. And yet it had been so close. What tiny thing was it which made the difference?

He saw the same rocks that he had seen before at the top of Tsodilo Hills.

'Perhaps I only saw ghosts?' the pilot whispered to himself.

He was losing height very rapidly and yet there was still some lift in the big wings above him. If only he could avoid that hill, if only he could lift them with wings, like a lift of the spirit. The mocking hiss of the warm air through which he was flying seemed to grow louder. Yes, he was still flying, he could still make it. There was no Okavango god, and no other god to save him, he had to fly this thing himself.

He looked up and saw the eagle above them, soaring higher. He touched the controls again, still leaning forward anxiously, trying to glide the aircraft away from Tsodilo. He noticed that both hands were sweating, he could feel the moisture on the controls as he sensed the limited response to his actions. The wings were still above him, but so flimsy, gossamer wings, so easily lost. Sudden loss of wings, loss of life, loss of innocence.

He had lost something in the air, he had lost something in the stranded aircraft, leaving a void. Then fear crept into the void, deep and immediate. It invaded his spirit, immobilized his hands. He would never find Julia, he would never find what he was searching for.

'I can't use my hands!' he shouted out to the clouds above Tsodilo Hills, to the eagle.

'The spirit!' he heard John Barotse say, perhaps as an answer from the clouds.

Then he lifted the nose of his unlikely aircraft, sensed some small response. He moved his weight back, away from the auxiliary pump and the rudimentary instruments. He pushed his head back, pressing with his feet on the thin metal bar.

'The wind will lift me!' he shouted in sudden relief.

The pilot felt the lift, was not sure that it would be enough, but it was a chance. He too lifted himself against his straps, willed his aircraft into the cloud.

In blind flying conditions the pilot tried to keep his record intact, he tried to keep the balance between take-off and landing. The lift of the clouds and the lift of the spirit were just enough to take him over the peak, to bring him out to the other side, out from the clouds and into the sun.

With his bleeding hand he again pumped viciously, rattling the flimsy housing on the framework. Life-giving fuel was finally forced through, the tiny needle of the new gauge wobbled. The Yamaha drank the fuel like an elixir and the big fan roared.

The pilot quickly looked for a forced-landing pad and he chose a cassava field below him. He glanced back towards the hills over which he had safely passed and he saw the distinct figure of a man running down a mountain path. The man was clearly waving to him, moving his arms above his head as he ran, as if calling for attention. The pilot lifted the snub-nose of the aircraft, aborted his landing and flew back to the hills. There on the path below him he saw the man very clearly. It was Pula Barotse. Lower down the path, near the opening to a cave, quite deep into the valley, he saw Julia.

It was clearly Julia and she was running too, but up the path, away from the shadow of the cave. It was the same girl, no doubt about that, and she was *running*. He was thrilled by the vision of the running girl, as he had been thrilled by her still and weakened body when he had first set eyes on her. There was such life in her, such youth, such animal vitality and promise. He leaned out of his machine to look closer, soared into the valley towards the dark shadow of the cave, and towards the glorious image of the running girl. He saw her stumble on the path, saw another man approach her from the shadow of the cave.

He sensed the sudden drama as if some ancient legend were being played out below him. Innocence in search of everlasting life, confronted by all the evils, was held in poignant balance below him. He was exalted to conceive such a primitive scene of conflict in such a lofty way. It was all so clear to him, the final scene. He, with his machine and his skill was destined to save innocence. He believed that he could do something about a crisis which he once again observed from on high. Once again, he flew in to the rescue.

21

The Hambukushu came out to collect the locusts and Bubi emerged from her cave to do the same. Bubi carried a skin bag slung over her shoulder and she too collected manna eagerly, thankful for new abundance. She made her fire on a rock outside her cave and she prepared to grill the fat bodies.

Pula and Julia hurried towards the rising smoke. They saw children running after hopping insects, catching them, stuffing them into their own skin bags. Pula took Julia's hand, led her past crawling bodies on the 'slippery slope'. He looked up again to see the smoke rising from the passage between rocks, and he sensed that Bubi was very close.

When Pula saw Bubi grilling locusts on the coals, he ran towards her, then stopped close to her fire. He seemed to Julia to bow to her. He talked excitedly for a moment, bent over her, and Bubi touched her greasy fingers to his forehead.

Julia approached more slowly, hanging back, watching the laughing people around her collect the squirming bodies. She saw some captured locusts claw their way out of a closed skin bag, saw children break legs off the locusts to drop the moving but deformed bodies into a calabash. One such calabash was very full and the bodies writhed in an awful mass. The child, successful gatherer, proudly showed the writhing creatures to Julia.

Bubi offered grilled bodies to Pula and then to Julia when she joined them, but Julia shook her head sadly. Bubi merely drew her sitatunga skin closer, crouched down next to the fire, took more locusts from her skin bag and placed them on the coals.

'You must be hungry. I have cassava for you at home,' she said.

Julia was hungry, and when Pula insisted that she try the choice body of a locust grilled to golden, she took it. She bit at it with long teeth. She found she liked the taste, and smiled. Bubi clapped her wrinkled hands.

'Good. Later you can have cassava.'

She called to some children nearby and they approached her cautiously. She told them that Pula was the son of the rainmaker, that the white girl from the aeroplane was his bride. Other women joined the children , even some men, and now Bubi had the tribal audience she needed.

'Pula Barotse has returned with his bride!' she declared.

Julia did not understand what Bubi had said but she accepted the cheers and shuffled dancing of the smiling crowd around her. Pula was silent, as he stood by Bubi.

Bubi thrust out a hand to Pula's throat, her palm flat on his skin. On the back of her hand lay the rainmaker's necklace.

'Where is he?' she accused.

'This is not a time for rejoicing. It is a time for mourning. The rainmaker died in the flood.'

The small crowd stood in shocked silence for a moment and then Bubi let out a shrill sound which was picked up by the other women. The sound of their lament echoed in the Hills, the ululation soared as it had done during those awful days in the aeroplane. In front of Pula and Julia Bubi began a shuffling dance. She scuffed bare feet in the dust, moving in the rhythm of her sounds. She shuffled to the edge of the fire, scattering coals and locusts. She scooped up hot ash from the edge of the fire, threw it in the air so that grey powder rained down on her head. She intoned words to the gods, to the *mugrodi*s of the past, she repeated the name Kupenda, Kupenda.

Then she suddenly stiffened. She stood rigid before Pula. Bits of ash burnt her hair, dust still clung to her face. Pula could smell the burning hair and again he was with her in the aircraft. What would

Bubi do now?

With surprising agility she then sprang into the air in front of the new rainmaker, flapping her cloak and emitting loud expletives and explosive sounds of her despair. She took live locusts from her bag and threw them over Julia's head, macabre confetti. She sprang up in front of Julia too, swept her cloak across her face and then turned to the witnessing tribe.

'Pula Barotse is the rainmaker,' she declared. 'We have a new *mugrodi*.'

Julia still did not understand much of what Bubi said but she did sense that the witch was very serious in her purpose. She also knew that Pula had at last done what he had come to do. He had told Bubi about the tragic event in the mud, he had reported back to his own people.

Julia scraped away a few remaining locusts, took a deep breath, lifted her shoulders to take charge of herself. She would not be intimidated by this woman in skins.

'I must go back to Shakawe,' she said and Bubi only laughed at her in shrill ridicule.

'They will be looking for her,' Pula said, seriously. Bubi only laughed again, and swung round in her skin cloak so that dust rose from the ground, swept by the hem of it.

'Of course, did you not see the aeroplane?' Bubi asked. 'It came to fetch her! The locusts drove it away!'

'That was the pilot!' Pula said, as if to defend Julia against Bubi's ridicule.

'The one who will teach you to fly! Of course, you will take the new *mugrodi* up into the air and she can touch the clouds and help you in your duties.'

'I will fly one day!' Pula said, and at once regretted his indiscretion. How ridiculous he sounded, to Bubi and to his own people. And what would his father say, what would the gods say? *Seramapetlo* would also laugh.

'I must speak to the elders of the tribe. I must tell them what happened in the mud,' Pula added with some authority, to regain his position amongst the women and the children.

Bubi took Pula and Julia to her hidden cave and there she offered cassava porridge to Julia, as well as clear water in a calabash. The water came from the stream which flowed freely at one end of the cave. Away from the one glowing fire it was dark and dank in the cave. There was a high bed in the flickering shadows, and a bundle of blankets near the fire. Bubi told them to sit on the flat stones near the fire and she told them to eat and drink. Later they could sleep. In the morning, together, they would decide what was to be done.

'I must thank you, Bubi,' Pula said, 'I am glad that we found you.'

'It was the locusts. They brought me out.'

'Thank you, Bubi,' Julia said very quietly.

'Yes, you should thank me. Who saved you from Potlako Lereng?'

Julia recoiled at the sound of the name. Pula put an arm around her. He gave her the carving, made her take it in her hand, hold on to it.

'Bubi will care for you here. You must rest well tonight,' he said.

'But where will you be?'

'I have to talk to the men. They will be waiting for me.'

'I came here with you, now you must go back with me. To Shakawe!'

'In the morning. Tonight Bubi will look after you.'

'In the morning we will start our other journey?'

'Early. Get some sleep, we will start in the morning.'

Bubi would indeed look after the new *mugrodi*. She would be given special meals. Everyone had to eat and drink.

Into Julia's water Bubi placed a few drops of *muka* made from honey and *rumbansi*, the dagga plant. Bubi put her to bed in the special place which she had prepared for her.

The primitive bed which Bubi had so carefully prepared deep in her cave near the source of water, was raised to form an altar. Around it, to the very edge of the flow of clear water which came from the rocks, were strewn numerous ornaments of Bubi's hidden home. There were gourds and ostrich eggs, feathered spears and small shields, necklaces and tiny bells, rattles and flutes made of wood, tortoise shells and dried bodies of brightly coloured lizards. At the head of the bed was the tiny cup of the skull of the last infant sacrificed in the proper way. Inside the cup the Hambukushu diamond lay on desert sand. The huge pear-shaped gem made a hollow in the fine desert sand in the cup of a child's skull, and it was framed by a copper bangle, a crocodile eating its own tail.

Bubi picked up the bangle, showed it to Julia. Julia recognised it at once.

'Potlako is dead,' Julia said in dreamy whisper. 'He was eaten by crocodiles.'

'Like Pula's father.'

Bubi put the bangle on the sand inside the cup of the last sacrificed child of the last true *mugrodi*, Kupenda.

'Kupenda!' Bubi intoned respectfully. 'She did the proper thing. She produced thirteen children for sacrifice so that the rains would come. After each sacrifice, just before the rains were due, she would offer herself and they would begin to make next year's baby. The children she made were sufficient sacrifice for the season.'

'Why do you tell me these terrible things?'

'As soon as Pula is out of mourning, I will arrange a great ceremony.'

Deeply aware of her own vulnerability, Julia felt trapped on her high bed. In the light of the fire in the centre of the cave, she saw again the shadows around her, the things of the bush, the alien mysteries. There was a curled snake on a shield, its head touching a feathered spear. She believed the snake to be alive. The legs of her high bed were the legs of a giraffe, cut off, the pattern of the skin shining as when it lived.

Near the water was a huge bullfrog and Julia was sure she saw it open its mouth, catch a beautiful bird, a carmine bee-eater. The bird disappeared down the frog's throat and Julia sat up in alarm. She was now terrified of the things of Bubi's home, the things in the cave in which she was to sleep for the night. She was also very drowsy, very weak, but Bubi continued to taunt her.

'The firstborn of a white child may even be better for today. You white people control so many things, perhaps your children can control the rains.'

'I want to see Pula!'

'Tonight he has to talk to the old men. He now has special duties. He told you.'

'I will not wait until the morning!'

'Tomorrow you will see him but you will not be able to touch him. First he must cleanse himself.'

'What on earth are you talking about?'

Julia lay anxious and uncomfortable in her high bed. When she closed her eyes, she fell into a drugged sleep.

22

In the morning Bubi appeared with a hot broth and she offered it to Julia, but Julia would not drink it. Bubi was confident that the girl would remain slow and drowsy for most of the day. She was so drugged that she did not even ask for Pula. She lay still on the bed, Pula's carving beside her like a weapon.

Bubi went to crush grain on a stone. Working on her knees, swaying backwards and forwards in the grinding rhythm of a song of the Hambukushu, Bubi smiled at her new patient. Her song was usually only sung at threshing time when the final product of the harvest fell on to stone and the husks were blown away. Now the grain was there in the hollowed stone, like an abundance in her cave. She would make a powder of it. She would feed the new *mugrodi*.

'Wind, Wind do not go away,
Wind, Wind do not go away,
Your mother has died a long time ago.'

The low chant and the grunt of grinding grain was an awful sound to Julia, like the consistent rumble of the running stream. It was as if demons hummed to her, mocking her. She was trapped in the cave of a wild person. Her father had said that Pula was really a wild person, living the way ancient people lived. She imagined cave-people drawing figures on stone like the ones she had seen on the peak of Tsodilo. They never painted crocodiles.

John Barotse was also a wild person. Her father had respected him so deeply. He had compared the wild men to Gilgamesh, living in the distance at the mouth of rivers. He had talked about a search for immortality, about ancient gods.

Now she could hear Bubi's song and smell the fumes of the open fire on the floor of the cave. The smoke reminded her of Pula's skin, his warmth and his closeness as he had held her on the mountain. He had protected her from the swarm. She closed her eyes and could feel his kisses on her hair. If only I could sleep and dream, at peace like a wild person, at peace with all the gods.

She forced herself to look about her, she opened her eyes to reality. Her head was still heavy, she was still drowsy, just as Bubi meant her to be. She was also Bubi's prisoner, but for what purpose?

Kupenda! The *mugrodi* who produced sacrificial children!

Julia sat up in her high bed, shaking her head to clear it of images. She had to get away from the cave, she had to escape. Now, she had to do it now, while Bubi was busy with an everyday chore.

She lifted *feitiço* in her right hand, slowly swung her legs off the bed, then picked up the skull which was filled with desert sand. On the sand lay a rough pear-shaped stone. Julia saw the stone lying in the frame of the bangle and recognised the copper crocodile once again. She looked at the big diamond. The skull in which it lay seemed to throb in her left hand. She held a staff and an orb, royal and ridiculous, ready for the *Nalikwanda*.

'Pula! Get me out of here!'

The grinding stopped at once. So did the song. Bubi sat back on her haunches, leaving the pestle stone in its hollow mortar. She struggled to her feet, shuffled to Julia to lead her back to bed.

'You must not touch those things,' she scolded, 'they are sacred.'

'I hate them!' Julia screamed, lifting *feitiço* as if it were truly a fighting-stick. She threw the skull, the diamond, the bangle and the sand at Bubi. The skull hit Bubi on the forehead, she was stunned for a moment, as much by the omen as the bone. She saw the bangle roll away like a toy wheel. She could not see the diamond. She cursed Julia, a terrible curse in her anger, in which she offered the young girl to Pula so that she would produce sacrificial children. All her children would be buried in the sand to catch the rain. As for the son of John Barotse, he would lose the use of his hands, he would never carve again. The swamp would run dry after all, the people would suffer just as Pula had feared long ago. There was only one fate for those who denied the gods.

Julia attacked her then, wielding Pula's carving by the thin legs. Bubi moved away quickly, she lifted the spear which stood near the shield and the snake and backed away, closer to the flowing water. She grasped the snake's head too, and pointed it at Julia as if the mouth were spitting. The snake's body hung limp from her hand.

Julia watched the hand which held the spear, ignored the snake and then rushed at Bubi with her own weapon. Bubi threw the spear at Julia's chest and Julia hit it away with *feitiço*. Then she attacked again, and they both tumbled into the water which flowed near the altar-bed.

Julia rose above Bubi, repeatedly beating at her with the heavy flat head of *feitiço*. She swung the weapon with all her strength, the hard edge of the flat head cut into Bubi's temple and she dropped into the water. She lay still, she could not rise from the water. Julia sobbed above her, continued to swing the hardwood weapon with great anger. Her blows splashed near Bubi's head.

The hardwood stick felt like a steel rod in her hand, even more deadly than a thin sword. Julia sensed a sudden dominance over Bubi, a coming victory, a flash of acute recognition that she had until now been too timid, too weak, too intimidated. Why had she not fought before?

But now Bubi lay still. Blood trickled from a wound high on her temple, her nose bled. The blood streaked away with the flowing water.

Julia looked down at Bubi's body in the water, then dropped to her knees beside her. She lifted the limp body in her arms, sensed that there was still life in it. As she did so she felt the immediate presence of another person in the cave. In sudden alarm, in the draining guilt of being observed, she looked downstream. Her staring eyes followed the slick of blood in the water, until it disappeared into a dark tunnel.

She saw a bent figure loom out of the tunnel into the cave. He was walking in the water, stooping below the rock roof. The man straightened up. Still sloshing through water, he approached Julia.

Even in the half-light of the fire, after so long, Julia recognised the ghost's walk, the arrogant man's stride. She felt Bubi's body stir, but it might have been the movement of the water. To her horror, the apparition now confronted her in her guilt.

'Your friend Pula carved that stick,' Potlako Lereng said, 'with it you have killed Bubi.'

Potlako stood before Julia and he thrust an accusing hook of a hand at her. The hook was a curled finger, rising from the stump of a hand. There were no bangles on the wrist.

'Bubi cared for injured people,' Potlako Lereng said. 'Now you have killed her.'

Julia sat slumped in the water with Bubi in her arms. Her weapon was now ridiculous in one hand. Potlako reached down with his good hand, grabbed her one arm to pull her to her feet. Julia held on to Bubi and the body rose too. Potlako released her arm and smiled.

It was the same awful smile of expectation, but now it was deformed. A raw and livid slash of ugliness closed one eye, disfigured his nose.

'Where is the big diamond?' Potlako demanded.

Julia vividly recalled earlier occasions on which she had defied Potlako Lereng. When his friends had held her down; when he had first showed her the cattle-killing weapon. He had thrust it into a monkey apple. Sharp, penetrating, killing with a smile. She had turned away in disgust. She tried to pluck up the courage which had enabled her to do that, to turn away in disgust. Then, she had treated him like a child, as if a child should not have such power over anyone. Now she knew that defiance would need to be backed by her own power. She needed some kind of power to escape this thing, some spiritual support from outside herself. She needed more than mere defiance, she needed the help of some external agent, some god of the swamp.

'Pula has it,' she said, trying to calm the terror within her.

'You have killed Bubi. Now the Hambukushu diamond belongs to me. So do you.'

'She is not dead!'

Julia tried to hide the weapon behind her back in a futile gesture and she again recalled the rapier, the sharp spoke. If she had that in her hand, would she be able to use it?

At that moment Bubi's body moved in her arms, it lifted very slightly, as if stirring itself once again to join the creatures of the swamp. Perhaps she was moved by a change in the flow of the stream. Potlako stepped at once into the water to lift Bubi out of it.

'Pula came to her, I came to her. But this is what you do!'

Potlako carried Bubi to Julia's high bed, he bent over her, listened for a moment to her still-pumping heart. He touched the wound on Bubi's temple, collected some of the oozing blood with gentle fingers, sucked it from them.

When Julia saw him do this, she also saw again the awful gash across his face, the teeth that were exposed by the wound that Pula had inflicted in their terrible fight. She saw the vivid scar, one staring eye which accused her, as if she were the reason for the violence on that day. You mix with wild men, the eye said. Then she saw in the flash of that challenge, a far greater threat: a growing hate. It was a wild passion, all other possible passions distilled into hate. Potlako would, in turn, kill her.

Julia began to shiver slightly, as if some drug was wearing off. She still held her carving, and she watched the deformed face of Potlako sucking Bubi's blood.

'You killed her,' Potlako said, turning again to the body on the bed.

Holding the weapon very firmly Julia lifted it once again and brought it down with both hands and with all her strength on the back of Potlako's head. The weapon glanced off Potlako's skull, thudded to his hunched shoulder. Julia turned and fled.

She ran out of the cave, away from the water and the darkness, out towards the rocks of the Tsodilo foothills. She followed the worn path which now led her away from the cave. She clambered up it, gathering renewed energy.

She held her weapon like a baton and charged up the path towards the flat rocks above. In her confused mind churned images of Potlako chasing after her and her thoughts swung wildly, like the baton she carried. She too was wild, like Pula who lived at the mouth of a river.

She looked back and saw Potlako standing at the entrance to the cave with a spear in his hand. It was the spear which Bubi had thrown at her, the one she had knocked aside with her own weapon.

As she ran in panic, Julia looked back down the path. She saw that Potlako now followed her with the spear in his hand. He was charging out of the cave like a wild bull and he clambered up the steep path towards her.

Still holding *feitiço* like a knobkerrie, swinging it above her head, she ran away from Potlako, and from Bubi on the bed which was like an altar. In her panic was some burning realisation of the evil of her own deed, some burgeoning guilt that might itself overwhelm her. What right had she to take such action? To kill a woman, destroy a witch? Now she too would be destroyed by this man who approached her. The ugly bull would knock her down and trample her into the desert sand, he would paw at her, feast upon her, tear her flesh. He would curse her while he did these things.

She heard Potlako shout at her from the path and already the words were a curse. The curse echoed in the distant desert and the sound of it was like the rushing flood. The flood should have taken her. What had she been doing wandering over strange pastures?

She could see the awful teeth revealed in the scar of Potlako's face, she could feel the hook hand scratch at her like the claw of a scorpion. She could hear his curse, which was a bellow of ancient rage risen from a dark cave: *You will make your bed on the dunghill at night and by day you will stand in the wall's shadow.*

Julia dropped to the ground, exhausted. She tried to shut out the confusing noises in her head but they grew in crescendo until she could hear her father's voice telling her that there was no eternity. Everlasting life was not your destiny. Because of this do not be sad at heart, do not be grieved or oppressed; he has given you power to bind or to loose, to be the darkness and the light of mankind.

Then she heard another distinct voice coming from the mountain and it was not the voice of her father. It was the voice of John Barotse, blessing her. Then it was still the voice of a Barotse, it was Pula telling her to choose.

He was there above her, coming down the worn path towards her. He was shouting something to her and she looked back to see that Potlako had stopped behind her in the path, that he had raised his spear to throw it. He was too far from her, too far from Pula, to attack with a spear or with anything else, even a thin sword. It would need to be very long, a lance of sudden and evil magic, the demon sting of an almighty scorpion.

Pula still ran towards her. Behind him, way above his head, near the clouds which gathered over the peak of Tsodilo, she thought she saw a huge bird hovering. It was an eagle of some kind, riding the thermals, and she was convinced that it could see her. It was a most unusual bird, with huge wings like some creature out of a story book, and it soared into the clouds and was gone. Would it come to earth on the other side? Was it a bird of goodwill, with powerful wings? Was it the pilot coming to save her?

Pula reached her then. He had only his small knife in his hand. What was such a thing, made for carving, against Bubi's spear or the sting of an almighty scorpion?

'Take this as well!' Julia said, giving him the carving which he had created, the god-model.

Pula took *feitiço*, and he charged down the path to face the man-scorpion. Julia watched the wild man run with the fantastic weapon in his hands. In it is all the strength of the Hambukushu, she said to herself in hope, hearing the words of Bubi.

Legend might say that Pula Barotse, the new rainmaker, killed the scorpion, beating its head with a club made of *moselesele*, crushing his heart with a rock which was the Hambukushu diamond. It might record that lightning struck the place where the forces met, that sparks flew from the spear of Lereng, that the rains poured down, that the wind howled around the fighting men, that a thunderbolt from the mountain crashed between them.

In the Mountain of Night there might be mourning for the passing of the old order, for the witches which were dead.

Julia got to her feet as if Pula had held out his hand to help her up, but now there were no voices, only the incredible roar directly above her and a sudden rush of wind. In some confusion she saw that Pula was still running and he was still shouting and pointing to the sky. Behind him, straight above his head, well below the clouds which gathered over the peak of Tsodilo, she saw the huge bird once again, hovering. It was an eagle of some kind, riding the thermals. She was convinced that it could see her on the path. It was a most unusual bird with huge wings, a creature out of a story book. It soared over her head, just as Pula stopped with *feitiço* in his hand, ready to attack.

She wished it were an axe that he had in his hand. She had a vivid vision of Pula's father with his axe, attacking crocodiles in the mud.

At that moment a sudden rush of wind almost blew her off her feet and she saw the microlight drop from the sky, she saw Potlako throw his spear at the descending bird and then the bird was on top of Potlako, like a swooping hawk. It had no talons but its head crashed into Potlako as if to butt him off the path, like an angry goat. Potlako fell but so did the bird, with a thud and in a cloud of dust.

Julia could not see Pula, who had been so close to the sudden explosion, and she hurried to him, stumbling down the path. She scrambled back towards the cave from which she had escaped. She saw that the wings of the bird were still waving in the dust. Smoke rose from the engine which pinned Potlako's body to the path. At the end of one wounded wing a feather fluttered. Through the haze of smoke she saw the pilot move, saw him rise from his flimsy seat, flick his harness from his shoulders and slither away from the wreck like an insect, using his strong arms, dragging his legs.

'Stay back!' the pilot shouted as he tried to move the heavy radiator nose from Potlako's chest. He had no power, no leverage, and he burnt his hands on hot metal. He pushed on one wing from his helpless position and Pula ran to help him.

'Petrol!' the pilot warned. Pula saw that something had attached itself to the pilot's flying jacket, it moved as he moved, waved like a spear lodged in the pilot's chest.

Pula tried to move the light craft away from the path to release the body beneath it. He saw petrol pouring from a primitive tank. He abandoned his useless task and dragged the pilot away from the wreckage. Now he could clearly see a length of aluminium sticking out of the pilot's chest. A snapped strut, supposed to support wings, had pierced the pilot's body.

As the metal framework settled to its original position, small rocks dislodged from the edge of the mountain path, made small sparks which found the petrol. With a thud almost as loud as the crash itself the petrol lit just as Julia reached them. Pula dragged the pilot further away from the explosion. Julia screamed as the flames spread over Potlako's body and she witnessed the final sacrifice. She pressed her knuckles to her teeth, watched in horror as the flames devoured him. She saw the dark cloud of smoke rise into the still air and was strangely calmed by it. As if dark clouds rose only to be whisked away by the wind; as if dark nightmares in a cave were miraculously lifted.

Pula hurried to help the pilot to his feet. He saw the piece of metal move in front of the pilot's chest, saw one leg thrust out at an unnatural angle. He did not try to lift him but settled him on the rocks at the edge of the path, away from the flames. The pilot lay flat on his back for a moment, then his hands rose to pull the offending piece of metal from his body. He touched it but the will failed him. His hands dropped to his side just as Julia reached them.

Pula wrapped his arms around Julia as he had done on the peak of Tsodilo. He pressed her head to his chest to shut out the sacrificial images.

The pilot lay for a moment close to the couple, his legs useless beneath him. He now tried to lift himself up, both hands on the ground behind him, but collapsed at their feet. He lay there like a creature brought down, a wounded bird. He raised an arm, appealing to be lifted out of his helplessness. He spoke directly to Julia.

'Forgive me, Julia. Pilot error,' he said.

Julia dropped down to his side, made him lie back on the path while she tried to move the spear which had entered his body. The broken strut was deathly cold in her hands. When she lifted it blood throbbed from a neat hole, covering the pilot's shirt. With his knife Pula cut away the shirt. Urgently Julia helped him rip it apart. She wrapped some of it around her hand, pressed the swab to the wound. Her hands could feel the naked flesh of the pilot's chest, feel the movement of his continued breathing. She glanced at his leg which lay at an unnatural angle, saw the bone protrude, saw more blood.

'Lie still. We'll strap you up. We'll get you to a doctor.'

'I misjudged,' the pilot said. 'I thought I could hit him with my wheels.'

At that moment there was a movement amongst the flames and Potlako's body appeared to rise in final agony, just as Bubi had moved in the water. Pula saw the movement. In horror he dropped *feitiço* and the pilot saw the carving fall to the ground.

The pilot was lying on this back, his eyes were open and now he looked up at the clear blue sky above Tsodilo Hills. He spoke directly to Pula. 'Let me hold it.'

Pula picked up his carving, gave it to the pilot who held it with both hands. He managed to turn it against the light of the sky. He stared fixedly at the revolving form of the young and the old man, the lizard and the chameleon.

'I kept your sable,' the pilot said, still staring at the carving in his hand. 'You will make many more beautiful things. Much better than flying.'

He tried to turn on to his side to give the carving to Julia, holding it by its feet.

'He is no model of God. There is only one God for all of us. Is that true, Julia?'

'Of course.'

'Is that true, Pula? The unknown One to whom all the gods report. The real Pilot.'

'You yourself came out of the sky like a god!'

'We will use it as a splint,' Julia said, taking the long carving from the pilot and placing it along his leg. She prepared more strips of cloth to bind it tight.

'I found you first,' the pilot said, as Julia worked. 'Before your father.'

'We must get you to him.'

'He said that Pula is a wild man. He lives in the distance at the mouth of rivers.'

'He understands.'

'I will reveal to you a secret, I will tell you the secret of the gods. First, some water!'

'Water! Pula, he is asking for water.'

'When you come to the waters of death what will you do?'

'Lie still. Pula will get you some water.'

'Woman, I promise you another destiny.'

'You are hurt. You must lie still.'

'The devil is dead.'

'Because of you.'

'I will teach Pula to fly.'

'Of course.'

'Do you think he will teach me to understand his river?'

The pilot winced as Julia pressed firmly on the wad of cloth swabbing his wound. He grabbed her hands with his own, held them very firmly. They were alone and Julia thought of the injured Bubi in her nearby cave, of Pula fetching water from the deep spring.

'We need a helicopter!' she said in anxious jest, 'to take you out of here.'

'Stay with me, Julia.'

'I'll bind you up. We will call men to carry you.'

'Promise me that we will fly again.'

'Of course we will.'

'And Pula will continue to carve beautiful things?'

'That must be his destiny.'

'He will fly away from darkness, into the light?'

'That too.'

The hands which held hers suddenly stiffened as if in spasm with the rest of the damaged body, or in urgent emphasis.

'There is only one God, of love,' the pilot said, squeezing her hands for the last time.

'Do any of us know him?'

'Maybe Pula?'

The spirit left the body and Julia felt the very moment. She knelt there for a long time, alone, so close to two people who had died in sudden violence. Now the images were stilled, there were no voices in the wind. In silence in the desert, she knew that she had the power to choose what she might do with her own life.

She sensed Pula running towards her up the same path along which she had herself escaped from the cave. She looked up to see him approaching awkwardly with a large calabash in his hands, like a mantis carrying a pot. He had fetched the water from the spring.

With the large calabash in both hands Pula dropped to his knees beside Julia to offer water to the pilot. He recognised death at once. He poured a little of the water on to the body of the pilot, an anointment. He slowly raised the full calabash to his own lips, sipped, then offered the calabash to Julia.

'We must both drink from this cup,' he said.

APPENDIX

The author acknowledges reference to certain works and would like to add a few further notes.

The Epic of Gilgamesh – An English Version with an Introduction by N K Sandars (Penguin Books, 1972).

Central to this story is the flood, as in *The Story of the Flood* in *The Epic of Gilgamesh,* created five thousand years ago. I gratefully acknowledge the source of some Gilgamesh quotations which I use in this book. The river of the original epic was the Euphrates which opened into the Persian Gulf, not into a desert. The Gilgamesh epic antedates Homer's *Iliad* by some 1500 years, and so does the story of the flood. The people of that ancient Sumerian civilisation believed that flood and deluge were sent by the gods. Adad was the ancient raingod.

> *For six days and six nights the wind blew, torrent and tempest and flood overwhelmed the world, tempest and flood raged together like warring hosts. When the seventh day dawned the storm from the south subsided, the sea grew calm, the flood was stilled; I looked at the face of the world and there was silence, all mankind was turned to clay. The surface of the sea stretched as flat as a roof-top; I opened a hatch and a light fell on my face.'*

The Hambukushu of Okavangoland – An Anthropological Study of a South Western Bantu People in Africa. D.Phil. thesis by Louis Lourens van Tonder, 1966.

The last *mugrodi*, or rain-mother, of the Hambukushu, was reported to have died as recently as 1963. She was the wife of Chief Dijeve and she had produced many sacrificial children. Chief Dijeve allowed one baby boy to live. I would like to acknowledge the source of my fictional hero Pula Barotse, who lives at the mouth of a river.

Other than referring to the *mugrodi* Kupenda, I have not quoted directly from this thesis. The following passage will, however, offer some background to certain events in *Okavango Gods*.

> *When the* mugrodi *had a child, male or female, it was taken to the* mbundi *by the Chief and the oldest* hekurua fumu,

male and female. Here its throat was cut and its blood mixed with other rain medicine, mvashe, *which was obtained from the* mvashe *tree and the giraffe. The skull of the infant was then cut open, the top of which was kept. The baby's body was then taken to the island where the Chiefs were buried. The little body was rubbed down with castoroil and buried in a standing position with its sawn off head above the ground, looking west ...*

*The ritual and sacrifice conducted to bring forth rain (*sivaka so mvura*) in Mbukushu was developed into a cult of tremendous proportions and fame. Its significance was so great that the inspiration derived from it spread beyond all boundaries into distant lands. Mbukushuland became the centre of the creation of rain with the Chief the sole officiant of this divine service. The ritual and sacrifice necessary to bring forth rain could only be conducted by the Chief, in his capacity as tribal* nganga. *In this he was assisted by the oldest living male and female* hekurua fumu. *One of the Chief's wives was chosen to spend all her child-bearing days giving birth to sacrificial babies. This woman was known as the* mugrodi *which means 'the rain woman', and 'mother of the tribe'.*

The last mugrodi *in Mbukushuland was the wife of Chief Dijeve. Her name was Kupenda and she only died in 1963. During her time as wife of Dijeve she gave birth to many sacrificial babies. Because of the great number of infants that were sacrificed, Chief Dijeve decided to spare the life of one boy baby.*

Basutoland Medicine Murder – A Report on the Recent Outbreak of 'Diretlo' Murders in Basutoland. HMSO Cmd. 8209, April 1951.

The links between the African countries of Botswana and Lesotho are well known, but perhaps the word *diretlo* requires some explanation. These paragraphs from the White Paper presented by the Secretary of State for Commonwealth Relations to Parliament by Command of His Majesty in 1951, may be helpful:

25. There is also a very considerable and widespread belief in the efficacy, the power, of human flesh and blood when used as an ingredient in some of the most important of these protective medicines. It is claimed by some that this belief is a modern innovation, by others that it is an ancient super- stition that has persisted underground, and which is only now coming to light through improved police methods and increasing willingness on the part of the victims or their relatives to report such things. Neither of these views are supported by the facts, anyhow as far as Basutoland is concerned. It seems more probable that it represents a recrudescence, but in an altered form, of an ancient belief ... one finds in areas where it is customary to sacrifice animals to achieve a desired result, that people may resort to human sacrifice should the normal sacrifice produce no result, or should a particularly impressive result be required ...

30. But there is considerable difference between ditlo *and* diretlo. Ditlo *is the traditional name for flesh and other parts obtained from the body of an enemy killed in the normal course of warfare.* Diretlo *is a new term, an extension of the word used for slices of flesh cut from the body of an animal killed for eating, and* diretlo *is obtained not from the bodies of strangers or enemies, but from a definite person who is thought to possess specific attributes considered essential for the particular medicine being made. Such a person is usually a member of the same community and is frequently a relative of some of the killers. He is killed specifically for his* diretlo *which has to be cut from his body while still alive.*

ABRACADABRA the Magic of Medicine – Wellcome Institute for the History of Medicine. Arnold, Baldwin, Mack, 1966.

> *Medicine is virtually always inextricably bound up with aspects of the spiritual and psychological, and dwelling on the consequent implication that illness and treatments cannot be dealt with in isolation often seems to raise the curtain on the magic of medicine. If any sort of maxim has emerged from this strategy of bringing together science and art, ethnography and history, medicine and folklore, it is that medical magic lies most clearly in the eyes of those who behold it.*

Anthony Fleischer
Cape Town

AFRICASOUTH & FICTION STOCKLIST

Farida Karodia – AGAINST AFRICAN SKY
Hugh Lewin – BANDIET
P Lanham & AS Mopeli-Paulus – BLANKET BOY'S MOON
Hjalmar Thesen – BOND OF THE SEA
C Hooper – BRIEF AUTHORITY
Douglas Blackburn – A BURGHER QUIXOTE
Bessie Head – THE CARDINALS
Anthony Fleischer – CHILDREN OF ADAMASTOR
Todd Matshikiza – CHOCOLATES FOR MY WIFE
Hjalmar Thesen – A DEADLY PRESENCE
CJ Driver – ELEGY FOR A REVOLUTIONARY
Richard Rive – EMERGENCY
Richard Rive – EMERGENCY CONTINUED
I Vladislavić – THE FOLLY
Miriam Tlali – FOOTPRINTS IN THE QUAG
ZK Matthews – FREEDOM FOR MY PEOPLE
Sindiwe Magona – FORCED TO GROW
Gerald Gordon – FOUR PEOPLE
John Howland Beaumont – THE GREAT KAROO
Denis Hirson – HOUSE NEXT DOOR TO AFRICA
Tatamkhulu Afrika – THE INNOCENTS
Nadine Gordimer – JUMP AND OTHER STORIES
Guy Butler – KAROO MORNING
Pauline Smith – LITTLE KAROO
Sindiwe Magona – LIVING LOVING & LYING AWAKE
Menán du Plessis – LONGLIVE
Etienne van Heerden – MAD DOG & OTHER STORIES
Perceval Gibbon – MARGARET HARDING
Ivan Vladislavić – MISSING PERSONS
Nadine Gordimer – HOUSE GUN
Nadine Gordimer – MY SON'S STORY
Mandla Langa – NAKED SONG & OTHER STORIES